THE
9 MM
MURDERS

THE 9 MM MURDERS

A DS MADDOX NOVEL

STEVE PACKWOOD

Praise for The 9mm Murders

"Gripping, emotional, and full of authentic police detail—*The 9mm Murders* is for fans of Ian Rankin, Ann Cleeves, and *Line of Duty*."—Gabriel Valjan, Anthony-nominated and Shamus Award-winning author of the Shane Cleary mystery series

POLICE RANKS

Uniform Branch	Criminal Investigation Department (CID)
Police Constable (PC)	Detective Constable (DC)
Police Sergeant (PS)	Detective Sergeant (DS)
Inspector	Detective Inspector (DI)
Chief Inspector	Detective Chief Inspector (DCI)
Superintendent	Detective Superintendent
Chief Superintendent	Detective Chief Superintendent

GLOSSARY OF TERMS AND EXPRESSIONS

Actual Bodily Harm (ABH)	A minor level of assault
Arsenal, Spurs, The Eagles	London Football Clubs
ARV	Armed Response Vehicle
Belt Rig	PC's Quick release equipment belt
Bit of a Kicking	Slang, attacked/beaten up
'Blues and Twos'	Police car's blue lights and two tone sirens
Caution	Formal warning for minor offences
Clod-hopping	Heavy footed/stomping without regard
Conditional Discharge	A non-custodial conviction
Diplomatic Protection Group	Police Armed Protection Dept
Do a number on	Slang, teach someone a lesson
Estate Agent	Realtor, Property Salesperson
Family Liaison Officer (FLO)	Link officer for crime victim
Filled his boots	Slang, took full advantage
Form	Slang, previous criminal convictions
Furry Exocets	Police Dog/K9 Unit
Getting on your tits	Slang, causing irritation or annoyance
Ghostbusters	Officers trained to effect forced entry
Grief	Slang, trouble, irritation or hard work.
Guv'nor/Guv	Informal title for inspector or above
Haymaker	Powerful wide swinging punch
Homely	Domesticated, maternal, a home-maker

Hot Splosh	Cup of tea
H.R.	Human Resources. Personnel Dept.
The Hump	To feel offended, angered or upset
India 99	Radio call sign of the police helicopter
Jessie	An overly sensitive person, a 'softie'
'The Job'	What Police Officers call The Police Service
Joshing	Gentle teasing or banter
Lifted	Slang, placed under arrest
Main Set	A powerful radio in a police car
MP	Member of the British Parliament
'MP'	Radio Call sign of Met Police
Mr Floppy problems	Erectile disfunction
A Nick. To Nick	Noun: a Police Station. Verb: to arrest
OIC	Officer in the Case
Old Bill/The Bill	Slang term for the London Police Service
Old Sweat	Slang, an old and experienced person
Over the side	Slang, extra-marital affair
Piss taker/taking	Slang, taking a greedy advantage
Playing away	Slang, extra-marital affair
POLSA	Police Search Advisor
Porking	Slang, engaging in sexual intercourse
Post-mortem/PM	Forensic examination of a body
Prot Team	Armed Protection Officers, bodyguards.

Pumping her tyres up	Slang, sex with a woman
Puppy Walker	Senior PC mentor to a Probationary PC
Rule 43 (in prison)	Segregated at risk prisoners
Shag/shagger	To have sex/a person who frequently has sex
SIO	Senior Investigating Officer
Skipper/Skip	Slang, informal title for a sergeant rank
Slot	Army/Police slang, to shoot someone
SOCO	Scenes of Crime Officer. (Forensic)
Sprog	A newcomer, youngster, inexperienced person
STD's	Sexually Transmitted Diseases
Tear a new arsehole	To seriously admonish or criticise
Territorial Support Group	TSG, public order officers
Toe-Rag	A low-life, worthless person, often a thief
Trouser Worm	Penis
The Tube	London slang for Underground Train System
Wuss	An overly sensitive person, easily moved to tears
X26 Taser	Electric stun gun

Foreward

He hated estate agents. He had good reason. A coven of the self-important parasites were guffawing at the bar, a slickly dressed, shiny faced wanker with gelled back hair was telling a joke, holding court, his audience of chinless pricks throwing their heads back as they hooted in unison. God, how he hated estate agents.

The initial shock had subsided. Just a little. Leaving him with a reality. He'd drifted to the pub for no better reason than it seemed what someone should do after such news. He raised his glass to no one in particular, a mock salutation, a scoffing snort rising from his throat and escaping through his nostrils. He shook his head from side to side, put the drink to his lips and quaffed deeply, feeling the cold of the liquid run from throat to stomach.

Lifting his eyes, he scrutinised the other occupants of the bar. At a table in a far-off, shadowed corner, two figures huddled close together, heads down and conspiratorially near. A married couple, but not to each other.

To his right were seated five ragged pensioners, circling a table larger than his own, its surface littered with dreg-stained pint mugs of mild, bitter, and bible-black Guinness. Each empty vessel standing as testament to their daily afternoon habit. Beer-wetted lips encircled mouths of loose-fitting false teeth and lolling tongues which spoke only of The Arsenal, Spurs, or The Eagles.

He looked around, from group to group. How could they be carrying on as if nothing had happened? How could the world be the same for everyone else when *everything* had changed for him?

It was the moment.

The world tilted on its axis. It was the moment realisation hit home with staggering clarity. He was free. He was untouchable. Two hours earlier, he'd thought he'd never smile again; now he couldn't take the grin off his face.

Chapter One

6 Hours 35 Minutes.

"Evenin', Crispy."

"Evening Tiddles, you alright?"

"Not really, the leg is playing up." PC Rory Caplan took two painful steps to the weapons rack and removed a Glock pistol, which he twisted to note the white Tipp-Ex'ed number 16 painted on its underside. He'd limp for the rest of his life, the leg injury acquired after an on-duty motorcycle accident three years earlier.

Rory Caplan should have been medically retired on a much-reduced pension, but a sympathetic senior officer found a job for him to see out his full thirty years of service. As the armourer at the Diplomatic Protection Group base in central London, he cleaned, maintained, and issued weapons to the firearms officers. The armoury and canteen encompassed his whole working world; his duties never took him past the front door, onto the streets of London. Rory Caplan was the 'Station Cat' and, as everyone knows, all cats are called Tiddles.

"Glock number 16 and thirty-four 9 millimetre rounds. Taser?" Tiddles asked as he pushed the handgun and two charged magazines towards Sean.

"Yes, please."

Tiddles grasped the Velcro-covered webbing straps and holster which contained the X26 Taser and pushed it into the well under the glass screen to rest next to the pistol. "Taser number 15 and four cartridges. Sign."

PC Sean Crisp raised a quizzical eyebrow at the armourer's brusqueness but put it down to the pain in his leg. He checked the details in the Firearms Register were entered and timed correctly, glancing up at the clock, 10.45 pm, excellent, he could get a cuppa before parade at 11 pm. He signed the Register, taking possession of the two weapons.

Sean selected a charged magazine and superstitiously ran his thumb across the brass casing of the 9mm bullet seated at the top of the sixteen others beneath it. Government Home Office rules of engagement were *very* simple and *very* clear and impressed on each of the very few specialist officers who carried guns in London. An officer may only discharge a firearm if he or she has an honestly held belief that there is an *imminent* threat to life. That threatened life could be his own, a colleague's, or a member of the public. Sean looked at the bullet; it would be the one, if the moment ever came, which would be fired. He ran his thumb over it again.

In a well-practised choreography, he cleared the handgun, loaded it with the magazine of seventeen rounds at the adjacent sand-filled bay and pushed the weapon firmly into the retention holster. Removing the cartridge from the front of the Taser, he flicked the power lever up, noting the display showed an 87% charge and the 'LL' setting for both laser-dot and flash-light modes was engaged. Pulling the trigger, Sean smiled at the gratifying crackle of 50,000 volts jumping across the terminals. Satisfied the Taser was operating correctly, he reattached the cartridge and departed the issuing bay to allow the next officer to enter.

5 Hours 10 Minutes.

As the sergeant's car rounded the sweeping bends of Belgrave Square, PC Sean Crisp released his seat belt and stretched to recover his flat cap from where it was wedged under the windscreen. "Thanks, Chris, see you in two hours."

"Will do. Looks like it'll be cold but dry." The sergeant guided the car to the kerbside outside the darkened Turkish embassy as the officer on post, PC Gareth Took, emerged wraith-like from the shadows of the front door portico and descended the three steps to the pavement, a grateful grin on his face.

"Hiya Crispy, nothing to tell you, all quiet and colder than a well-diggers arse."

Sean laughed. "Nice image. I've just farted so the seat is lovely and warm for you."

Gareth laughed. "You're too good to me, Crispy. Now get up those steps so I can sod off and warm through."

Sean scanned the deserted street as the passenger door slammed shut and the car sped away. He patted the weapon at his side, checking the retentions on the holster hadn't been unlocked during his manoeuvring into and out of the vehicle. Content that the Glock pistol was secure, he followed the same procedure for the X26 Taser secured to his upper thigh.

With a sigh which showed up as white condensation in the cold night air, Sean Crisp ascended the three steps into the murk of the embassy door and turned to look out over the gardens in the centre of the Georgian square. The Turkish embassy received twenty-four hours a day armed protection from officers of the Metropolitan Police's Diplomatic Protection Group and for the next two hours was Sean Crisp's post.

2 Hours 10 Minutes.

Sean dropped the weights onto the mat and appraised the sweat-drenched figure in the mirror of the small gym on the ground floor of the DPG base. 'Not bad,' he thought. He was forty-five years old, six feet tall with an athletic build, but Sean's distinctive feature was his bright ginger hair. Teased mercilessly throughout his childhood, Sean embraced his colouring on achieving manhood, grooming his facial hair in the manner of a 17th-century cavalier. He shaped and curled upwards the ends of his red moustache and tapered the beard to a sharp and dramatic point, Sean Crisp gloried in his resemblance to a ginger King Charles I.

Gareth Took had relieved Sean from his post in Belgrave Square at 2.20 am after two dreary hours. "Colder than a witch's tit," Sean declared as they swapped places.

"I've returned your earlier favour" Gareth replied, "and farted on the seat, warmed it up for you."

"Anymore farting in *my* car and you can all start walking, you disgusting bastards." The sergeant countered, but the amusement in his voice was obvious.

At the base, Sean questioned the absence in the armoury of the station cat, Rory Caplan. "The guvnor let him slide off early, complaining about his leg hurting…again," a PC moaned. Sean shrugged, unconcerned, heading for the gym.

His workout concluded, Sean slumped in the TV room, hugging a mug of hot splosh, and watched some late-night rubbish on television before heading out for his final 4.20am to 6.20am stint on post. Sean was a happy man, after so many years of domestic turmoil, admittedly mostly of his own making, he finally felt settled. If only he could connect with his eldest son, Callum, his contentment would be complete.

He thought of his younger son, Casper, who'd be staying over with him that night. After snatching a short sleep during the day, he'd collect the boy from school to spend the evening together in the small flat in Feltham he shared with Lizzy. He'd have the joy of putting the eleven-year-old to bed and cooking him breakfast in the morning before dropping him at school. Simple, commonplace pleasures. There was just one untidy matter to be resolved, one person who needed to understand it was finally over. His solicitor's letter had provoked a predictably furious phone call, and he foresaw more difficulties ahead. But at last his selfish, egocentric, turbulent days were behind him. Now he sought what so many took for granted, a normal family life.

1 Hour 1 Minute.

"It's colder than a politician's heart," Gareth greeted Sean when he resumed his post in Belgrave Square a few minutes early at 4.17 am.

"Great! Good job I've got long-johns on, isn't it?" The two friends laughed.

"Anything to report? All quiet still?"

As the relieved officer squeezed his form, made bulky by multiple layers of clothing, cumbersome body armour, and protrusions of weaponry and equipment, he called to Sean, "nah, just a weirdo wandering around. I saw him near Wilton Crescent, by the statue earlier, but he's gone now. Probably a vagrant looking for a warm corner."

"Description?" Sean called as the car door began to close.

The officer shrugged. "Male, dark hoodie. Hope it doesn't bother you that you'll still be here with ice cubes for bollocks when I'm home, snug and warm in bed. Byeee!"

7 Minutes.

He thought he saw movement across the road at the corner of the gardens, close to the statue. A shadow moving amongst the foliage that tumbled over the metal railings enclosing the locked grounds. Sean shook his head, dismissing the figure, most likely someone having a crafty piss in the darkness, or even the vagrant he'd been informed of.

4 Minutes.

After nearly an hour on post, Sean was shuffling from foot to foot, occasionally stamping, trying to get some warmth into his body. He rubbed his hands together, blowing warm breath into cupped fingers.

2 Minutes.

The dark, hooded figure emerged from the shadows and crossed the road to the footway a short distance from the embassy. Sean scrutinised him. He was hunched over, his hands thrust deep into his pockets, the cowl of the dark fleece hoody pulled forward, shrouding his face. From his size and movement, Sean judged he was male, of slight build and medium height, perhaps 5'9" tall.

The figure reached the pavement about twenty-five yards to Sean's right; he looked slowly around and walked towards the embassy.

1 Minute.

Sean stepped down onto the pavement, emerging into the street light and called out. "Oi. You. Come here, I want to speak with you." The figure halted at the sudden appearance of the officer and looked around once more. Sean considered the figure was perhaps a person with mental health issues, maybe someone in need of help on a cold night.

"You're not in trouble. I just want to speak to you," the figure walked towards Sean. The street lighting in the square was poor; what light there was didn't penetrate the depths of the hood.

Sean instinctively adopted the officer safety 'thinking policeman stance'. Left foot forward, right foot back, balanced and ready to react, the sidearm on his right side furthest away from the approaching figure. His left hand across the chest cupped under the right elbow, the right arm vertical, with the hand near the face. An unthreatening posture of defence with the ability to deflect or attack as necessary. A posture second nature to a street cop.

"What you up to, mate? It's a cold night to be out." Sean asked the approaching man. When the figure was only a few feet away, he lifted his head, the light cutting across his features, Sean's eyebrows rose with the surprise of recognition, and with recognition, his guard dropped. His mouth opened, preparing to speak, but no words escaped his lips.

It felt like a punch to the left side of his neck, only when he saw the glint on the wet metal did he realise he'd been stabbed. The second plunge of the broad-bladed knife came a split second later, striking with such force that the tip passed through the width of his throat, severing his windpipe and exiting the right side of his neck. He tried to push the attacker away before, by a reactive instinct, clamping his hand across the ripped wound, struggling and failing to find the emergency transmit button on his personal radio. Already his consciousness was reeling, the shock overpowering. The next stab passed through his hand, which was pressing down on the wound, penetrating, once again, into the critical veins and arteries of the neck. Sean felt his knees buckle, his vision swimming.

At some point, **every** police officer pictures the manner of their own violent death. *Will I see it coming? Will I die with dignity? What will my final thoughts be?* Sean always assumed his last thoughts would be of his youngest son and the loss of guiding the boy he loved to manhood. Rugby matches not shared, the first beers together foregone, the milestone of teaching him to drive unfulfilled. Everything denied. As Sean Crisp lay haemorrhaging on the ground and urgent hands dragging at his belt rig, all he could think was, *'No.'*

Zero.

The assailant's raging voice was distant and echoing. The words unintelligible.

His vision was blurred, the dearth of oxygenated blood to the brain rapidly shutting down his senses.

The muzzle of his pistol swam in and out of focus a few feet from his face.

PC Sean Crisp was unaware of the concussive sound of the handgun's discharge, which travelled like a thunderclap around the deserted square.

The nine millimetre bullet, stroked by his thumb, for luck, six hours and thirty-five minutes earlier, exploded through his right eyeball. The projectile, travelling at over eight hundred miles an hour, inflicted catastrophic tissue cavitation and fluid shock on its victim's brain. Death was instantaneous.

Chapter Two

Although it wasn't yet 8am, the CID office was humming industriously with its usual background of manmade noise. A scanning observer would note small knots of officers conversing with each other in intimate huddles, while singletons chattered into telephone mouthpieces, unaware of their gurning faces and jabbing fingers, emphasising points as if the listener were sitting opposite and not miles away. One officer chewed the end of a ballpoint pen, staring blankly at a computer screen, hoping inspiration would leap through the glass into our world like a cartoon character, whilst another's face toggled back and forth between hand-written notes lying on her desk and a statement held fan-like in her hand, a grin forming on her face as an awareness coalesced.

In the glass-walled office, the tall, gangly figure of Detective Chief Inspector Paul Winter paced back and forth behind his high-backed executive chair. Periodically, he would halt, grip the seat back with both hands, and lean forward, his head dropping and slowly shaking from side to side. The other participant in his conversation was hidden from view by the office's wooden door, but from Paul Winters' demeanour and facial expression, the topic under discussion was not one which brought any joy to their early morning meeting.

* * *

At eighteen years of age, Detective Sergeant Grant Maddox had served during the Falklands Conflict as a Royal Marine. At twenty-three, he'd solemnly attested to hold the office of Constable in London's Metropolitan Police. Twenty-eight years later, aged fifty-one, he was still well over six feet tall, but his waistline was spreading, his hairline receding to the point of extinction, and he found himself routinely sounding off at the various aches and pains his body inflicted on him. Grant had learned his policing craft in uniformed response duties before serving eight years as a specialist Armed Response Officer, during which time he'd taken promotion to proudly wear three chevrons on his sleeves. For domestic reasons, he'd transferred to the CID, where he'd forged a reputation as a tireless investigator, a peerless role model, and humanitarian. Grant Maddox was a man who'd been tested in the crucible and not found wanting. He was respected by his seniors and feted by his juniors who sought his approval and guidance, which he always gladly gave. In the understated vernacular of The Job, Grant Maddox was a 'Good Lad'.

Grant scrutinised his guvnor through the glass as unobtrusively as he was able, watching with interest as DCI Winter ceased his pacing and came to a halt behind his chair and clasped the back rest once more, his head sank until his chin was resting on his chest. It was a posture of abject sadness and resignation. The door to the office opened and the dark-suited figure of the Area Detective Chief Superintendent exited, his face a picture of focused misery. He closed the door behind him and, with a few emotionless nods to the officers of the Major Investigation Task Force, he departed without further ceremony. Grant couldn't guess what the visit presaged, but from the body language of the two senior officers, it was nothing good.

The answer came within a few minutes. It didn't appear to be the work of any one person but rather a process of osmosis. The news passed from person to person, moving through the office like an incoming tide composed of disjointed snippets of information. *'A police officer'*, *'dead'*, *'murdered'*. As the words reached him a sigh of profound sadness left his body, officers *were* murdered, it happened, it had always happened, but it was such a mercifully rare occurrence in Britain that when it did, the response was always shock and incredulity. It was an appalling feeling and one which invariably elicited the same thought, 'it could have been me'.

Grant looked across the width of the office and saw that Paul Winter was on the phone, the receiver wedged into his neck, his tilted head holding it to his ear as he wrote on a pad with his right hand and flicked through a copy of The Almanac, a police resources directory with the other. Grant decided not to disturb his friend for the moment, he would communicate his news and the Task Force's role when he was able. In the meantime, the urgency was to garner more details, what had happened, where did it happen and most important of all, who was it?

DC Nagur Padda, a new arrival to the Task Force, emerged from a knot of officers, slumped in his chair at the desk opposite Grant and passed on the most recent news. "Early hours of this morning in Belgrave Square, a Diplomatic Protection Group officer, apparently," he offered. Adding as an afterthought, "a bloke, not a girl."

Grant nodded, "Right. Any word on a suspect? Have we got him?"

"No skip, and no victim name yet. D'you know anyone on DPG?"

Grant searched his memory. "Yes, a couple. From my firearms days." Grant offered by way of explanation. "We'll have to wait and see." He cringed inwardly; it was a feeble assembly of words, *we'll have to wait and see.*' But until the DCI exited his glass box and addressed the Task Force, waiting and feeble words were all he had; he wouldn't descend to idle speculation.

The main door to the office opened, and Grant saw his young colleague, DC Amber Bennett, reverse into the room, forcing entry with her backside, each hand clutching a large mug of steaming liquid. She twisted and headed towards her DS, her expression betraying that she, too, had heard the news.

"You know?" She asked as she lowered herself into the chair beside Grant, placing his coffee on the desk. He nodded. "It's on Sky News on the canteen TV," she continued, "they've a helicopter above Belgrave Square filming. It's all cordoned off, and a tent is over the scene. All they're saying is a PC's been murdered, not yet named, no arrests, and then the usual wild speculations." Amber carefully sipped her coffee. "It's horrific."

"The Area Detective Chief Superintendent has just walked out of the DCI's office." Nagur offered. "Gotta mean it's coming to us. The investigation, I mean." Amber turned to Grant, raising her eyebrows, looking for an opinion.

The Detective Sergeant stretched his aching body, feeling his back clicking with the effort. He'd slept badly the night before. Connie, his eldest daughter, had failed miserably in placating a screaming, teething baby, Saffron, in the Maddox household. He rubbed his eyes and sighed heavily for the second time in a few minutes.

"Nag's right." He dipped his balding head towards the young DC. "It makes sense, this'll be a very high-profile job." He winced inside at his own words, reducing the death of a comrade, maybe a personal friend, to a mere 'job'. "The press will be all over it like a fucking rash. The venue alone will have the media in a frenzy of speculation, and then there's the specific circumstances of the victim." The two DCs looked to each other, mystified. Before either could ask, Grant explained. "Protection officers carry guns. The press will want to know how an armed officer came to be killed *and* what's happened to his weapon?"

Amber's mouth dropped open. The enormity of the event had blinded her to the few details which were already known. Before she could speak, the door to the DCI's glass box opened and the tall figure of Paul Winter emerged.

"Ladies and Gents, listen in please, I've some terrible news."

Chapter Three

An unfamiliar hush descended on the office. Those standing turned to face the guvnor, those sitting twisted to see. All knew the basics; now there was a universal holding of the breath as each officer awaited the grim details and wondered, 'Is it someone I know?' The numbers in the room, their combined service, and wide geographical experience made it statistically likely that someone would know the victim.

"Ladies and gents, I have to give you the worst news an officer can ever report in this job of ours, the death…the *murder* of one of our own. Shortly before 5.30 am this morning, whilst on protection duty outside the Turkish Embassy in Belgrave Square, Police Constable Sean Crisp was attacked by person or persons unknown. He suffered grievous stab wounds to the neck and throat and a single gunshot to the head. It seems likely the officer's own weapon was used."

As Grant searched his memory without success for the name Sean Crisp, he heard a tiny, muffled squeak from his right and became aware of a sudden movement in his peripheral vision. He slowly turned to his right to see Amber holding both hands to her face, the fingers splayed over her eyes, her shoulders convulsing, and her chest heaving with emotion. He understood immediately.

"As you'll have seen, the Area Chief Superintendent has just departed; this one is ours. The scene is preserved and forensics are doing their job and ladies and gentlemen, we are going to do ours. We are going to find the person who did this, and we are going to put him away forever, that's a promise. Now, will you all stand with me and give a minute of silence for our colleague."

The clatter of chairs being moved and the shuffling of bodies finding space to stand heralded the silent tribute.

"Members of this Task Force," Paul Winter broke the silence sixty seconds later. "*That* was the last minute that anyone will stand around doing nothing until this case is concluded. Right, Kerrigan and Chamberlain, get your arses to the DPG base, everyone from the night-shift has been held, I want to know anything and everything about last night and this morning. I don't care how tired they may be or what commitments they may have, I want initial statements while it's fresh in their minds, we can drag more detail out later." The two DCs, Pat Kerrigan and 'Dirty' Don Chamberlain, nodded their heads and answered "Guv" in unison.

The DCI directed his next words to his Detective Sergeant. "Okay, Granty, I've called DI Yorke and she's cutting short her annual leave and will be here this afternoon. She carries the rank to liaise with the Diplomatic Protection crowd, the Embassy, and the Home Office. As you can imagine, this isn't just a London story, or a UK story; this is an international incident. In the meantime, I want you and Amber down at the scene, find out what you can without treading on Forensics' or the local CID's toes. They may feel a bit sensitive about the Task Force charging in and taking over. We need everyone on board with this. Build bridges, you know what to do." Grant nodded. "Amber," Winter continued, "CCTV is going to be crucial on this one. I want you to oversee the locating and collation of all cameras and all recordings. I want you like a chimp on a banana hunt, grab that evidence, it's far too common that recordings are automatically wiped and re-recorded after 24 hours. We can't lose a second of tape, that's critical." Amber nodded her understanding. "I want a meeting at 6 pm to bring everyone up to speed and for DI Yorke to be able to have an overview. She's going to be the conduit for info in and out; she'll need to know everything. Padda, I want you to get onto H.R. and pull Sean Crisp's personal file. I want to know all about him, okay?"

Nagur put a forefinger to his head and flicked an acknowledging salute. "Will do, Guv."

Turning once more to Grant, he said. "Granty, I want you to re-jig and re-assign the case-loads of the officers I've actioned. I need a core freed up to be on this until we're up and running and properly resourced. I don't want anything we're dealing with now to suffer, but this is our priority. Got it? Can you do that?"

Grant smiled resignedly, nodding and answering. "Yes, Guv. I'll sort it."

"Good man, thank you, Grant. Now, the first thing we need to establish is why *this* victim? Was this man killed because of where he was and the political sensitivities of his role? Was this an attack on the structure or dignity of the embassy, an attempted incursion which was thwarted or abandoned? Was he killed simply because he was a police officer? We've seen that often enough in the USA and even here in the Raoul Moat case. Or was he murdered to facilitate the theft of his firearm? I can tell you now that his pistol and his Taser have been taken. Or was he killed because he was Sean Crisp? Was *he specifically* targeted? We need to know everything about everything to answer this question of motive. That's our starting point, the rest will follow on from that. So all of you, as well as your assigned actions, find out about this officer."

Amber Bennett's voice cut across the room. "Sir, may I speak with you, please?"

* * *

Detective Constable Amber Bennett was a striking figure, just passing her mid-twenties; she was tall, dark-haired, and pretty. With approaching six years' service and less than a year in the CID, she had matured considerably under the tutelage and patronage of her DS, Grant Maddox. The trauma and horrors of their last major case, sensationalised by the media as *The Dissection Murders*, had pushed the two closer together, forming a bond much closer than mere work colleagues. Amber and Grant were friends.

"Please, sit down, Amber." Paul Winter waved a hand at one of the two chairs opposite his desk. Grant sat beside her without seeking an invitation. He and his guvnor went back a long way, and stiff hierarchical formalities, which were observed outside the DCI's glass-walled office, fell by the wayside once the door was closed. "I'm guessing from the look on your face and your reaction that you knew Sean Crisp."

Amber nodded, running the edge of a finger under an eyelid, fearful of a forming tear overflowing to wreak havoc on eyeliner. "Yes, sir. He was my Street Duties Tutor for ten weeks when I first started on Borough. I knew him well, although we eventually fell off each other's radar after he transferred to Diplomatic Protection." Grant slid a hand holding a folded tissue from his pocket and passed it across to Amber, holding it low, near her lap, not making a big deal of it. Amber took the tissue gratefully and dabbed her eyes softly.

The DCI's voice was soft and empathetic. "I wish it wasn't true, but as rare as it is for us to lose a colleague we know personally, if you're in The Job long enough, it's likely to happen. I know how you're feeling, and so does Granty here." Maddox nodded solemnly, his mind flying back to a truly terrible day. "What can you tell me about Sean?"

Amber Bennett started to laugh, the sound mixing with a catch of emotion in her throat. "Well, Guv, first off, he was a funny guy, I mean, he made people laugh. He was more than a bit eccentric, too. He had bright red hair and grew a pointed beard and a moustache, which he turned up at the ends. He looked like the Laughing Cavalier, you know, the painting, or even King Charles the First, a proper dandy he was. He was a good copper too, active and knew his stuff, a bit rigid at times, he didn't give much quarter, not a great believer in discretion, but straight down the line and by the book. He was a good choice as a tutor for that reason..." Amber halted.

"I feel a 'but' coming on." Paul filled the silence. "He was a good choice... but?"

Amber shrugged. "Well, he was a 'bit of a lad', that's all. He was a good-looking bloke, went to the gym, kept fit, looked after himself, and well-groomed. He was funny, personable, and entertaining to have around. But he was a womaniser." Amber looked to Grant. "Not a saddo like Dirty Don, an habitual loser with women, Sean was *successful* with women, his track record and private life were amazing. Unbelievable really. Us girls looked on in wonder, how did he find the time *and* come to work?"

Paul Winter reached for a pad and lifted a pen, which he tapped on the paper's surface. "This is what we need. Tell me as much as you know."

Amber smiled at the memories. "I hope you've lots of paper, Guv." The tension was broken by the joke. "Sean was married to Deborah, they had a son, Callum, he must be around twenty now. Debbie had to put up with a lot. Sean was *never* faithful, by his own admission. He just couldn't keep his trouser worm zipped up. Eventually they split, at the time I knew him they hadn't divorced, maybe they have by now. The split was very acrimonious, lots of arguments about money. He took up with Sienna, they had a son together. What was his name now?" Amber shook her head for a few seconds. "*Casper!* That's it, like the friendly ghost. Sean really loved that boy, he must be ten or eleven by now. Lavished time and money on him, which didn't help with the relationship with Debbie or Callum, that was always grief with a capital 'G.'"

Paul was scribbling furiously with the pen, nodding encouragement with each set of facts. "Okay, so married to Deborah, son about twenty called Callum. Acrimonious. Took up with Sienna, son called Casper, ten or eleven, whom he doted on. Okay, got all that. Keep going, Amber, this is good stuff."

"It didn't last with Sienna either. Their split was more civilised, for the sake of the little boy. But it was the same old reason; he couldn't help himself. He tried it on with everyone; he even made a pass at me, twenty years younger, and he *still* had a go. But he'd a way with him, Guv. When he made a pass, it wasn't sleazy, it almost seemed a bit of fun. I just laughed at him and said something like, 'in your dreams,' he laughed, and that was the end of it. He wasn't a stalker type, or creepy in a leering, underhand, slimy way. Does this make any sense?" Amber turned to Grant for reassurance.

Grant laughed. "Yes, Amber, we all know the sort. You paint a good picture."

"Well, anyway." Amber opened her hands and shrugged again. "The last I heard, he'd settled down with someone and was trying to turn over a new leaf. Then you gave his name this morning…and it's all over. He's gone. It doesn't seem possible."

Paul and Grant caught each other's eye, exchanging a knowing look. With over fifty years of policing between them, they knew *anything* was possible.

Chapter Four

Grant asked Amber once again, giving her a last chance, now that they stood at the outer cordon tape and could see the white pop-up tent and the activity around it. "Are you sure you want to do this? No one, least of all me, will think any the less of you if you'd rather find something else to do, we're not short of jobs."

Amber stared across the short distance, a white-suited figure, hooded with a blue face mask, stepped out of the tent into the bright winter sunshine. He put his hands on his hips and arched his back, stretching off the effects of working in a confined space, movement limited to minimise any disturbance to the scene. "I'm sure. It's my job, and doing my job is the only thing left I can do for Sean. I'll be alright. After seeing what happened to Paula Bingley, I think I can cope with anything."

Grant shuddered at the memory of the gruesome series of murders during which he'd forged his close relationship with Amber. "Okay. But when it's someone you know, it could be different." Grant decided he'd pressed the point far enough, he didn't want to nag. "You know your own mind, and I respect your motives. Let's go."

The pair reached the inner cordon, where their attendance was noted by a PC in the Incident Log Book. They donned blue elasticated shoe covers, face masks, and rubber gloves, and followed a course pointed out to them by the records officer towards the tent. Ten yards from the small shelter stood a short, rotund, olive-skinned figure, in a dark suit and similarly accessorised about the feet, face, and hands with scene preservation equipment. He was making notes in a booklet from which he dragged his attention at the approach of Grant and Amber. "Major Investigation Task Force?" he asked, his tone betraying his foreknowledge of the answer.

Grant answered. "That's right, DS Grant Maddox, this is DC Amber Bennett. How're we doing?"

"Better than the poor bastard in there." He flicked his head towards the tent. "Best description is butchered. A total mess. I'm DS Panayiotis Kalamatianos, out of the Borough CID office. Call me Panos, it's easier."

Grant replied quickly, "Panos, you should know the victim, Sean Crisp, was known personally to Amber here."

The Greek-Cypriot DS winced. "Ah. Fuck. I'm really sorry, I didn't mean to sound insensitive. But the fact is, it *is* a mess, like a classic case of overkill to me, but you'll see for yourself." He twisted to face Amber directly. The tone of his voice soft and well-meaning. "Are you sure you want to see your friend like this? What's to be gained?"

The steel in Amber's decisive, single-word reply surprised the spherical DS and Grant Maddox both. "Motivation."

* * *

The three detectives stood a few yards from the open side of the tent which sheltered the body of Sean Crisp. DS Kalamatianos had taken on the role of tour guide, his local knowledge described the Turkish embassy building, its geographical orientation, and its hours of operation.

As the group closed on the tent-covered scene, Panos conveyed the otherworldliness of this particular corner of Belgravia, a district of a bustling Capital city, largely bereft of residents or commercial premises. Once the sun set, pedestrian and vehicular traffic fell to near nothing. Panos swept a hand in a broad arc and recited, "embassies of Turkey, Malaysia, Trinidad and Tobago, Ivory Coast, Bahrain, Serbia, Norway, Finland, Austria, Ghana, Portugal, Syria. Need I go on?" He needn't. "This is embassy central, our best bet is the CCTV, which is plastered all over the place." Grant and Amber stood in silence. "Don't you think?" Panos paused. "The CCTV?" he pressed.

The two Task Force detectives *were* listening. What he was saying *was* good information, but the officers were absorbing the first view of the brutal scene, only partially visible to them, blocked as it was by forensics officers going about their grim business. The restricted view was enough. The amount of blood which had stained the ground, pooled under and around the sprawled body, sprayed in arterial gushes across the flagstones and ran down the sloping footpath, over the edges of kerbstones to collect in sickening puddles in the gutter, was astonishing. Grant heard Amber whisper to herself. "So much blood." There was wonder in her voice.

Grant observed the systematic process of examination. Whilst one forensic officer held a sterile pad beneath the body's left hand, another scraped under its nails, the collected residue was bagged, sealed and labelled, the details of the procedure and itemised number recorded by a third who oversaw the process. It was all part of the chain of evidential continuity to stymie the most simple and obvious challenges by a defence counsel. *'What is this and where is it from?'* and *'Now prove it.'* Grant nodded with unconscious approval. The possibility existed that before he was incapacitated, the victim may have scratched or grabbed at his attacker. DNA, fibres, or some other trace evidence may be recovered, evidence which could slam a cell door on a killer for the rest of his life.

Even from this distance, Grant could see the pale bluish discolouration to the hands and fingers, which were the focus of the examiner's attention, peripheral cyanosis caused by the lack of blood to the extremities. The reason was obvious, splashed all over the ground. One of the figures in the tent shuffled his position, and for the first time, the officers saw the face of Sean Crisp clearly. Grant felt the weight of Amber lean on his side for a moment as her body rocked in reaction to the image which would be forever seared into her memory.

Under the dried, reddish streaks of gore, Sean Crisp's face was alabaster white. His mouth open, stilled mid-word. His undamaged left eye gazed, unseeing upwards, its last earthly act, only hours before, to view the myriad of stars on display on the clear, freezing, winter's night. There was a time not so long ago, Grant knew, that the police photographed the eyes of the dead, believing the last image they saw, of their killer, had been captured, imprinted, and fixed on the retina. If only it were true. The right eye was a dark chasm, the entry point of the bullet which had finally ended the efforts of Sean Crisp's heart to circulate blood about his body, unaware the liquid was coursing from the carved open remnants of his throat and neck.

"The camera's sighted on the underside of the portico, looking down the steps to the pavement. Can you see?" Panos's words shook Grant and Amber from their reverie; they looked in the direction of the pointing hand to examine the camera. "The whole thing will be recorded. Most of the buildings around here are CCTV'd up to the hilt. It'll be a trawl, but it should all be on film." The DS seemed almost cheery. "How often does that happen? This should be easy, we'll have the fucker who did this in double quick time."

"Yes, it should help enormously." Grant conceded. "We appreciate your input and local knowledge, I hope we can work closely on this." Grant heard the sounds coming out of his mouth but sensed Panos's word, 'easy', was ill-judged. "Okay, the processing of the scene is ongoing, we'll let these people do their jobs, you and I need to plot out the venue. Panos is quite right, Amber, our best tool is CCTV, and as I recall, the DCI gave you that job."

"Yes, skip. Let's get started."

Chapter Five

The gurney, with an elasticated white cover concealing its passenger, began its short journey to the waiting black van, the words 'Private Ambulance' written across its rear doors. The few officers and civilian staff present stood respectfully still and upright as PC Sean Crisp finally left his post, watched by a knot of media men and curious members of the public held behind metal barriers at a discreet distance.

The quietude of the spot, such a short distance from Hyde Park Corner, one of London's busiest and most frenetic intersections, was preserved until the significance of the trolley and its mortal cargo came into view. The throng of waiting humanity held at the cordon suddenly shuddered and swelled like a single entity awakening, as at first photographers sprang into action, the synthesised electronic clack, clack, clack of virtual shutters violating the peace. Next the shoulder-mounted cameras of a dozen news channels swung in unison towards the scene, like guns on a battleship pivoting towards their target.

Evidently, someone in the press throng was in contact with the circling helicopter because as the group wheeling the trolley reached the rear of the ambulance, its doors opened from inside by an unseen hand, the machine descended and banked alarmingly, manoeuvring in a tight circuit of the square, the better to film the events unfolding below. Grant had just exited the Adriatic Cultural Institute, a few doors down from the Turkish embassy, an evidence bag holding an archaic VHS tape from the building's security cameras gripped tightly in his hand. He watched the unfolding scene with distaste.

Ironically, the most important venue for CCTV evidence was the one to which they were still forbidden access. Although the body of Sean Crisp had been removed to the mortuary for close forensic examination, the scene of the crime, the steps leading to the front door of the embassy, and the area on the footpath immediately outside were still being examined. Whilst this process was underway, the embassy remained firmly shut. Grant was relieved to hear via his personal radio that embassy security officers were aware of his presence and access to the all-important video recordings were preserved and would be available to him.

Amber Bennett crossed the road towards Grant as he stood staring up at the helicopter which wheeled away to track the departing ambulance, he shook his head in irritated bemusement. Amber held up a large property bag which contained many smaller containers. "Half a dozen discs and memory sticks from last night and this morning, listed, named, numbered, and exhibited."

"Good work, any issues or problems?" Asked Grant.

Amber shrugged. "Three needed authorisation from a supervisor who isn't available at this precise moment to release copies of their recordings, but there are no objections, just red tape. Everyone knows to secure the CCTV evidence, no re-recording, and the three will be available for us within twenty-four hours. Another three buildings are locked up and uncontactable, understandable considering..." Amber nodded to the cordon tape and uniformed officers strategically placed all around the square.

"Did you view any of the film?" Grant enquired.

Amber shrugged. "Only to confirm the correct times and dates, not the actual..." she paused. "I'll use our facilities back at base to examine them properly, the priority was to rush around the buildings and get our hands on the stuff."

Grant nodded his approval and was about to report his progress when the portly shape of DS Panos approached the pair, declaring, "Well, as he's on his way now, I thought I'd give you an update."

"That's good of you," Grant responded, "I know you're busy, liaison on a case like this can be a thankless job, but there's little that's more important.

I've been there, don't think you're not appreciated." It *was* true, but Grant was oiling the wheels of co-operation as requested by the DCI. A little bit of flattery and gratitude directed to the locals could only help in the long run.

Panos positively glowed as he responded, a little flustered at the unexpected praise. "Well, yes, right. You're welcome." He consulted an A4-sized pad and scanned a page within its many leaves. "Okay, this is all initial stuff and subject to verification. My control room has spoken with the embassy, who've viewed their tapes; they *do* have the attack recorded, timed at 05.18 hours." Grant sighed with undisguised relief as Panos continued his report. "As soon as the scene is signed off by forensics, you can enter and view it; that shouldn't be long now. The initial scene report from the attending doctor is grim. The victim suffered catastrophic, multiple stab wounds to the left side of the neck and throat, which were made with such force that the knife exited on the right side of the neck." Panos paused to let the shocking details sink in. "Like I said before, it indicates rage, fury, and overkill, and the side of the damage indicates a righty, not a lefty. The post-mortem will give much more, but she felt that the weapon must have had an incredibly sharp and broad blade to have caused so much penetration and tissue damage, on the way in *and* on the way out. The victim had a defence wound to his left hand; it looked as if Sean had clamped his hand over the wound to his neck. Panos unconsciously held his hand to the side of his throat. "The next stab went straight through the back of his hand. *Every* stab wound was a fatal injury on its own," Panos shook his head sadly, "but it wasn't enough for our guy." Panos's voice dripped with restrained anger. "It looks like the ultimate cause of death will be a single gunshot to the brain, the entry point through the right eye. A 9mm casing was found a few feet from the body, apparently ejected from the weapon, so an automatic not a revolver. At this point, common sense says it was Sean's own Glock 17 handgun, which is missing."

"Ammunition?" Asked Grant.

"The spare magazine was still in its pouch on his belt-rig," Panos replied.

"Hmmm." Grant pondered out loud. "He missed a trick there, either he didn't know about the spare mag or was in a hurry, panicking maybe?

Stabbing and shooting a police officer to death isn't an everyday occurrence. So, he has a Glock with sixteen rounds left in the magazine out of the original seventeen."

"And the Taser. He took the Taser too," interrupted Panos.

"How many cartridges has he got?" Panos turned to observe Amber, who'd asked the question.

"Just two. The one fitted for immediate use and the spare, which is set in the handgrip. The other two were still held in their Velcro pouches on Sean's belt."

"You must be right, skip, this guy was in a desperate rush to get the hell away from the scene. If the only motive was to take the weapons, surely he would have grabbed as much ammo as he could?"

"We have a partial shoeprint." Panos dropped the information casually but was fully aware of its significance. "Imprint of a training shoe, in blood as you'd expect. Giving the decamp direction as South East towards Upper Belgrave Street. Distance between the diminishing traces indicates he was running, as well he might."

"That's good news." Grant couldn't disguise his satisfaction. It was at least some tangible evidence that could be linked to a suspect, pending the bulk of forensic reports. "The central database should be able to give us make, style, and size from the tread pattern. If by any good luck it's a rarity, we may even be able to track down a manageable number of purchases to sift through." Grant balled his hand into a fist and shook it enthusiastically as he spoke. "One other thing, Panos, regarding the recovered shell casing, we need it sent to ballistics asap, to examine it for the firing pin scrape mark, it'll be as unique as a fingerprint."

Panos grinned. "Already on its way." Grant grinned back. The little fat fellah seemed to be on top of his game.

Chapter Six

Sometimes foreknowledge isn't enough. Amber and Grant stood side by side in the security office of the Turkish embassy behind the seated guard who operated the buttons controlling the images on the bank of monitors before them. They both knew they'd be viewing the murder of a police officer. They knew that. They even knew the probable sequence of events and certainly its conclusion. Still, that foreknowledge wasn't enough to dilute the shock and pure horror of what unfolded on the screen before their eyes.

Amber was surprised at the no-frills dinginess of the décor as soon as the ornate public area of the embassy was left behind to traverse the private corridors of a utilitarian, working building. They followed the grim-faced security officer to what he called 'the box' down several staircases to the basement. 'The box' was a small windowless room, in which nine monitors displayed the pick-up from internal and external CCTV cameras.

The guard was waiting at his seat when the two detectives and their escort entered. He twisted and offered his hand and, in halting, accented English, said, "I sorry this happen here. All here sorry." Grant accepted the hand and the sentiment graciously. "Ready?" The guard asked.

Grant looked questioningly to Amber, who nodded. "Ready," Grant said.

The camera was seated high in the portico, looking over the steps to the street level and out across the road towards the central gardens of Belgrave Square. Although the film was in colour, the lateness of the hour, the drabness of the scene, and the poor quality of the street lighting provided a near monochrome reproduction.

The silhouette of a police officer's head and shoulders came into view, the face under the flat cap in profile as the officer looked left and right, then down to examine something to his left.

"He's looking at his watch," said Grant. The time shown in hours, minutes, and seconds ticked onwards, overlaid in white at the bottom of the recording. "See, it's 4.16 am. He's due to be relieved soon."

Amber read from her notebook, "It's PC Gareth Took, he was the early start officer, sharing the post with Sean." Grant nodded, acknowledging the information without looking away from the screen.

The film ran on. From the right, lights illuminated the roadway in the top half of the screen, and moments later, a marked police car came into view, halting immediately in front of the embassy.

Amber glanced at her notebook once more, reading the transcribed information which had been relayed to her mobile from DC Pat Kerrigan, who, with 'Dirty' Don Chamberlain, was collecting evidence from Sean Crisp's traumatised colleagues. "That'll be Sergeant Christopher Fallon dropping Sean off at the post."

Grant and Amber watched as the figure of Gareth Took skipped swiftly down the steps towards the car, wisps of white, exhaled air marking his descent to street level. Amber blinked swiftly, sudden emotion threatening to spill out as tears at the sight of Sean Crisp exiting the car. She could see him smiling, a broad grin across his face with its distinctive pointed red beard and swashbuckling moustache. He hadn't changed a bit in the years since they'd worked together. Amber watched as Sean and Gareth exchanged banter, both in profile for a few moments, both laughing. Amber knew her friend only had an hour to live. She felt a ridiculous urge to warn him, to change what had already happened, to save a life already lost. The timer in the corner of the screen showed 04:17:46.

The observers watched as Sean Crisp adjusted his clothing and kit, his head turning left and right, scanning the environment, apparently satisfied, he ascended the steps until he too, like Gareth Took a few minutes earlier, was a silhouette of head and shoulders. Grant and Amber watched intently as the figure shook vigorously for a few moments.

"What's happening?" Asked Amber.

"I think he's stamping his feet, he's just left the warmth of the base room, he's freezing," suggested Grant. "Fast forward, please, to a few minutes before the attack." The operator complied.

The minutes and seconds on the timer counted onwards to 05:11:15. Sean's figure suddenly moved to the left, body leaning forward, his head turning to the right. "He's seen something, he's opening the angle to look at something or someone on the right, out of shot." There was a tremble in Grant's voice, anticipation mixed with distress. Was this Sean's first view of his murderer? They watched and waited, only seconds later they saw Sean shake his head to himself and resume his position in the centre of the portico, apparently satisfied he'd just experienced a case of 'night duty eyes', a common condition amongst police after dark, seeing all sorts of suspicious shapes and figures in the shadows.

The timer indicated 05:14:33. Once more, Sean Crisp's attention was drawn to something out of sight of the camera lens over to the right of the square. They knew this was it, the final few moments of a life, ticking away. After a minute of observing, Sean descended the steps of the portico, turned to his right, and looked out along the path. The watchers could see he was calling out to someone, he took several steps forward, moving to the right-hand edge of the monitor where he halted, assuming a 'bladed stance', left foot forward, right foot back, the holster with his weapon furthest from the point of contact with a possible threat. He raised his arms, one across his front, the other up to his chin.

"Thinking Policeman's pose, standard officer safety posture. But he looks relaxed, Sarge, ready, but relaxed, he's not perceiving any real threat." Amber was right, Sean Crisp wasn't anticipating the reality of the next few seconds. He had no idea what was coming.

The darkly clad figure emerged from the gloom on the right side of the screen at 05:17:04. He, and from the height, build, and posture, it seemed a reasonable assumption the figure was a 'he', approached Sean slowly. He was wearing a hoodie which was pulled up and forward giving no hint of the features that were hidden within, most alarmingly, both his hands were thrust deep into his pockets as he moved slowly towards the waiting officer. Amber wanted to scream out her warning, 'Draw your weapon, run away, do something!' Instead, she silently watched the tableau unfold. It was a sudden and slight movement, a change in the demeanour of the officer, the slightest movement of his head, a dropping of his hands a fraction. It was apparent to the viewers that Sean had been surprised by something, but the dark figure, as close as he was, hadn't moved in any threatening way; his hands were still thrust far into the pockets of his hoodie. Whatever had surprised Sean Crisp, it *still* wasn't something that he perceived as a threat.

05:17:20. Foreknowledge *wasn't* enough. When it came, Amber jumped with surprise. Grant felt his muscles suddenly strain and his hands rise, an automatic action of vicarious self-preservation, very human responses to the suddenness and horror of the attack. The dark shape that was the hooded figure changed in an instant from a still form into a lightning-fast blur of violence. The right arm withdrew from the pocket and swung in an accelerating arc, slamming with colossal force into the left side of Sean's neck. The transfer of such momentous kinetic energy pushed the stricken officer to his right, his cap flying backwards, his right arm flung upwards. Such was the speed of the attack and the angles involved, it wasn't until the hand withdrew that what it contained became visible. The blade was wide, its long belly narrowing to a savage point. Grant and Amber recognised the distinctive profile of a chef's knife.

The blade plunged into Sean's neck, slicing as it went into flesh, carving as it exited. The victim clamped his left hand defensively, across a savage wound, it was pierced, penetrated as if it wasn't there. Amber's hand was over her mouth, her chest heaving, her heart pounding. Grant's face was taut, mouth narrowed, lips strained and tight, teeth clenched. The seated guard lowered his head, he'd watched the recording several times before, he felt no need to see it again. Behind Grant, the escorting guard softly whispered foreign words; it sounded like a prayer.

Sean Crisp's knees buckled; he sank rather than fell, the arterial spray of blood pouring liberally from his throat and neck as he did so. The attacker stood back, his face still hidden, but his body heaved, his shoulders rising and falling, evidence of the physical effort generated for the assault. The dark pool began to spread, the poor light sparing the viewers from the lividity of the liquid's true redness.

The assailant gathered himself, pushing the shining knife back into the right pocket of the hooded jacket. Grant forced himself to observe and see as a detective, looking for evidence from the horror film playing out. "The pocket's a cut out, a sheath set in the bottom to hide a knife that big. He'd prepared for this, it wasn't a spontaneous act." It was a telling observation. The killer lunged forward, stretching over the stricken body, grasping Sean's handgun, still secure in its holster, and shook it violently. "He's not familiar with retention holsters; he's struggling to remove the gun," Grant commented, his efforts to disassociate his emotions from his job finally taking over. A few moments after he spoke, the weapon came free, and the hooded figure took a step back.

"He's right-handed," observed Amber. "It looks like he's screaming at Sean. God, I wish we had sound. Look at his body language, he's raging." Amber's words were superfluous; anyone with eyes to see couldn't fail to recognise the fury in the figure waving the gun in the face of the prostrate policeman.

Then he stilled. The handgun held steady. The arm flexed. The weapon's muzzle pointing directly into the victim's face. The soundless flash. The recoil. The shooter's hand flung upwards and to the left. The victim's head driven back. The stillness of several seconds as if someone had hit the pause button. It was done. The timer on Sean Crisp's life displayed 05:18:22.

The Task Force's detectives watched as the figure pulled the X-26 from its holster and, with a pistol in one hand and the Taser in the other, disappeared off the screen, leaving its left-hand side, heading southeast, towards Upper Belgrave Street.

In the small room they called the box, there was silence, eventually broken by gentle words. "Are you okay?" Grant's question was near to a whisper.

"No." Amber managed to reply. "Not even close to okay."

Nor was Grant.

Chapter Seven

The world outside the Task Force office was one of flags at half mast, of tributes by politicians, senior officers, and grim-faced news channel presenters. At the cordon surrounding Belgrave Square, uniform officers accepted extravagant bouquets, humble bunches of flowers, and single blooms from well-wishers wanting to pay their respects. Blossoms of every hue were laid at a forensically approved point against a wall fifty yards from the site of the murder, the flowers interspersed with teddy bears, children's crayon pictures, and religious tokens. The shrine, what else could it be called, grew in size by the hour, and once the Met's Press Bureau released Sean Crisp's personal details on the late afternoon of his death, the flow of tributes increased dramatically.

The world inside the Task Force office was one of frenetic activity. The core officers of the team were joined, or more often re-joined, by others whose daily duties were based in CID main offices scattered about the stations of The Met. As familiar faces passed through the office doors, hands were gripped, backs slapped, and determined expressions exchanged. As the complement of officers took shape, as DCI Paul Winter assigned tasks and investigative actions in the first few hours after the murder, the atmosphere was one of concentrated, relentless determination. It was a mood Grant Maddox, in all his years of policing, had never seen or felt before. It felt right.

In the corner of the office, Charlie One and Charlie Two were at the centre of much of the activity. Charles Buller, in his mid-fifties, had spent nearly fifteen years as an Admin Officer, then an Executive Officer, in the civilian administrative branch of the Met Police. Civil Service AOs and EOs provided the backbone of the police support staff, and Charles had worked in numerous diverse roles and locations before hitting a career brick wall by failing to reach the Higher Executive Officer rank. In his mid-thirties and needing a fresh impetus, he re-trained as a Crime Analyst and later as an operator of the computerised system excruciatingly named the Home Office Large Major Enquiry System or 'HOLMES'. A shameless nod to Conan Doyle's great detective.

The contrivance of the system name hid a huge leap forward in investigative processes, replacing the laborious and inefficient card system of logging intelligence by hand. In the 'bad old days', prior to HOLMES, press-ganged officers, invariably women who were viewed as less useful than men on the streets, acted as 'Indexers' and were required to literally write, file and cross-reference record-cards with all the attendant personal variations, complications and opportunities to lose information. In a major investigation, it became impossible to access the mass of available evidence, and no single person could ever oversee the whole operation.

HOLMES changed all that and became the repository of all intel and data relating to an investigation, the go-to point to retrieve information on victims, suspects, associates, vehicles, addresses, telephone numbers, and any links between any of these inputs. The D.R.E. 'Dynamic Reasoning Engine' facility of the later, upgraded versions of HOLMES, was even able to self-analyse and suggest lines of enquiry previously unconsidered by the human components of the enquiry. Little wonder, then, that detectives considered the operators of the system as proponents of the dark arts. Charles Buller was the Task Force HOLMES operator and, until the arrival of Charlotte, naturally enough, was simply called 'Charlie.'

Charlotte Trent was known as 'Charlie' by all her family and friends since early childhood. She was a native of Birmingham in the heart of England's Black Country, and spoke with a strong West Midlands accent. On hearing Charlotte, many Londoners stereotyped her as being less than sharp, but Charlie was blessed with a superior, analytical mind; the ridiculers soon learned they couldn't have been more wrong.

Charlotte had been gripped at a young age by television's obsession with all things forensically themed. From reruns of *Quincy M.E.* to every incarnation of *CSI*, from *Waking the Dead* to *Silent Witness*, Charlotte lapped it all up. She wasn't alone. When she attended university to take her degree in Forensic Science it seemed everyone wanted to be a Sam Ryan, Nikki Alexander, or Mac Taylor, small-screen characters who, in immaculate white coats, glared determinedly at a DNA sample, obtained in under three minutes, which miraculously provided the name, current address and inside leg measurement of the suspect, who was *always* at home when the police called. As Charlotte's degree course concluded, the chief executive of the Forensic Science Service commented on the abundance of Forensic Science graduates, '*I'm not sure where all these people are going to work?*' He was right. Stymied in her ambition to wear a white coat and stare at a test tube, Charlotte Trent instead re-directed her enthusiasm to computer-based crime detection, winning her place beside the vastly experienced Charles Buller in the Major Investigation Task Force. It seemed only natural, to avoid confusion, that whilst the incumbent should become Charlie One, she should be known as Charlie Two.

* * *

The twenty digits that belonged to the two Charlies were a blur as the initial input data, which would form the baseline of the investigation into Sean Crisp's murder, was entered onto the system. The crowd of detectives, wads of papers in hand, stood with varying degrees of patience at the shoulders of the typing analysts, voicing the importance and therefore priority of *their* information compared to a compatriot in an attempt to jump the queue.

Charlie Two, although the younger and least experienced of the pair, was the calmer and more affable personality. "Guys, we'll get to you all, how about a bit of patience, eh?" She offered by way of placation.

Charlie One, grumpier by nature and having spent his working life surrounded by the blunt profanity of police officers, had become infected with the same condition. His response to the bustle markedly different from his partner's, he turned on Pat Kerrigan, whose exasperated sigh was a little too loud. "Wait your fucking turn and give me a fucking break. Inconsiderate bastard."

Grant, sitting at his desk observing the mêlée, allowed himself a smile at the scene; it was always thus at the beginning. He realised it was the first time he'd smiled that day, feelings were still raw, that would ease, and the funniest job in the world would reassert itself eventually. It always did, it was one of the best features of his chosen career, that and the satisfaction derived from doing what he perceived as 'good'. It made each day a worthwhile effort.

He'd read and re-read the last line of the scene-of-crime summary he was typing several times over, a sure sign he needed to rest his old eyes and take a break. His synopsis would form part of the progress meeting in thirty minutes. It needed to be accurate, contain all relevant information, but be succinct enough for the facts to be retainable to minds already being jammed full.

Amber's desk, next to his, was piled with clear plastic evidence bags. Full of discs, tapes, and memory sticks. She was mumbling words and numbers to herself as she looked from the exhibit list she was compiling to the contents of each bag. The tip of her tongue peeked out of the corner of her mouth, a sure sign of the concentration level as she compiled her inventory, noting each item, its origin, its exhibit number, its property book entry, and, until properly viewed, its likely content. It was a laborious task, but one if properly completed would make life much easier in the days, weeks, or months ahead. Legal challenges to continuity of evidence, provenance, authenticity, and admissibility could be batted away if this chore was properly undertaken. Vital it was. Glamorous it was not.

"They never show some poor bastard wading through all this lot in the Hollywood versions of policing, do they?" observed Grant. His interruption was an error.

"Sorry? What are you talking about?" she turned to her sergeant, a frown of deep concentration being joined by irritation at his intrusion.

"Sorry. Carry on, ignore me." Amber turned her attention back to her lists and her bags and her exhibits, shaking her head as she did so. Thankfully, the arrival of Detective Inspector Heidi Yorke provided the excuse he needed to vacate his seat, stretch his muscles, and leave Amber in the peace she needed to complete her work.

Heidi Yorke cut a striking figure as she strolled into the Task Force office. She was smartly dressed in a dark suit over a pale blue blouse; the skirt, which hugged narrow hips, reached below the knee. She wore practical, low-heeled black shoes and, apart from gold stud earrings, was devoid of jewellery. Heidi, in her mid-forties, kept her blonde hair cut short and neat, what little make-up she wore was concentrated about her blue eyes. Her most conspicuous feature, however, was her height, six feet two in her bare feet. Slim and athletic, she couldn't be described as beautiful, but Heidi smiled easily and was devoid of meanness or self-importance, which made her attractive. Possessing enough confidence to seek advice from those who knew more than she did, whatever their rank, DI Yorke was also prepared to challenge the bully-boys and misogynistic dinosaurs that still roamed the hinterland of the police service.

Grant strode towards Heidi, who was acknowledging the greetings of the assembled officers she knew and saying hello to those she didn't. "Good to see you, Guv." He offered. "Annual leave cancelled and back to find a cop-killer. You must be thrilled."

The Detective Inspector shrugged. "Hiya Granty, it was only a visit to my dad in Cornwall, he'll survive, and coming back to find the bastard who did this… well, is there a better reason to cut short a break?"

"Put like that, no, of course not. The DCI has the first progress meeting at six, but we'll get you up to speed before that. He's in the glass box, and I'll bet he's still on the phone."

Heidi smiled, "I bet he is, all day, I'm guessing." The two made their way towards Paul Winter's office. Grant noted a feeling inside, a feeling of completeness now that Heidi was back. As the case had begun to unfold, her absence in something so big was palpable.

DI Yorke *had* been a member of Surrey Police; her investigation into the brutal murder of Martine Walsingham had crossed over with the Major Investigation Task Force investigation into what the media named The

Dissection Murder case, at the conclusion of which Heidi had transferred to the Met. The day Heidi had walked into the office as a permanent member of the team was one of Grant's favourites. He tapped the door to DCI Winter's office and entered. Paul *was* on the phone.

Chapter Eight

Paul scanned the group of officers and civilian support staff, his look traversing the room, taking in each face, making contact with every person. He took a deep breath and began. "Ladies and gents, for those of you who don't know me, I'm Detective Chief Inspector Paul Winter. I will be heading up this investigation into the murder of Police Constable Sean Crisp. This is Detective Inspector Heidi Yorke. She will be my deputy and involved in most of the day-to-day supervision and guidance of all your efforts." The DCI swept a long arm towards Heidi, who stood a short distance away, she nodded in acknowledgement. "Over there," Paul pointed to Grant, "is Detective Sergeant Grant Maddox. He's a very experienced investigator and, unlike the DI and myself, will be spending most of his time out there," Paul jabbed a finger several times towards the office windows, "on the street. Consider him your Section Sergeant and be directed by him." Grant stood at the mention of his name, waved awkwardly at the assembled group to identify himself to newcomers, sitting down as soon as was polite to do so.

"Now, ladies and gents, although we obviously all have a personal connection with this case, the victim was one of our own, do not lose sight of the fact that we do as we always do. We follow the evidence to wherever it takes us, we leave no stone unturned, we act without fear or favour, and we act within the law. If, when we get our hands on this bastard, I find that he slips through our fingers in court because someone has taken a shortcut, bent the rules or gilded a lily, I will personally fuck you right up. We owe it to Sean Crisp, his family, friends, and to everyone in this family of ours we call the Metropolitan Police to get this right. Got it?" He paused and a low mumble of assent rolled around the room.

"Good. That's out of the way then. Now I want to flag up that our victim, Sean Crisp, was known personally to one of our team, DC Amber Bennett, who has given some relevant information about him. Is there anyone else here who knew him, in any capacity? Anyone?"

A hand rose from the group in the centre of the room. "I was on the same basic firearms course as Sean. I knew him from there. A good lad. Funny. I liked him." Grant saw it was DC Craig Lines who had come to the Task Force after a spell on the Robbery Squad.

Another hand rose from the rear of the room. "We served together at Chiswick, not on the same relief. I was a sprog while he was an old sweat area car driver, so we didn't really rub shoulders, but he was very well thought of. Like Craig said, a funny guy, good company." The speaker, DC Pat Kerrigan, hesitated. "He was a bit of a ladies' man, did well on that score, if you know what I mean."

Paul Winter smiled. "My information is that he was an habitual shagger!" The tension broke, nervous laughter swept around the room. "Look, guys, I'm not condoning that behaviour, but none of us is an angel. We've *all* got history, and we've *all* got secrets. Sean Crisp is going to be no different, but if we're going to do him justice, we need to dig out his secrets, learn his history. If he was killed because of his extracurricular activities, then we need to know about it. Our priority is to find out if *his* murder was incidental or deliberately targeted. If what he was, or where he was, or what he possessed, was the motive. Was this an attack on a nameless, faceless police officer, simply because he was Old Bill? Was this connected to the Turkish embassy or Turkish-related policies at home or abroad, a politically related act? Was this a murder/robbery in order to take his weapons? Or was this the murder specifically of Sean Crisp?" Paul paused to let his words take effect.

"Okay… DC Nagur Padda here," Paul pointed the officer out, "has been delving into Sean's personal file with Human Resources. What can you tell us, Nags?"

The young detective, gripping a wad of papers, nervously stepped forward to stand before the Task Force and began to detail Sean Crisp's career path from his probation, his development courses, commendations, disciplinary history, and his eventual arrival at the DPG, the elite Diplomatic Protection Group. It was an enviable record. The only very minor blemishes on a twenty-three-year service profile were the receipt, on two occasions, of 'words of advice', the least and most minor of reprimands possible. One for forgetting to note mileage in a police vehicle log book and another for inappropriate language directed towards a member of the civilian support staff. It was piffling stuff. Of far more interest was the limited but revealing record of Sean Crisp's private life.

"The personal details held are limited, of course," imparted DC Padda. "The Job can only ask for and record details which are relevant to the subject's professional role, so next of kin, spousal details, partners, children, dependents, etcetera, are documented for contact or welfare purposes and for payment of any benefits, pension, Police Federation group insurance, and the like. What I'm saying is that what we have in the HR file is Sean's official activities, if you like, not what the guvnor called 'extra-curricular activities'." There was a murmur of low laughter around the office. The officers were starting to get a handle on their victim's personality.

"Anyway, this is what we have…officially. Sean Crisp married Deborah Spurgess twenty-one years ago, near the end of his probation period. She gave birth to their son, Callum, three months after the wedding. Sean and his family lived in police provided accommodation in Acton, West London, until he left his wife seven years later and rented privately in Brentford. He was working at Chiswick nick at the time. From the file of communications, reports, and appeals which relate to this time, it appears the break-up was *extremely* acrimonious. Deborah Crisp made repeated accusations of physical abuse and financial negligence, all of which were investigated and found to be baseless. The enquiry went all the way to Central Complaints at Tintagel House, overseen by a Detective Superintendent, so it was taken *very* seriously and dealt with thoroughly. The SIO concluded that Deborah's accusations were malicious and spiteful, intending to harm her husband's career and relationship with his new partner, Sienna."

Nagur looked down, consulting his notes before continuing. "The file shows Sienna Windham as cohabiting with Sean at the Brentford address and as being his next-of-kin in the case of emergency. Eleven years ago, they had a son, called Casper. Unfortunately, the relationship with Sienna came to an end six years after Casper's arrival, and Sean moved out of the Brentford property and into another rented flat in Staines, near Heathrow Airport. Three years ago, Elizabeth McKillop moved into this apartment with Sean. Sean's contact details were updated, and she was listed as his next of kin, as of that date up to today." There was a collective sigh around the room, which Nagur acknowledged.

"Yep! I know. A bit complicated, and as I said, that's just the official records. The curiosity is that Sean never divorced Deborah; it seemed to be a way around keeping her and Callum housed in free police accommodation. Strictly speaking, she was disqualified from that privilege, but she had made such a fuss, made so many allegations, and continued to make complaints about maintenance payments for her and Callum, that the relevant department felt it was easier to just leave her there. In the meantime, Sean was paying the rent on Sienna's property in Brentford *and* the flat he shared with Elizabeth in Staines. It seems that Sean was paying a satisfactory amount of maintenance to Sienna for Casper, with whom he had a good relationship. But his outgoings must have been phenomenal."

"Did the relationship with Deborah improve over the years?" Faces turned to the questioner, Heidi Yorke.

"No, Guv," responded Nagur. "Worse if anything, even Callum got involved. Eighteen months ago, Callum confronted his father outside the DPG base about paying for his university attendance. It turned into a punch-up, Callum ended up laying his father out. He was arrested, of course, but Sean refused to give a statement or substantiate an allegation against his son. So that answers your question."

"It does." Heidi was still rubbing her chin, thinking. "But Sean *is* still married to Deborah, right?"

"He wasn't planning on that being the case much longer." All heads swivelled to the speaker, DC 'Dirty' Don Chamberlain. "Pat and I went straight to Sean's DPG base this morning to question the team on duty last night, and this morning, we can fill you in on all that later, but this snippet of info is relevant. Sean Crisp had just got engaged to Lizzy McKillop. Sean's solicitor had informed Deborah he was finally divorcing her, a few days ago."

"Am I right in thinking," Heidi continued, "that as Sean has died *now*, before a divorce, that Deborah, as his wife, no matter how estranged, will receive the Police Pension death in service grant *and* the Police Federation group insurance payout *and* an index-linked police widows' pension for the rest of her life. Is that right?"

Don Chamberlain nodded, "That's exactly right, boss."

Chapter Nine

For a few pregnant seconds, silence descended on the assembled group. The catalogue of benefits listed by the DI to which Sean's long-since discarded wife would be entitled amounted to a considerable sum. The group insurance payment alone would be in six figures, the death in service lump sum, certainly as much as that again. As for the widow's pension, calculated on Sean Crisp's final salary, it would pay a monthly amount to Deborah Crisp for the rest of her life, index-linked. Who knew the financial value of that? Everyone was thinking the same thing: that quantity of money was certainly a motive to murder, and the bad blood between Sean and his son only added to the disturbing possibilities.

Heidi Yorke brought the team back. "Thank you, Nagur, you've painted quite a picture and we've a lot to look into. Okay, Don, as you've touched on what you've found out at the DPG base, do you and Pat want to take the floor?"

DC's 'Dirty' Don Chamberlain and Patrick Kerrigan addressed the Task Force, Pat speaking first. "All this information will be transcribed onto the daily sheet and will *eventually* be available to scrutinise on the HOLMES database." Pat glanced malevolently across at Charlie One, who'd so recently called him an 'inconsiderate bastard'. Charlie One wasn't winning any friends recently; impatience, mood swings, and a sharp tongue had become his default settings of late.

"Sean Crisp was working the late start, night duty shift," Pat Kerrigan began, "that's 11 pm last night to 7 am this morning. This was a rest day, he was working, for overtime, as we've heard Sean had a lot of reasons to be an 'overtime bandit'. If anyone went sick, if any new post came on, or an incident involving a hospital guard required extra hours at short notice, Sean Crisp was always at the front of the queue to work overtime. This caused some resentment; a couple of people, very discreetly, told us that he took more than his fair share. They understood he was under pressure financially but that was his own fault and a result of his lifestyle. The tour he worked last night was because an officer went sick yesterday afternoon. Sean was informed night duty was light by one man, and he called the duties office to offer his services. The point is that until 5.35 pm yesterday afternoon, no one knew that Sean Crisp would be working last night and this morning."

"Who told Sean there was an overtime shift going begging?" Heidi asked.

Don Chamberlain answered. "The night-duty section sergeant, Christopher Fallon. He's an old mate of Sean's and knew for certain he'd willingly come in at very short notice. Sean was always happy to take on the Turkish embassy, which wasn't a popular posting; it was described as 'gutty, dull and boring, with nothing and no one to look at'. Sergeant Fallon jiggled the duties, put Sean on his usual spot at the Turkish on Belgrave Square, freeing up the rostered bloke there to do something more interesting. Everyone's happy."

"So," Heidi concluded, "no one knew Sean was working that night until late afternoon, *and* until Sergeant Fallon jiggled the duties, no one knew that Sean would be posted at the Turkish embassy. Do we know if Sean told anyone when he was working or where?"

DC Pat Kerrigan answered. "Obviously, his partner Lizzy must have known, and any officer at the base with access to the duty roster." Pat consulted his notes, "PC Gareth Took told us that Sean mentioned he'd arranged to pick up his son Casper after school later that day, and he'd be staying overnight. So he must have told Casper's mum, Sienna, he was working. We can ask that when we start interviewing and accessing Sean's phone records."

"Okay, let's do that. Carry on." Heidi nodded her encouragement.

"Right," Pat continued, "we've said the Turkish embassy on Belgrave Square was considered a graveyard post, the area is very quiet at night, not much vehicular traffic, very few pedestrians, few residents, lots and lots of embassies, societies, institutes and associations are based in Belgrave Square, but they shut up shop and go home at 5 pm. As for last night, PC Gareth Took shared the posting with Sean, two hours each from 10.20 pm onwards, Sean was killed on his second stint, an hour after relieving Gareth."

"Did Gareth Took report anything unusual, anything suspicious?" The DCI asked.

"Sort of, Guv." Kerrigan equivocated. "He says he saw what he took to be a vagrant wandering about at 3am-ish. It was a freezing cold night, and he was a little surprised that this guy hadn't found a dark corner to settle down in. The description wasn't up to much, probably a male, wearing a dark hoodie, dark trousers, hunched walk, he walked slowly, bent over. No view of his face and doing nothing suspicious, just wandering around for a while, then he disappeared. Gareth says he handed the info over to Sean when he was relieved."

"Amber and I have seen the CCTV of the attack recorded by the embassy camera." Grant's voice cut across the room. "It's not a great description, but it *does* match the attacker."

"We need to find out how he got to the square, how he left, and how long he was waiting. Was he watching for Sean to arrive? We need to search the CCTV in the area, looking for this guy; we may get lucky and see his features. Also, we need to question the DPG officers. Has anyone else seen this hooded guy hanging around?"

"I'm on that, Sarge," Amber responded. "I'm on CCTV duty, it makes more sense for one person to coordinate it, leave that with me."

"I've obtained a list of all the officers in the past fortnight who worked on Belgrave Square. I'll work through them." Pat Kerrigan offered.

"Thank you, Amber, thank you, Pat." DCI Winter smiled encouragingly. "Carry on, what did you find out about Sean from his colleagues?"

Dirty Don took a deep breath, "As mentioned, Guv, Sean was very active with the ladies. It seems even when he was settled with a partner, he was playing about. However, his sergeant, Chris Fallon, an old friend, said Sean had confessed he was fed up with living such a complicated life. He said he'd just finished with someone, and she was the last one, ever. He'd decided to settle for Lizzy and Lizzy alone. Sean had proposed and started the process to divorce Deborah."

"Do we know who he'd just finished with?" Heidi asked.

"No. Sergeant Fallon didn't know, or didn't want to say."

Heidi nodded. "Okay. That's on an increasingly long list. Granty, can you tell us about your day?"

Grant stood and faced his colleagues. "The murder is captured on film, colour but poor quality. You'll all see it. It's grim. The attack itself is extremely sudden and extremely brutal. The suspect seems to have been seen by Sean, off camera, to the north west of the embassy. Sean appears to call to the suspect who approaches, he's only visible on the edge of the screen, but he matches Gareth Took's description of the 'vagrant' he saw earlier in the evening. As he gets closer, it looks as if Sean drops his guard slightly; he doesn't appear to perceive any threat whatsoever. The suspect pulls out what looks to be a chef's knife from the right-hand outside pocket of the hoodie. The length of the blade means the pocket must be a cutout, which indicates premeditation to me. Sean is stabbed three times in and through the left side of his neck. The injuries are catastrophic, and the degree of blood loss has to be seen to be believed. The victim collapses, and the suspect takes his sidearm. He visibly struggles with the retention holster but removes the weapon, a Glock 17 semi-automatic pistol, and shoots Sean through the right eye whilst apparently shouting at the victim. The film has no sound." Grant paused in his dispassionate description. Every face around him wore a fixed, taut expression.

Grant sighed deeply, then spoke again. "Obviously, it is very early days, we'll have forensic evidence to examine and chase up in the next twenty-four hours. We've got a footprint with a tread pattern in blood at the scene, which we can check against the database, and we still have hours of CCTV to examine. This is going to be a mammoth task which Amber is dealing with, I think too big for one officer, Guv, maybe Nagur could assist her?" Grant raised his eyebrows questioningly in Heidi's direction.

"Definitely. Nagur, you're teamed up with Amber," answered the DI.

"Thanks, Guv," Grant responded with a smile. "The tape of the attack needs some cleaning up and enhancing. We need to get a better look at the suspect's clothing and the knife in particular."

"I'll liaise with the techies on that." Amber offered.

"One last thing, boss," Grant looked to the DCI, "There's a local DS, called Panos, just Panos, his surname is unpronounceable. He knew his stuff and the area, could be an asset, a temporary attachment maybe? Perhaps a phone call?"

"Detective Sergeant Panos Unpronounceable? I'll see what I can do." Paul winked. "Okay then, people." DCI Winter's voice communicated the conclusion of the briefing. "I have a meeting with our Press Officer to put a release and an appeal together, and then a press conference which our people want to go out on the ten o'clock news bulletins. Heidi, will you arrange to meet with PC Crisp's family, past *and* present? Maybe you can untangle the complicated life of our victim. It'll need delicate handling, but we need the full story, warts and all. Grant, sorry, but someone has to do it, the post mortem, it's scheduled for 9am tomorrow. As for the rest of the team, DI York will assign your actions and tasks. Carry on. Thank you, everyone. Let's get going."

Chapter Ten

Grant Maddox heaved his exhausted body from the car. It was close to 2am, and he was due back in the office, a forty minute drive away, at 7am. As he staggered to his front door, sorting through the keys on the ring, trying and failing to find the right one, he pondered on his fate. Taking into account his military service, he should soon have been able to retire and enjoy a comfortable existence with his beloved wife, Lydia. Fate, his devotion to his family, and the actions of a low-life scumbag, had put paid to that. The scumbag in question, was his eldest daughter's husband, who'd deserted Constance only weeks before the birth of their daughter Saffron. Now Connie and Saffy lived with Grant and Lydia, the scumbag leaving his child and grandchild homeless and near destitute. Even as his youngest daughter, Monza, had left home to begin her career as a police officer, Connie had moved back in, and with a small, perfectly formed, bow-lipped mouth to feed.

Grant felt not an atom of resentment at this turn of Fate; supporting his family, emotionally and financially, was his duty and his joy. Grant Maddox was a family man through and through and proud of the fact. During his promotion interview, he'd been asked what his hobbies and interests were, he'd give a single word answer. 'Family'. The upshot of the present situation was the impending prospect of his retirement had faded to a point in the far future. Downsizing the house, moving to the seaside, and basking in what was nowadays called 'me-time', was no longer discussed.

Having eventually found the correct key, Grant approached his front door, directing it towards the brass circle marked 'Yale'. To his weary bewilderment, the key never seemed to get any closer to its intended target. His mental faculties, so depleted by fatigue, failed to register the reality that the door was opening before him, still attempting to engage the key in the hole, he nearly fell through the doorway.

The light from the streetlamp passed over his shoulder to illuminate the soft features of his wife, Lydia, peering around the edge of the door. Grant's body relaxed; he was home.

* * *

Although he could almost hear his bed calling to him from upstairs, he sank onto the armchair in the sitting room, gripping the mug of tea which Lydia had prepared for him.

"Poor you. It's been all over the news, it's too awful, terrible." Lydia's face was lined with sadness and worry. "I knew you'd be dealing with it, as soon as your text said, 'sorry, I'll be late', I knew what it was. Did you think I wouldn't know?"

Grant shrugged resignedly, his eyebrows rising to express his helplessness. "I *never* want you to know, I never want you to worry. It's bad enough as it is without details you don't need to hear about."

Lydia shook her head slowly. "The news report said he had a partner. I thought about the poor woman, saying goodbye last night, kissing him bye-bye. Exchanging a few words about the following day, things to do, shopping, seeing family, normal mundane stuff, and then getting the knock at the door. *The* knock."

Grant stretched across the space between them and squeezed his wife's hand. "Oh, Lyddy, you mustn't torture yourself. We both know terrible things happen in this world…" Grant winced inwardly at his words, looking to see if his carelessness had reawakened memories of the 'terrible thing' which had happened in *their* world. The terrible thing that had happened to his Lydia. The thing that was his fault. He continued, not missing a beat. "…But we all have to carry on, do our best, live our lives." Grant winced again. How many more meaningless platitudes could he slip into one sentence?

He sighed and slumped back into his seat, staring down at his tea.

Lydia nodded, her face giving no indication that her husband's words had brought back the memories of the pivotal moment of her life, the day she'd received *the* knock on her door and heard the worst words imaginable. But the words were lies, part of an elaborate ruse to take her, to hurt and debase her, to punish her husband with an act which they would both carry with them forever. It had worked.

* * *

Grant recognised from the earliest days of their relationship that Lydia had been what his mother described as 'delicate'. Lydia's nervousness didn't bother Grant an iota; he'd fallen in love with her in an instant, and the more he found out about her, the more convinced he became that his initial judgment that she was 'The One' was confirmed. Lydia was feminine, kind, quiet, always considerate of others, humane, forgiving, loving, warm and homely. Grant wanted a wife who needed him, who wanted to care for him, and for whom he could care, protect, and provide for in return. Perhaps these weren't very modern views or desires, but they synced with each other, their relationship worked, and they were happy.

Grant's active service as a Royal Marine in the Falklands War and his tours of Northern Ireland at the height of 'The Troubles' were subjects he rarely spoke of with Lydia; she didn't need to hear of the horrors seen or the terrors experienced, and Grant didn't feel the need to speak of them out loud. They'd married as Grant's probationary period as a constable had ended, and the baby who would be their first daughter, Constance, was kicking up a fuss in Lydia's expanding tummy.

Grant's previous military experience had led him inexorably towards a career as a police firearms officer, and he served with great distinction on Armed Response Vehicles for eight years, taking promotion to sergeant in the process. If he was honest with himself, he knew the toll of worry and stress his work was taking on his wife, but he was revelling in his role as a specialist and knew he was doing some good, too. The turning point came on a tragic day in a shopping mall with his colleague and close friend, Babatunde Okafor, when the rampage of a mentally disturbed person resulted in numerous stabbings of shoppers. Called to the scene, Grant and 'Babs' confronted the suspect, fearing for the life of an unarmed police woman. Both armed officers chose to shoot the suspect, but Babs fired first, killing the troubled knifeman.

Grant made an awful mistake, he'd told Lydia the shocking story, mentally she imagined a different result to the incident, one which ended with the knock every police wife or husband dreads, the one where the open door reveals a grim faced senior officer and the words, 'May I come in?'

He'd made a huge error in telling her. Her mental fragility, the subsequent tears and hysteria, the questions, and ever more gruesome conjectures of her febrile imaginings poured out. Grant realised that something had to give, for the sake of his wife. What gave was his career as a firearms officer. Within the week, he'd applied to the CID. The rationale that a chiefly desk-bound position would remove the anxiety suffered by Lydia regarding her husband's chosen profession. It should have been…but then there was Saleh Cesar, and everything changed.

The vast majority of the time, Lydia functioned perfectly normally. She was a dutiful and caring mother to their two daughters, was affectionate and loving with her husband, and a peerless keeper of their house. However, Lydia rarely ventured beyond the front threshold, became immobilised with dread if the doorbell rang unexpectedly, and despite knowing and battling her inner demons, needed and relied on Grant utterly.

It was the trauma of that terrible twenty-four hours, of Saleh Cesar, that shattered the happiest of marriages as a bullet would a mirror. The shards could never be repaired to be as before. The physical side of Grant and Lydia's relationship had ended that day, a tragedy for Grant, who loved and desired his wife as much as the day he'd placed a ring on her finger, but the love between them was strong and enduring. Despite all, there was a happy and contented marriage. There, too, was hope. Time healed.

* * *

Grant looked up from his tea to the pretty face of his wife. "The officer who died," he chose not to say 'murdered' or 'butchered'. "It was quick. He didn't have time to know what was happening or to suffer," he lied. "Single gunshot, 9mm to the head." He snapped his fingers. "Quick and clean. If you've got to go, it's as good a way as any." Grant shrugged. He couldn't hide the reality of Sean Crisp's murder, but he could try and diminish the savagery of it. "We'll get who did it. Okay?"

Lydia smiled weakly. "Okay. If you're on the case, you'll get him…But Grant. Promise me, give me your word, you won't take any risks. I couldn't bear it, no risks, promise. Not like last time. Promise." Lydia's eyes welled to overflowing.

"Of course, Lyddy, I promise." He reached across and squeezed her hand once more. "I really need to sleep, my gorgeous, I have to be up at silly o'clock, let's go to bed. And no more worrying, okay? I'm a desk jockey, safe as houses."

Lydia squeezed his hand back and smiled. She knew when her husband was lying, and she'd just heard a whopper…and loved him all the more for it.

Chapter Eleven

He was still breathless. The adrenaline rush hadn't fully abated. The fact was, the *physical* high point had been the act of withdrawing his hand, grasping the knife, and plunging it into yielding flesh. But the *emotional* high was the instant preceding that irretrievable step which had been almost sexual in its mounting excitement and anticipation. Once the hand was out, once the dull street lighting had glinted off the exposed steel, the plunging with all his might of the blade into that bastard's throat was irrevocable. The deed *had* to be done.

The nerve-jangling moment of decision was the peak, but his adrenal glands continued in their frantic exertions, pumping their stimulant into his system as he stretched over the expiring body and struggled to release the handgun from its holster and fire a bullet into that ridiculous moustachioed and pretentiously bearded face. The fight and flight hormone coursed through veins and arteries as he fled the scene on his circuitous, pre-planned route home.

He stealthily closed his bedroom door, sinking onto the bed, shrugging off the black rucksack from his shoulders, and rubbed his face. The act of closing the door was the symbolic moment of safety; he'd done it and got away with it. The breathlessness eased.

He wanted to unzip the rucksack, wanted to savour his prizes, but his meticulous and systematic mind inhibited the act. He needed to review his progress to this point, looking for mistakes which could be rectified, seeing through the eyes of those who would be hunting him, trying to stop him before he was finished. Finished in all meanings of the word.

The stolen cycle was sure to be found, possibly, no, *probably*, stained with the policeman's blood. So be it, there would be nothing of his on it, certainly no fingerprints. He'd worn two pairs of rubber gloves, in case one should tear, exposing a betraying fingertip of ridges, whorls, and valleys for the experts to search for and find in their records. The gloves were disposed of separately in four public wastebins far from the scene of his crime. As he'd anticipated, his training shoes had been spattered in blood on their uppers and soles. Hidden in a plastic bin bag, he'd tossed them into a skip to lie beside countless other such waste sacks. Those shoes had been bought with cash at Shepherd's Bush Market, with no incriminating CCTV that he had seen, and besides, his face was hidden by the hoodie and a stooped posture. Even if found, they wouldn't lead a detective to him. The pre-placed bag, hidden in the park, had contained new training shoes for him to wear, bought in a similar manner but from a different location. As for the clothes he stood up in, each item would be disposed of. Scattered around West London, nothing could be traced back to him. Satisfied, he unzipped the rucksack.

He laid the gun and the Taser next to each other on the bed cover and stared at them reverentially. He lifted the handgun, the Glock 17, a semi-automatic pistol. He knew about this weapon, made in Austria, it held a magazine of seventeen 9mm bullets, the number '17' being a manufacturer's designation and having nothing to do with its ammunition capacity. Each round would leave the muzzle travelling at over 1,200 feet per second, near to 850mph. It was a simple, reliable, and lethal weapon, he'd already proved that. A sudden image of Sean Crisp invaded his thoughts, his body jerking backwards as the small projectile slammed fatally into his face.

He pressed both trophies back into the rucksack, which he pushed under his bed. He was suddenly very tired; he needed to sleep.

Chapter Twelve

The constant background thrum of office chatter was intermittently pierced by a call across the room, a question, a statement, or a banter-based comment, rising above the rest of the hubbub. The early few days of any major investigation followed the same hectic pattern until the relevant investigative areas of responsibility, the various lines of enquiry, and the targeting of the likeliest suspects emerged from the chaotic mist in an organised and tangible form. For now, the Task Force members were sorting themselves out. Phones were pressed to ears as appointments were made for interviews and statement taking. Tasks were dished out or swapped about to suit skills, interests, or just plain convenience. Fingers tapped computer VDUs with satisfaction, annoyance, or exasperation as the glowing screens did or didn't provide the information its viewer demanded of it.

Grant was once more reviewing the complex personal life of Sean Crisp as he sipped at a piping hot coffee, which was injecting a degree of consciousness into his flagging mind and body. He'd gotten less than four hours sleep before the alarm told him it was time to drag his carcass to the shower and start the process of getting to work. As he drove into London, the traffic still light before the rush hour proper, he'd speculated on his major role of the day. The post mortem to be performed on Sean Crisp's near bloodless body at 9am.

Grant had lost count of the number of these procedures he'd witnessed over the years. From the heart-wrenching sadness of the pathetic little body of a dead child, to the horror of a full-burn victim, blackened, unidentifiable, with arms and legs bent and contracted into the so-called pugilist posture, to the disgusting, stomach-turning, nasal-assaulting repugnance of a decomposed cadaver. He'd seen them all, over and over again. Today, he'd attend the forensic examination of a freshly deceased body, violated by an act of savagery for sure, but not intrinsically a horror when compared to much that had gone before. The difference was this was 'one of ours'. His thoughts flew unchecked to the imagined scenario which could have been a reality a dozen times over, of a *different* Detective Sergeant, driving to work, musing on the task ahead of him, attending the post mortem of Grant Maddox.

Amber Bennett had barely spoken to him since his arrival, totally absorbed as she was with a hand-drawn, rough map of Belgrave Square upon which she was peppering dots with a bright pink highlighter pen. Also bent over the sketch and an A4 sheet plastered with scrawled notes, was DC Nagur Padda, the top of his head almost touching the top of Amber's as they scrutinised the complex task of finding and preserving CCTV recordings. The importance and immensity of the task was obvious, and Grant left his friend to her undertaking, quaffing down another dose of life-enhancing caffeine.

Grant marvelled at the serpentine complexities of Sean Crisp's 'official' relationships that the investigation knew about, how complicated would it become once the rumoured scores of 'unofficial' liaisons were factored in. The most recent of which had only been just been terminated and precipitated the engagement with Lizzy McKillop his live-in partner of recent years. The split with the mystery lover, the betrothal, and the notice of divorce to Debbie, were all tightly clustered in time to each other and the murder. Was there a connection? A shadow was cast over his desk, causing Grant to look up and see the smiling face of a short, round, olive-skinned man. "Panos!"

"The same. How are you, Grant? This looks like a madhouse." The DS scanned the room and waved an encompassing arm. "So this is the fabled Major Investigation Task Force, is it? Bloody hell." He laughed.

"You got the call? Good. I thought your local knowledge would be a valuable asset to us, I hope you don't mind; I thought a temporary attachment might make a change for you, too." Grant raised a questioning eyebrow.

The excitement and enthusiasm on the DS's face fell for a moment on hearing the words 'temporary attachment', but he recovered quickly, not wishing to disclose his jealousy of those permanently assigned to the Task Force. "Glad you did, thanks. I've got some major incident history, way, way back, as a DC, but since promotion, I've mainly been the office manager at the local nick. This'll be good, good to have a change, good to have a challenge, and good to help get the animal who did this. And who knows…?" With covetous eyes, he looked around the room, alive and buzzing with activity and purpose.

Grant smiled, missing the envy. "Come on, I'll introduce you to the bosses, Paul Winter, the DCI, and his Deputy, DI Heidi Yorke. They're both good."

* * *

It was 9.12am when Grant and Panos, clad in plastic gowns, shoe covers, paper hats and face masks exited the locker room and faced the chilled air of the examination room in the mortuary. After the introductions in Paul Winters' office, it had been suggested that Panos accompany Grant to the post mortem, to assist with continuity and be exhibits officer for the anticipated forensic gold resulting from the examination.

No matter how many times he entered this place, it took Grant a few seconds to assimilate. The white tiled room was dominated by the double row of shallow steel trays, half of which contained a human body, prepared by mortuary technicians for examination by the pathologist. Each waxwork-like cadaver lay on its back, the head supported by a small plastic block, the torso opened wide with the familiar 'Y' cut from shoulders to pelvic bone. Not for the first time, Grant vowed to never let a loved one of his endure the dreadfulness of a post-mortem examination unless it was a legal requirement.

Grant and Panos made their way towards the white gowned figure at the end of the row of examination tables, who stood on the other side of the unclothed body of Sean Crisp.

"Welcome to 'Rose Cottage', gents." Grant recognised the hospital euphemism for the mortuary and acknowledged the greeting.

"Good morning, doctor. I'm Detective Sergeant Grant Maddox, and this is Detective Sergeant Panos…" Grant hesitated.

"Kalamatianos." Panos rescued his colleague.

"Yes, what he said," concluded Grant, trying to keep his eyes away from the body laid out before him.

"Did you get that?" The pathologist directed his question to the note-taking female assistant, similarly robed, a few feet away. To the surprise of the officers, the figure nodded calmly, replying.

"Panos Kalamatianos, got it, Panos short for Panayiotis, I take it, usual spelling?"

"Er, yes. That's right." Panos couldn't keep the surprise from his voice.

"Greek Cypriot." Explained the pathologist offhandedly. "Right, let's get on then, gents."

The body of Sean Crisp had not yet been subjected to the dissectors' scalpel. He lay naked, unwashed, arms at his side, skin pallid and waxy. Other than some blood spattering, the area below mid-chest was unmarked and clean. The female assistant took her place next to the pathologist, and holding a small recorder in her hand, looked at the body from top to toe. The action seemed to free the officers to do likewise, liberating them from the ghoulishness of scrutinising their dead colleague.

Grant noted with some surprise, considering the family history he was aware of, that two names were tattooed on Sean's upper left shoulder, 'Callum' and 'Casper', woven about with leaves, branches, and angels. His eyes were drawn to the ravaged neck and throat before him, the ginger pointed beard and the coiffured moustache were heavily stained with blood. The knife had sliced holes through the flesh, larger on the left side, but still significant wounds at the exit points on the right. The burst, smashed right eyeball was a dark, congealed mass blighting Sean's face; the damage below its surface could only be guessed at for now. Grant knew soon enough the top of the dead officer's cranium would be removed and the bright lights from above would show all too clearly what a 9mm bullet could do to soft human flesh.

"He was blessed downstairs." The female assistant's voice disturbed the reverie. "Well hung, and shaved balls too, very considerate, no one, and I mean no one, likes ginger pubes."

Chapter Thirteen

"Are all Greek Cypriot girls so…" Grant struggled for a word. "…forthright?"

Panos shrugged. "They can be. She *was* a little…" Now Panos struggled for words, settling on "…laid back." Panos wanted to defend a fellow Greek Cypriot, but it was difficult. "She did mention his big cock more than was necessary, I suppose."

"*More* than was necessary? The woman was *obsessed.*" Grant couldn't disguise his discomfort.

"Obsessed or not, she knew her stuff, so did he, and this is an outstanding stroke of luck." Panos cheerily held up the sealed evidence bag, which rocked back and forth with the small but weighty object within. "This is almost pristine; the ballistic guys'll love this. Should Crisp's Glock *ever* be used again, we'll have a baseline comparison."

Grant, far from cheery, had to concede Panos was correct, but the impact of viewing the bullet's recovery from the near-liquified brain of the dead officer lingered in his thoughts. The effects of tissue cavitation and fluid shock on the organ were staggering. It occurred to Grant he may be going soft in his old age; those about him seemed to be less moved than he was by the last thirty-six hours. "Yes, you're right," was all he could offer, but the tone of his voice betrayed his irritation.

Panos picked up on Grant's mood. "Look, forgive me for saying, I don't mean to sound flippant, I'm not, I want the bastard who put Sean Crisp on that steel table, and I'm sure they do too." He flicked his head back towards the mortuary door through which they'd just exited. "It's just words, words

used to disguise feelings, to project an image and get through the day, look at their actions. It's been a while since I attended a PM, but I don't recall it lasting that long or being that thorough. Our guy went to the top of their work schedule, the examination was top-notch, and we've walked out with the preliminary report *already* printed off and in our hands. Is that normal service? How long would you usually wait?"

Chastened, Grant turned to look at the rotund DS. "You're right, I'm being oversensitive. I think it happens as you get older, emotions, you know. Sometimes I'm watching the human interest stories on the news, and I find the tears running down my face. What a wuss!"

Panos pocketed the bag containing the 9mm bullet and nodded understandingly. "The kiddie stories they tell. The ill children, you know, that are looking for organ donors, or special, expensive treatment abroad. I weep like a baby." He shrugged helplessly. "Tell you what, I won't tell anyone we're turning into big jessies if you don't."

Grant couldn't help but laugh out loud and feel a release of tension and gloom that had been festering inside him since the news of the murder. The slaughter of Sean Crisp was an attack on the brotherhood of police officers everywhere, but it was also a job of work. The efforts and stresses, the highs and lows, the triumphs and failures, would be the same as *any* case, as would the commitment of the investigators, and being a black-humoured, cynical old bastard was part and parcel of being a copper.

"Come on." Grant patted his colleague's back and waved the pathologist's initial report. "Let's get back, and the Two Charlies can get this onto the HOLMES database. And you know what?"

"No, what?"

"She was right, Sean Crisp really did have a huge cock."

Chapter Fourteen

Leaving Panos to oversee the post-mortem data entry onto HOLMES by the two Charlies, Grant waved a photocopy at the glass of Paul's office, entering at the DCI's enthusiastic nod. As usual, Paul had a phone pressed to his ear, Grant entering mid-conversation. "That's fucking brilliant, Amber, well done, great work! Sorry, but Granty's back from the mortuary and I need to speak to him...Yes, I will. Bye."

Good news, Guv?" Enquired Grant.

The DCI pointed to the chair opposite for Grant to be seated. "That was Amber; she and Nags made a systematic plan to track our suspect from the scene."

"Yes, I saw them first thing morning, like two conspirators."

"Well, whatever their plan, it's worked. They've a vast amount to trawl through in the long run, but for speed of evidence gathering, they leapfrogged from one CCTV camera to the next, picking our suspect up with one at the point where another one lost him. They've only got his route out! That's all!" Paul slapped his hand down on his desk.

Grant glowed inwardly with pride. Amber Bennett had arrived in the office prior to the formation of the Task Force as a newly qualified detective. As an attractive and relatively inexperienced officer, she had been subject to some unwanted attention and unjustified scrutiny. Grant had taken her under his wing, where she'd thrived, proving herself to be highly intelligent, motivated, and professional. Furthermore, anything that Amber did well reflected on him, too. "That's great, tell me."

Paul examined his scribbled notes. "The embassy camera showed him decamping on foot South East on Belgrave Square, the next camera shows him turning left, into Chapel Street running North, that camera was old and grainy, so not much detail." Paul ran his finger down his hurried list. "The next shows him turning left into Montrose Place, which is at the rear of the embassy. A domestic camera, recently fitted with high definition and in colour, shows him running into the mews road, getting onto a light coloured, possibly silver mountain bike on which he pedals away in the same direction, to the junction with Halkin Street." Paul reached into a drawer as he spoke, pulling out an A-Z map book of London, and flicked through the pages. "Look, here." He turned the book to Grant, who eagerly leaned forward. "Can you see, he doubled back on himself, picked up the bike he'd left there. We can search the cameras for its placement later."

"Where did he go from Halkin Street?" Grant couldn't disguise the excitement in his voice. It felt like the chase was on.

"The quality camera filmed him turning right, towards Hyde Park Corner, she picked him up again on Transport for London cameras, pedalling like fury along the footway towards Park Lane. Another camera has him cycling into Hyde Park, through the Queen Mum Gates." Paul pointed to the location on the map.

Grant knew the spot and the ornamental structure of the Queen Elizabeth Gates well, he rubbed his chin thoughtfully. "Guv, those gates are locked overnight; the park doesn't open until 5 am." Grant counted off on his fingers, "the cutout pocket on his hoodie, the mountain bike stashed behind the embassy, and the route he's taking, it's all pre-planned. Once through the gates, he's off the CCTV camera grid until he leaves the park, which has numerous exits. But he *must* have known the park wouldn't be open until five, so he had to wait until his escape route was available *before* he could attack Sean." Grant mirrored Paul's earlier action and slammed his hand on the desk, shaking his head in frustration. "I don't know if that tells us he was waiting for Sean, particularly, or waiting until he knew he could get into Hyde Park? It's enough to do your head in."

Paul nodded. "I'll get onto Parks Police, they have a base in Hyde Park, Amber can go and liaise with them. We need to know who opened the gates and when, and if they saw our suspect. We need to find that bike, find the exit point, and start tracking him again. Give me five minutes to make some calls, don't go away, I want to hear about the PM on Crisp."

Grant drifted out of the glass box, appraised Panos of Amber's and Nag's progress, and decamped to the canteen to pick up a coffee and a sandwich. As he returned, he saw DI Heidi Yorke ascending the stairs. "Hey, you," he called cheerfully, "how'd it go with Sean's partner? Get anything?"

Heidi looked up, momentarily startled from her thoughts, and she smiled weakly. "Hiya Granty, yeah okay, I'm on the way to brief Paul, sit in, it'll save repetition."

From her tone, Grant knew she had news.

Chapter Fifteen

Grant's cheese and pickle sandwich was disappearing fast, as was the life-giving coffee, as Heidi related her meeting with Sean Crisp's partner, Lizzy McKillop.

"She surprised me a little," Heidi offered, "after all the talk of Sean's reputation, I expected a 'hot chick' but Lizzy was a bit plain, well-covered, I think is a fair description, quiet and extremely nice. She gave what I think is a fair assessment of Sean and his situation. She knew him well, warts and all, as they say."

"It must be tough," Paul commented, "it's still so raw."

Heidi nodded, "and will be for a long while yet. She's clearly devastated, cried her eyes red, and probably used ten boxes of tissues to blow her nose. The Family Liaison Officer is doing a great job in support. Her father is dead, sadly, but her mum is coming down from Newcastle to stay with her. The point is, I think she told it like it is."

"What did she say?" Grant asked, the sandwich finished, and the coffee cup drained.

"Going chronologically," Heidi began, taking a notebook from her handbag, "she knows that Sean has never, *never* been able to keep it in his pants. He admitted as much to her. From the early days when he was living with his wife, Deborah, he was always over the side. Lizzy said it was a compulsion but that he was emotionally faithful even if he wasn't physically so."

Paul was incredulous. "What a brilliant excuse! 'Sorry, honey, I know I screw everything with a pulse, but that's just physical. I'm *emotionally* faithful to you.' My bollocks would be in a jar on the wife's bedside cabinet if I tried to pull that one."

Heidi shrugged, "I'm telling you what Lizzy said and what I think she believed, it worked for her. Anyway, as we know, Sean and Debbie had a son, Callum, who's now twenty-one and studying at Surrey University in Guildford. He still lives with his mother in police accommodation in Acton and commutes to Uni for lectures. According to Lizzy, the poor relationship Sean had with Callum is totally manufactured by Debbie. She threw Sean out when Callum was seven years old, naturally fed up with his 'playing away', fair enough. But 'hell hath no fury like a woman scorned,' as they say, Debbie decided to do a number on Sean. Lizzy said Debbie made constant and malicious allegations of everything from physical abuse of her and Callum, to claims he was stealing from the scenes of break-ins he was reporting. She was incessant. The seriousness of the complaints led to a full enquiry into Sean, which *totally* exonerated him. On the date and times of most of her allegations, Sean could show he was nowhere near where she alleged him to be."

"We heard that from Nag's delving into the HR file. Did Lizzy shine any new light on the situation?" asked Paul.

"Yes, when Debbie failed to get him imprisoned or even just sacked, she turned her full spite onto Sean's relationship with Callum. Lizzy said Sean was a good and caring father, his relationship with Casper evidences that. But Debbie poured poison in Callum's ears. From day one, she said that Sean wasn't paying anything towards their keep, that he'd abused Debbie and didn't care for her or him. Sean had court-authorized access to Callum, but Debbie sabotaged that; she would turn Sean away from the door, saying Callum was ill, or out with friends. When Sean took action to *force* Debbie to let him see Callum, she would arrange a pickup time with Sean and tell Callum his father would come two hours *before* that arranged time. Callum would be sitting, ready and waiting, for a father who seemed to never arrive. When Sean did turn up at the agreed hour, Callum was so distressed at further proof of his father's disregard he'd refuse to see him. It broke Sean's heart, but he was powerless. In the end, he let Callum go, hoping one day he'd see the truth and come to him."

"And when he did, it ended up with him punching the snot out of his own father," Grant said sadly.

"That's right. Lizzy said Sean believed that Debbie kept everything he ever did, ever gave, or ever wanted to give, a secret from Callum. On that occasion, Debbie had told Callum his father had refused point-blank to pay a penny towards Callum's university costs. He'd wanted to go to Manchester or Newcastle, one of the party-town universities, instead he ended up living at home, with his mum and commuting thirty miles back and forth to Guildford, which Sean reckoned is exactly what Debbie intended all along. Callum was seething with anger and resentment at his father, and Debbie egged him on to confront Sean at work, you know the rest. Lizzy says, for the record, Sean *did* pay towards the keep of Debbie and Callum, admittedly the minimum required, he'd got other financial commitments by then, but Lizzy showed me bank statements to prove it."

"So," the DCI concluded, "We have an incredibly acrimonious separation, with Debbie trying and failing to ruin Sean, which can only have infuriated her even more. She instils the same degree of fury in her son, who blames Sean for a university experience which consists of living at home with his mum and missing out on all the good times, I'm sure his mates are all bragging about. What do we know about Callum? Any form?"

Heidi nodded. "Oh yes! Two cautions, then a conviction for cannabis possession. He couldn't take a hint, apparently. Another caution for a public order offence, shouting abuse at the window of an ex-girlfriend in the middle of the night, then a conviction for criminally damaging the car belonging to that girlfriend's father. There's a conviction for actual bodily harm on a barman who declined to serve him in a pub, got a conditional discharge for that, then, most recently, another caution for breach of the peace in a nightclub, refusing to calm down when advised to by a bouncer. He got a bit of a kicking off the doorman before police arrived and lifted him. He was drunk and probably high, too. Then, of course, there's the dropped charges for assaulting Sean outside his DPG base."

"Fuck me! A *very* angry young man," gasped Paul. "Okay, Heidi, the picture you're painting is of a man who's full of rage at the figure of his father, a man he holds in contempt and blames for most of his and his mother's woes. A young man who doesn't like to hear the word 'no' and can respond violently when he does. A young man who, when given chance after chance, doesn't take the hint." The long-limbed DCI stretched his arms over his head and exhaled slowly, puffing his cheeks out as he did so. "Phew. I know what a terrible thing we're all thinking. Is it possible? We've got to check him out on the strength of this."

Grant nodded in agreement. "I have the preliminary report from Sean's post-mortem. I'll save you the gruesome, finer details about the severing of external *and* internal jugular veins *and* carotid arteries *and* the bisected windpipe achieved by just *three* stab wounds to the neck, one of which went straight through the back of the victim's hand. And I'll skip over what the Glock's 9 millimetre round did to his brain and tell you what anyone who saw that poor bastard's body would know. The attacker was either a raving madman or someone motivated by an all-consuming rage and fury to inflict such catastrophic injuries. The truth is, there wasn't much more than his spine and some muscle tissue holding Sean Crisp's head on."

Chapter Sixteen

The officers sat in contemplative silence for a few moments. The ferocity of the attack could be read about in clinical reports, even talked about in shocked or appalled tones, but Grant's recent experience of actually seeing the reality was sobering for those assembled in the small glass box office.

Paul Winter broke the silence. "Carry on, Heidi, you were going through Lizzy's information chronologically."

Heidi glanced down at her notes. "Okay, so Sean left Debbie, rented a flat in Brentford, and Sienna Windham subsequently moved in, and they had a son, Casper, who is now eleven years old. Lizzy speaks well of Sienna and sympathises with her. She says Sean admitted to playing around even when Sienna was pregnant with Casper. Sienna and Sean split when Casper was six years old."

"Familiar pattern, about six or seven years, then on his way," noted Grant.

"The traditional seven-year itch?" offered Paul.

"Well, whatever it was, Sean couldn't stop scratching it," continued Heidi, shrugging. "Sean left Sienna in the Brentford flat but continued paying the rent to this day, *and* he paid maintenance for Casper *and* saw him as often as was possible. The split from Sienna wasn't happy, but didn't have the venom of his separation from Debbie. The relationship with Casper was the beneficiary; they'd a close bond, apparently. Casper often stayed overnight with Lizzy and his father, and did things with his dad, days out and such."

Paul leant forward. "What are the timings of all this? When does Lizzy come on the scene?"

"Sean rented yet *another* flat in Staines. I imagine he filled his boots with the freedom that gave him, but financially, he was pushed. Lizzy says they started seeing each other four years ago, and she moved in with him three years ago. Sean transferred to the Diplomatic Protection Group about that time, the potential for earning overtime was much greater than on response teams, it was a factor in his decision to move."

Grant nodded to himself but said nothing. His eight years on a Firearms Unit prior to joining the CID had been challenging at times, sometimes terrifying, often satisfying, but *always* financially lucrative. Where a shortage of in-demand, specialised skills existed, so did the potential to earn more money. It was as true for policing as it was in the commercial world.

"I think the fact Sean wasn't seeing Lizzy whilst with Sienna helped the latter immensely. The two women spoke amicably to each other on the phone regarding Casper and arrangements to pick him up, drop him off, or generally mind him, they even met for handovers if Sean was still at work. It was a situation that would have been impossible to have with Debbie. But…"

"Ah, the dreaded 'but.'" The DCI nodded knowingly.

"Indeed, the dreaded 'but.' *But* Sean was still playing about. Lizzy said, to use her expression, 'he didn't rub my nose in it,' but she knew he was seeing other women on and off. She didn't challenge him; she truly loved him and believed he loved her. She said, 'he'll get it out of his system one day,' and it seems he did. He confessed to seeing someone who he'd finished with, apologised, cried like a baby, and then popped the question, promising to get divorced from Debbie and make an honest woman of her." Heidi looked from Paul to Grant and back. "And now another 'but'. Sean kept his promise, and Debbie had a solicitor's letter informing her of the start of divorce proceedings five days before Sean was murdered. *But* someone was sending poison pen letters to Sean and Lizzy's address *three weeks* ago…and someone had been damaging Sean's car, starting about the same time. Three instances, carving obscenities into the paintwork twice, and on the *night* of his murder, two of his tyres were punctured. A sharp object stabbed into two tyres in a side street close to the DPG base. A low-loader brought the car back as I was interviewing Lizzy."

"What did the letters say and where are they?" Grant asked.

"They were abusive and threatening. Abusing Sean, lots of 'c' words, calling him a user and abuser of women, threats to 'sort him out'. Some were addressed to Sean and some to Lizzy. They told her to get checked for STDs, told her Sean was screwing prostitutes, male *and* female, and telling her she was a slag for living with him. Pretty unpleasant stuff. The threats were reported to Surrey Police based at Staines, and they have the letters. The damage to the car was always overnight, committed when Sean was at work. The local nick for the DPG base is dealing with the damage reports and linking them to the threatening letters job."

"Callum has a previous for damaging a car," observed Paul.

"Yes, he does. But this occurred *before* the divorce from Debbie was mentioned, so might be more to do with the mysterious woman whom Sean confessed to dumping just before he proposed to Lizzy."

"We mustn't forget about the financial benefits Debbie would gain on his death, but was going to lose when Sean divorced her. That's a real motive for her or a proxy, like Callum, to do something drastic." Grant reminded the group.

"Okay." Paul clapped his hands together. Let's get the system updated with all this information. Heidi, good work, can you follow up on the next of kin, get something from Sienna, and God help you, talk with Deborah Crisp please. I want Callum checked out. Let's get him eliminated or included one way or another. Christ! What a complicated mess."

"O, what a tangled web we weave when first we practise to deceive." Two faces span to stare at Grant, who reacted, *"What?"* The two faces raised synchronised, quizzical eyebrows. "Quote from Sir Walter Scott. What? D'you two think I never had an education?"

"Do you want that answered?"

Chapter Seventeen

The public image of Trade Union Chief, Bill Buckle, which he cultivated and encouraged, was of a bluff, plain-spoken, no messing, man of the people. Northern and working class to the core, he was defined more by what he was against than by what he was for. He was against the Tory party first, last, and foremost. If Jesus Christ himself stood for office on a Tory ticket, Bill Buckle would shout him down and spit in his filthy, fascist face. Bill was against privatisation, he was against management, he was against the police, the Royals, the upper class, and the middle class. He was against the biased right-wing media, the banks, capitalists, and reserved special venom for chinless, arrogant, stock market traders who populated the square mile of 'The City', making millions from the sweat of the working man.

He abhorred the class traitor, Tony *'Red Tory'* Blair, and had utterly detested Margaret Thatcher in life, and considering how often he referenced her, even more in death. He was the darling of the Labour Party Conferences; he was the 'Big Beast' who roused the crowd, summoning up the blood and eliciting standing ovations from the Party faithful year in, year out. *No one* sang 'The Red Flag' with more gusto or conviction than Bill Buckle as tears for the Workers and 'The Class Struggle' bubbled to the surface and ran down his face in torrents.

* * *

Bill Buckle was in his third month of retirement after stepping down as the leader of the Confederation of London Underground Drivers, a breakaway trade union from ASLEF, the mainstream train drivers' union. CLUD was an organisation conceived and created by Buckle to champion the small group of workers who daily moved over three million Londoners from home to work. It was said CLUD had one hand around the government's throat and the other cupping its balls. Dubbed the *'Cluddites'* by Murdoch's press for their anti-modernisation and militantism, Bill Buckle held the reins of his creation for twenty years.

In those two decades, he'd greatly increased the pay and massively reduced the working hours of his grateful drivers, such was their devotion to Bill Buckle that the nod of his head could bring the whole of the underground network to a shuddering halt. His most powerful and feared tactic was the instant and untelegraphed use of industrial action, usually at the earliest point of a dispute rather than as a last resort. Even as he walked, strident and acrimonious, through the doors to open dialogue with the detested management, thousands of his members would halt their trains at the first station they reached and walk away, bringing the system and London to a chaotic standstill. Bill Buckle was communicating, even before he sat down, 'that's for nothing, you wait and see what I'll do if you piss me off'.

The distress, inconvenience, financial loss, or emotional suffering this tactic caused meant nothing to Bill Buckle. When confronted with the publicised tragedy of Bruce Fancy, who, because of one of CLUD's 'lightning strikes', had failed to reach a central London hospital in time to hold his dying wife in his arms, Bill Buckle's response was typical. 'Of course I'm sorry for Mr Fancy, but the *real* issue here is the disgusting and prejudicial way in which my members have been persecuted by this Tory government. My members were *forced* to take action. Blame the Tories. They're responsible for the tragedy which has befallen this poor man, and if the Tories weren't selling off the NHS, Mrs Fancy would've received the treatment she needed. '

Bill Buckle missed his power but was adjusting to his retired life. Sixty years old, heavy of weight and scant of hair, he'd suffered a heart attack nine months earlier, receiving a life-saving stent. He was advised to alter both work-life and lifestyle if he wanted to enjoy *any* life at all. Bill Buckle swallowed the bitterest pill and let go.

In the 1960s and '70s, the Labour Prime Minister, Harold Wilson, famously paraded his working-class roots, values, and habits. He never let his strong Huddersfield accent slip or dilute, and famously puffed on a 'working-class' pipe, especially if a press photographer was nearby. This was a successful artifice, endearing him to the new politics of the era and throwing him into sharp relief when compared to the Eton-educated, landed gentry of the Conservative party. In reality, Wilson was from a comfortable, middle-class background, and when out of the public gaze, put the pipe away and cracked open a box of hand-rolled Cuban cigars. With Harold Wilson, what you saw was *not* what you really got.

As with Wilson, so with Buckle, what you saw was *not* what you really got. Bill Buckle was a lover of classical music, art, and the ballet. In the privacy of his home, he could be reduced to tears by the moving notes of Debussy's *Girl with the Flaxen Hair* or sob at the poignancy of Ravel's *Pavane pour une infante défunte* while the rising notes of Vaughan Williams' *The Lark Ascending* caressed his sensitive emotions with joy and hope. In Madrid, he stood before Picasso's *Guernica*, blinking furiously to abate the forming tears. In Malta, on a spurious 'fact-finding mission', he indulged the real reason for the visit and stood for an hour in Valletta's cathedral, agog before Caravaggio's *The Beheading of St. John the Baptist*. Open-mouthed in appreciative awe at the artist's vision and skill.

Bill and his wife Sandra parted following the tragic mental breakdown and suicide of their schizophrenic son, Leon, when he was just twenty-two, the death driving a wedge between the couple. Publicly, Bill Buckle raged against Tory cuts in mental health provisions, practically accusing the government of murdering his only child. Privately, he howled in pain at the loss, blaming himself. Subsequently, unknown to the public, he became active in the Samaritans helpline charity, taking calls at one of their centres, giving his free time in the hope that one day he might be there to help someone in need, as his son had been in need. That some parents may be spared the pain that he was not.

He quietly expanded his charity work, he sponsored guide dogs for the blind, and committed his union to financially support several good causes. On principle, he never let a single act of his kindness or caring be released into the public arena; his carefully constructed thuggish public image was sacrosanct.

After the heart attack and stepping down from control of CLUD, Bill Buckle thought the press interest in his life would subside, he'd devote his time to the pursuit of his joy in the arts and his pleasure in charity work. It was not to be. A mere eight weeks after closing the door for the last time at the tiny London flat he'd worked from, he'd answered the doorbell at his four million pound Weybridge home to be greeted by a reporter and camera crew. That evening, the wealth and comfort enjoyed by the Socialist, Working Class hero was exposed to the public on several news broadcasts. The next morning, the press ran headline stories featuring his surprised, then raging face, displayed on his doorstep. Features used expressions like 'Champagne Socialism', 'Do as I say, not as I do', and 'Keep paying your union membership comrades, I need a hot tub'. The unifying word of the articles was 'hypocrite'. All carried wide-angle, full colour pictures of his distinctive, mock-Tudor residence, emphasising its value and exclusivity, its location no longer a secret but known to all.

Bill responded the only way he knew how. He fought back. In several articles and a late-night TV interview, he produced his accounts, his mortgage details, and his tax returns. He claimed the attacks were politically motivated, personally offensive, and ultimately directed at the working men he represented, and yet another example of the Tory press's obsession with destroying anyone who stood up against them. Having made his rebuttal, Bill Buckle returned to his private life, but the privacy was gone.

* * *

Bill poured a glass of red and took the reheated, paper-bound supper from the microwave. He'd returned home after a four-hour evening shift manning the phones at the North West Surrey office of The Samaritans. On the way home, he'd treated himself to his favourite takeaway, a donner kebab. It was a freezing evening, the central heating was turned up too high, warming the huge house to a satisfactory temperature, until that happened, his thick, woollen pullover stayed on. The soporific harmony of *Benedictus* from Karl Jenkins's *The Armed Man, a Mass for Peace,* echoed through the living space as he prepared to unwrap and attack his kebab, in defiance of his cardiologist's advice.

The doorbell rang, cursing the interruption, he pulled himself from the armchair, glancing at the clock, which showed thirty minutes after midnight. The music played, the voices of the choir rose in exaltation, the strings and brass building towards a crescendo. Bill Buckle opened his front door, his teeth gritted in irritation, braced, ready to be confronted, even at this late hour, by yet another of the hated press. Instead, as his door swung inwards, the barrel of a gun was pushed towards his face, the dark chasm of its muzzle filling his vision. The impact of the 9mm bullet, exploding his right eyeball and puréeing his brain, was so sudden it didn't even register with Bill Buckle that he was being murdered.

The haunting theme of *Benedictus* echoed through the house, as unhearing, Bill Buckle's body crumpled and fell to the floor.

Chapter Eighteen

mber pressed the pause button on the remote control she was aiming towards the large flat screen, around which the assembled Task Force members were gathered. There was silence in the office. The 'Techies' had worked their magic with the embassy CCTV recording, processing, and improving the quality of the horror film, which had just played out.

"This cleaned-up version tells us much more than we knew before." Amber was trying to sound clinical and professional, unaffected by the image of her friend's last few seconds of life. "We still don't have a view of the attacker's face, but we can see he's wearing rubber gloves, which we hadn't picked up on before. We'd also missed the black rucksack, the straps had merged into the darkness of his top in the unenhanced film. As he twists, we can see a small logo on it. We've blown that up, it's the blue and red parallelogram of *Berghaus*." Amber held an expanded, printed image of the logo for her audience to see, fuzzy and blurred at the edges but unmistakable.

"We had a stroke of luck, a high-resolution camera behind the embassy, picked up our man, and showed this." The TV screen flickered for a few seconds before resolving to present a high-angle aspect looking along the length of Montrose Place. "Watch him." The words were wasted, the audience was transfixed.

The suspect ran to the porch of a building, cast in deep shadow, his back to the road, still clutching his plunder, the Glock pistol in the right hand, Taser in the left. Both weapons were placed carefully on the ground as the suspect shrugged off the rucksack and withdrew the long knife from his pocket. He squatted in the shadow, opening the bag into which he placed the three items before rising and slinging the rucksack back into place. "Moving swiftly, note, but no panic," Amber commented. "Practised? Rehearsed?"

The suspect pulled an object from his left trouser pocket, his actions confirming it was a key, stretched into the darkness of the alcove, emerging fully into the road with the silver mountain bike hidden there. He threw a leg over the crossbar and settled onto the saddle. "And this is a message to us." Amber's voice was a flat tone, controlling her antagonism.

Astride the bike, the black-clad figure, head down, raised his hand slowly, hoisting the index finger in an obscene gesture of defiance towards the recording camera. The office exploded, a mixture of gasps, swearing, and outrage.

Grant watched the rest of Amber's presentation with the same controlled fury as the rest of the team. Amber's compiled patchwork of recordings tracked the killer into Hyde Park through its open gates thirty-two minutes after the park ranger unlocked them. This fact, along with so much more, the cutout pocket for the long-bladed knife, the rubber gloves, the stashed mountain bike, the rucksack for the weapons, and most audaciously the presentation to the investigating team of the murderer's middle digit, spoke of planning and preparation. This was no impulsive act; every aspect of the crime screamed out that an intelligent, systematic, and forensically aware mind was at work. Grant shook his head slowly. Sean Crisp's killer knew what he was doing, but he'd make a mistake; they all did. The skill of the investigator was to spot it when it happened and pounce.

The major events of the previous day, Sean Crisp's post-mortem, the tracking of the suspect to Hyde Park, and the revelations concerning the victim's domestic circumstances and relationship with his son, had been mentally absorbed and filed by the team and electronically stored by the Two Charlies on the HOLMES system. Charlie One was still displaying a short temper and level of grumpiness that was pissing off several detectives. More than one asked his colleague, Charlie Two, what was wrong with the senior analyst; she could only shrug, as irritated and mystified as everyone else.

* * *

Amber's presentation was the first item of the daily 6pm review of progress. She'd concluded with the so far unsuccessful efforts of Royal Parks Police to track the suspect through the vast area of Hyde Park and adjoining Kensington Gardens to establish at which of the many gates he'd made his exit. The afternoon discovery of the discarded mountain bike, abandoned behind a large rhododendron bush, initially elicited great excitement. Forensically inspected, the examination had revealed bloodstains on handlebars and pedals as expected, presumably from Sean Crisp, but no fingerprints. The cycle's stamped-in serial number and post-code had traced the home address of the owner, who'd stated it was stolen from the bike rack outside Hounslow West tube station a week earlier. So common was such an event that he hadn't even bothered reporting the theft. His description and an alibi eliminated the owner from suspicion. Enquiries at Hounslow West garnered the news that the CCTV observing the bike rack had been vandalised the day before the theft and was still not working. Local CID officers were examining surrounding CCTV systems for a sighting of the thief, but the Task Force held out little hope that the suspect had let slip his painstaking efforts to avoid his face being seen.

'Dirty' Don Chamberlain announced the result of the search for the make and model of footwear whose bloody imprint had been found near the murder scene. "We have a positive ID, the print was from a left foot of a UK size eight Umbro 'Clean Tech' men's training shoe. That's the good bit. The bad bit is the shoe is cheap and really, *really* common. I looked it up on the internet, the main online suppliers and big sportswear retailers sell the Clean Tech from fifteen to thirty quid, and God knows how many market stalls sell them too. There was no significant wear on the sole to indicate the gait or posture of the wearer, they were too new. Obviously, that also means that the sole was very light on any good evidential marks or wear damage which could provide a comparative ID to a recovered shoe at a later date." Don shrugged helplessly. "I'd take a punt that the guy bought them brand new, for cash, wore them to kill Sean Crisp and then binned them at the first opportunity. It's what I'd do. It's what anyone who was really forensically aware would do."

Don's comment was met with assenting nods from around the room. "Any more news on our victim from the Diplomatic Protection boys, Don?" The question from DCI Winter.

"Lots of rumours, about Sean's 'activities', several sources confirming the difficulties with Debbie and Callum. One guy saw the altercation when Callum punched Sean. Said it was pretty brutal and Sean had no chance, Callum was ranting at him, then swung a haymaker which connected and laid him out cold. Sean obviously went to hospital, but was already saying 'let him go' before he got there. He was never going to let Callum be charged. It was known Sean was going to marry Lizzie, but no one knew anything about the mystery dumped woman Lizzie mentioned. We don't know who she is yet. Techies are checking his phone records, perhaps that'll throw something up."

The DCI nodded. "Any theories about the damage to Sean's car?"

Don laughed. "For the most part, 'serves him right', obviously that's guilt tinged now. But one guy said, 'You play with fire, you're going to get burnt.' The assumption is the damage was caused by a bitter ex-girlfriend of Sean's or a cuckolded husband."

"*Cuckolded!*" Pat Kerrigan's mocking call carried loud and clear across the room. "Fuck me Don. Recently returned from an assignment in the eighteenth century, have we? A scoundrel or vagabond hath defaced and spoileth mine mode of transport. Forthsooth, perchance it were one whom I hath cuckolded!"

The room burst into raucous laughter, it *was* a funny comment for sure, Grant noted, but the hilarity was in response to more than taking the piss out of Don Chamberlain. It was the bursting bubble of built-up tension. A feeling he'd noted in himself only yesterday at the mortuary. It was a sign the Task Force was moving beyond the personal affront of the murder and on towards the resumption of 'Normal Service'. It was a good thing, coppers wore size ten, clod-hopping boots, not ballet shoes, they weren't made for tiptoeing around tender sensibilities, it wasn't in their nature, and it wasn't good for an investigation either.

When calm returned, DI Heidi Yorke announced, "I haven't got to Debbie Crisp yet. She's holed up in the Acton flat, surrounded by press and camera crews looking for her first interview. Callum is with her, too. We've offered the services of a Family Liaison Officer, which was refused, as was my request to speak to her. A friend answered her phone, saying she'll speak to me when she's in a better emotional place."

"The heartless bitch and her druggie son are too busy adding up how much they're worth now Sean's dead, more like." The bitter voice belonged to DC Craig Lines, who'd known the victim.

Heidi responded firmly. "Unless the evidence takes us there, I think we should be very cautious in making assumptions and more cautious in verbalising them. Remember the DCI's warning at the beginning of this case. We must do *nothing* which could jeopardise the enquiry. If the press or, God forbid, Debbie Crisp were to hear of a comment like that, it could provide evidence of prejudice at a later date. Understood?"

Red-faced, Craig answered, "Sorry, Guv, you're right."

As Heidi reset, preparing to continue her report, the phone in Paul Winters' glass box office began to ring, irritatingly falling silent as Paul reached to answer. He shrugged, spun on his heel, and nodded to Heidi to carry on. "As for Sean's *other* ex," continued the DI, "Sienna Windham and her son Casper *have* gratefully accepted the services of a FLO who is fielding the onslaught from the press. I spoke with Sienna today. She's utterly distraught, and the state of the little boy is heartbreaking." Heidi looked aside as the DCI's mobile phone began to ring.

He pulled the device from his pocket apologetically, putting it to his ear. His face almost immediately registered shock. "Okay, yes. Understood. Yes, I will, no, we'll have the number. I will. Thank you." Paul's arm, phone in hand, slumped to his side. "Well, ladies and gents, that was Surrey Police. I've just been informed the ex-General Secretary of the Confederation of London Underground Drivers, Bill Buckle, has been found shot to death, shot through his right eye."

Chapter Nineteen

So recently, an officer of Surrey Police, DI Heidi Yorke, was the natural choice to reach out to the CID team investigating the murder, arriving in the chill dark of the evening to find flood-lights and forensic suited figures around the doorstep at the Weybridge home of Bill Buckle.

"Back so soon, Heidi? Couldn't stay away?" The words were spoken with the warmth and respect of long association by DI Evan Thomas as Heidi approached the cordon, holding up her warrant card to the keeper of the incident log book.

"Evan! Good to see you. How are you? How's Beth and the boys?" Heidi stretched out her hand in greeting.

"Beth is still going up the wall and complaining at the hours I work, and the boys are still parasitic vermin who never stop eating or asking for money. So everything's exactly as it's been for years, we're all very happy to see." Heidi smiled at her friend's words and the sing-songy lilt of the DI's Welsh accent. Evan was one of the happiest family men she'd ever met. "How's life in the big bad city then?" He asked, "keeping busy?"

"Hmmmm." Heidi's face saddened. "Too busy recently." She paused, "Sean Crisp." She let the name hang in the air.

Realisation registered on the Welshman's face. "Ah. Linking him with this, then?" Evan jerked his head over his shoulder towards the activity behind him.

"Maybe, what can you tell me." Heidi took out a notebook and biro, raising her eyebrows expectantly, the small talk over for now.

Evan smiled with helpless resignation, understanding there were bigger things than his ego. The murder of the nationally infamous Bill Buckle, the Left-Wing's 'Big Beast' and the Holy Terror of the long-suffering London Commuter, was a crime that had been committed on his patch. It would undoubtedly be the most high-profile case of his investigative career, but was potentially about to be whisked out from under him and taken by the Met's Task Force. Heidi saw what he was thinking. She understood and sympathised. It wasn't so long ago that a case of hers, the brutal murder of Martine Walsingham in a leafy Surrey village, was linked to an identical murder in London. *Her* case was absorbed into the bigger Force's investigation. Ultimately, she'd transferred to the larger, busier, London service herself, a decision she'd not regretted.

"Bill Buckle…no formal ID yet, but he's recognisable, so no issue there, besides, he's half in and half out of his own house. Lived here alone, divorced years ago, not long after the suicide of his son. No evidence in the house of shared occupancy or visitors, only the late Mr Buckle's clothes, personal effects, and toiletries. Just one, sad, lonely, top-of-the-range sonic toothbrush in the en suite. The wife was looking at one of those. A hundred and fifty quid… for a fucking toothbrush!"

"I don't think they can do that yet; they just clean teeth." Heidi winked mischievously.

Evan laughed. "But the 'man of the people' had a hundred and fifty quid toothbrush! He was found at 2.15 pm by the postwoman, on his back, front door open, legs on the path outside, torso in his hall. If you look, the view of the doorway is obstructed by the garden foliage, so a passerby wouldn't see the body unless they came up the path."

Heidi viewed the frontage, nodded her understanding, and noted the details. "The postie, statement taken, of course, anything to note, did she see or hear anything?"

Evan shook his head. "No, it all happened long before she arrived, we think late last night, maybe in the early hours. We've prelim' statements from neighbours, but the houses aren't close to each other, no one saw or heard anything."

"Hmmm. Silencer, maybe?" Heidi mused aloud.

"Maybe. But a bang, from a distance, if it was heard at all, well, it could be put down to several things, especially if you're in bed and half asleep. A car door slamming shut, or a fox knocking something over in a garden."

Heidi nodded. If what she suspected was the case, there was no silencer used for the shooting.

The Surrey DI continued his briefing. "The doctor did a core temperature test, which, even with the frost last night trying to mess up the maths, also matches the degree of rigor mortis in the body. He's just starting to loosen up, just a little bit. So, you know, around the 10 to 12 hour mark, so midnight to 2 am is the best guess. That's all the science stuff, the good old-fashioned common-sense, copper stuff supports that too. There's an unwrapped kebab on a plate next to a glass of red wine. I don't think that was his breakfast, plus his bed is made and unslept in, the curtains are open, and he has an *actual* record player with a real vinyl disc still spinning, and he's wearing a thick woolly pullover."

Heidi laughed, looking up from her notes. "I'm convinced. Killed late last night or early this morning. Keep going."

"Cause of death is pretty obvious, too. Single gunshot wound to the face. Entry point is through the right eyeball, not very pretty. We've recovered a 9mm shell casing from the grass about six feet to the right of the door. The natural assumption is an automatic pistol with a right-side ejection port." Evan grinned broadly. "Such as on a Glock 17? Like the one that Sean Crisp was carrying. Am I getting warm?"

"A single 9mm bullet through the right eyeball? Okay, Evan, this hasn't been released, so it's in-house for now."

Evan nodded, "Of course."

"Sean Crisp received multiple stab wounds to the neck and throat, all fatal injuries, but a 9mm through the right eye was what finished him off. His gun *was* taken and used on him; the killer still has it."

"I guessed you were linking the killings as soon as I heard you were on the way, but Christ! What's the connection between a London PC and a union bully-boy? I mean, it's a world apart."

"That, Detective Inspector Thomas, is *the* question." Heidi snapped her notebook shut.

Chapter Twenty

A car park opposite the station had been commandeered by the press corps. Outside broadcast vans with huge satellite dishes mounted on telescopic, elevating poles populated the space, whilst technicians and journalists scurried around between the vehicles like busy ants, comparing notes, speculating wildly, and moaning about the lack of information from the Met Police Press Office.

The murder of a prominent, public figure, on his own doorstep, shocked the nation and, for those old enough to remember, brought back memories of the assassination of the co-founder of the Guinness Book of Records, Ross McWhirter, by the IRA, gunned down at his own front door. The spectre of political assassination was evidently foremost in the minds of others, too, and it was a subdued DCI Paul Winter who slumped in his office chair the afternoon after the discovery of Bill Buckle's body. With DI Heidi Yorke away, liaising with Surrey Police, it had fallen to DS Grant Maddox to interview Debbie Crisp and her son Callum that morning, their reluctance to talk finally being mollified with persuasion and a mild threat.

Grant was writing up his notes of that particular visit as Paul Winter entered the Task Force office and, with uncharacteristically brief nods and acknowledgments to his team, made his way to his office and dropped into his seat. Overtly intending to relate his recent findings to his senior but with the ulterior motive of finding out why Paul had been called out so early that morning and returned so glum that afternoon, Grant approached the door and tapped it.

"Come in, Granty," Paul called.

"Hi, boss," Grant responded. "Thought you'd like to hear about how it went with Debbie and Callum Crisp this morning."

The DCI stirred from his reverie. "Yes, yes, of course. Sorry you got lumbered, but for obvious reasons, Heidi was the one to scoot over to Surrey to look into this Bill Buckle business."

"S'okay. Absolutely right." Grant smiled, paused, then asked. "Are you alright, Paul? You decamped this morning without saying much… don't worry, no problem, I had your notes on the day's actions and assignments and did the directing, but what was all that about? You look preoccupied. Is there a problem?"

Grant Maddox and Paul Winter went back a long way and enjoyed a relationship based on a deep mutual respect and a shared belief in how the job should be done. They were both officers from the 'Old School', a label often used pejoratively, but for these two men it was a badge of honour. Friends as well as colleagues, when alone, out of the earshot of other officers or the public, the two men comfortably reverted to informality and first-name terms.

The DCI sighed deeply, his shoulders sagging. "No, no. It's okay Grant. I'm really tired, late nights, early starts, you of all people know what that does and let's face it, we're getting a bit long in the tooth now. Most of this team could be our children. Have you ever noticed that?"

Grant laughed, understanding precisely. "What was the rush this morning all about? I saw you take a call, and your face was a picture."

"You don't miss much, do you?" Paul laughed. "Doh! You're a detective." Paul bumped the side of his head in mock realisation.

"I try."

"I was called in to Thames House." Paul let the words hang.

Grant gasped. "Thames House? MI5? The Security Service! Jesus, Paul, they didn't give you a suicide pill, did they?"

Paul laughed. "Not yet, but I may ask for one eventually. This case had complications before Bill Buckle, now it's even more so. I was called by *the* Big Boss and told to get my arse to Thames House and meet 'representatives' from the Home Office, Foreign Office, and the Security Service for a 'discussion'."

"Bloody hell, what's this all about?" Grant couldn't disguise the tremble in his voice.

"This is confidential, Granty, but there's some…anxiety. The 'representatives' are concerned about the possibility the murders were politically motivated, there's huge sensitivity about Turkey here, and the regime over there want to know what's going on."

"What did you tell them?"

"That Sean was shot by a cuckolded husband and Buckle by a pissed off commuter."

"*You didn't!?*" Grant's voice rose an octave.

"Of course I didn't!" Paul answered, grinning. "I told the truth; it's too early to tell for sure, but there's nothing yet to suggest a political motivation."

"It doesn't feel like it's that to me. The attack in Belgrave Square was directed wholly at Sean; the embassy didn't seem relevant at all to me." Grant offered.

"I agree, but the upshot is that I'm required to provide, personally, the progress of our investigation and any…*any* mind you, suspicions or indication that this is something which could affect national security or has the potential to cause embarrassment to H.M. Government. And on top of all that, I have the world's press screaming from over the road and the wankers upstairs breathing down my neck. *And* I have to prepare another statement and front a press conference this evening to discuss Bill Buckle's killing because someone, somewhere, told the press that a Task Force Detective Inspector investigating Sean Crisp's death attended the murder scene yesterday. Do you know what, I might ask for a suicide pill after all." The DCI laughed sarcastically.

"Paul, it's appreciated. The team knows you're out there covering their backs, letting them work, and they're grateful, I'm grateful. I can see why you're looking a bit beat. I'll leave you to prepare for your press conference, and I'll get a mug of strong coffee brought in for you."

"You're a good 'un, thanks, but what about the interview with Debbie Crisp?"

"It can wait; it didn't take us anywhere. No new doors opened… but none closed either. More digging needed."

"Right, go and dig then."

Grant closed the door after him, leaving Paul with his responsibilities. He shook his head resignedly, the thoughts racing through his head. A dead policeman, a dead firebrand union chief, and now MI5. What the bloody hell was going on?

Chapter Twenty-One

Grant scanned the written report from his meeting with Debbie Crisp. He'd phoned early that morning and spoke to a woman claiming to be a 'friend' of the family. "May I speak with Deborah Crisp, please? My name is Grant Maddox. I'm a DS investigating the murder of Sean Crisp." It seemed a reasonable and straightforward request, which should have elicited a reasonable and straightforward response of, 'yes, I'll pass the phone to her now.' Instead, a list of excuses to not speak had tripped off the 'friend's' tongue, all of which seemed petty and trivial pretexts to avoid the request. Recalling Heidi's failed attempts to communicate thus far, Grant decided on a new tack.

"My guess is that this is you speaking, Mrs Crisp, or if not, you have an ear to the phone and are listening to me right now. This is my message to you. This is a murder investigation and a story of huge, national, public interest. I know the press are camped outside your door, dripping sympathy and understanding for your terrible loss. But that could change. How long do you think the facts relating to your campaign to ruin Sean can be kept a secret? All those accusations against the heroic murdered officer, all proven to be malicious, Mrs Crisp. How sympathetic will the press be when they discover the financial gains you are set to receive because of your husband's death? What if it became known that you are refusing to assist with the investigation with a simple statement? The media are a howling pack of wolves, Mrs Crisp, that can turn nasty and tear you to pieces. The sooner I get a true account from you, the sooner we can say that we are getting full co-operation from you, and any hint of suspicion implied from certain scurrilous quarters is unfounded, the better. Don't you think?"

Less than ninety minutes later, the front door to Deborah Crisp's Acton flat was opened to DS Maddox, he was warmed to see a pot of tea and plate of biscuits laid out for him as he was welcomed in and invited to take a seat. There was no sign of any 'friend'.

Grant scanned the report he'd pass to Charlie One in a short while for data entry. Deborah Crisp had been something of a surprise to Grant, as Lizzy had been to Heidi Yorke. As much as Lizzy was best described as 'attractively well-covered', Debbie could be categorised as 'harshly angular'. In her mid-forties with closely cropped mousey hair, her frame was slim to the point of boniness, her face drawn, hard, and punctured with two deep-set grey eyes. Debbie was not an attractive woman.

Grant ran his fingers down the section of questions and answers he'd directed to Debbie once her son, Callum, had been banished to his bedroom. 'I'll interview you separately,' he'd stated, not up for discussion. Once the preliminaries had been observed, sympathy for loss, tea sipped, biscuits nibbled, welfare enquired of, Grant began to ask questions and was surprised at the frankness of her responses.

"Where were you and Callum the night Sean was killed?"

"Here, at home, all night, and so was Callum."

"So, you're each other's alibi then?"

"Yes."

"How would you describe your relationship with Sean?"

"Disastrous. How would you describe it? He philandered from the moment we met, up to, during, and after the birth of our son. His behaviour was intolerable, he left Callum and me without a thought for even the roof over our heads. I fought tooth and nail with the Met's Welfare branch to keep this flat. Have you looked at it? One double bedroom and a box room for Callum, one sitting room with a kitchenette in the corner, and a bathroom the size of a wardrobe." Grant had to concede, the living conditions for two adults were less than perfect. "I've had to struggle alone, stacking shelves in a supermarket and cleaning for an agency. *Two jobs,* Detective! Just to make ends meet." Debbie extended her work-worn hands for inspection.

"I'm telling you, whatever anyone else is saying, and I've seen the papers and watched the news, Sean Crisp was a selfish piece of shit."

"What was your reaction to Sean's solicitor's letter, the notice of divorce?"

"*Fury!* Blind fury. After all the years of arguing and wrangling to keep this flat, I could see the struggle starting again. These are 'married quarters', Detective Sergeant, *married*. I could see a notice to quit from your precious Job the day after my status as married to an officer ceased. So I was furious, I called him and told him so." Grant had nodded; the facts of the story were as relayed by Lizzy McKillop to DI Yorke.

"I understand Sean was receiving abusive and threatening letters. What do you know about those?"

"Nothing. Sean called and made all sorts of accusations, but that was weeks before the divorce letter and before he was..." Grant was stunned to see Deborah Crisp's eyes well up and her voice crack and fail. She pulled a tissue from her pocket. "Surprised?" She asked Grant. "He was an utter bastard, but he was my husband and the father of my child. And no, I didn't still love him. I hated him. But I didn't wish him dead. Never that. Alone and cold on a street." Debbie sniffed and blew her nose, regaining control, jabbing a bony finger towards Grant's notebook. "You can write *that* down."

Grant dropped the transcribed report on his desk and reached for the second, relating to Callum Crisp's interview. Grant had hoped Callum would be incredibly tall or unnaturally short, or fat, or anything which would immediately physically eliminate Sean's son from being the five feet nine figure of medium build who'd ripped Sean Crisp's throat out and fired a bullet through his eye. He'd been disappointed. Callum Crisp's height and build fell within the parameters of the suspect caught on the CCTV cameras.

Grant had tapped on the bedroom door and entered on hearing a resentful 'yeh'. The room was as described, a box room, the single bed took up over half the floor space. The room was plastered with posters, one of a giant cannabis plant leaf, another of the 2003 Rugby World Cup-winning England team.

Grant pointed at the poster. "Jonny Wilkinson, drop goal less than thirty seconds from the whistle in extra time to win the World Cup. I'll never forget it, I went crazy."

"My dad had gone, and mum was at work, I watched it on my own. I was seven."

"That's tough." Grant conceded.

"He'd played a bit and got me into rugby, bought my first ball, took me to a junior team. It's the only good thing my dad ever did for me."

"Do you still play?" Grant pointed to the muddy boots lying under a yellowed, flaking radiator."

"Yeh, West London Ruffians." Callum didn't seem keen to explain further.

"I've heard of them, Shepherd's Bush way, aren't they? Good team at the moment?" Grant asked, trying to tease a conversation from Callum. It didn't work.

"You wanted to ask me questions? About dad?"

The questioning went as Grant expected; Callum and his mother were alibis for each other on the night of the killing. Callum hated his father, resentful at his abandonment, the treatment of his mother, and their perceived financial suffering, which he laid at his father's door.

"You've got a bit of form, Callum. Want to tell me about it?"

Callum shrugged. "You already know, don't you?"

"I know one side, tell me yours."

Callum shrugged again. "Bit of cannabis, got a caution and an almighty bollocking off my dad, which pleased me no end. When it happened again, he went even more ballistic, and I was even happier. I wanted to hurt him. Stupid, I was immature, I've grown up since then."

"You punched him unconscious only eighteen months ago."

"Yeah, that was the last straw. He'd refused to support me at Uni, I wanted Manchester, fun times, and a degree. Look what I got?" Callum waved his hands around the tiny, squalid room. "I lost my temper. I was wrong. That's it, over."

"You've lost your temper a few times…haven't you?"

"You know I have, I told you, that's in the past, after seeing my dad hit the floor, hearing his head hit the concrete, it scared me. It was ages ago. I've changed."

"Sean's car was vandalised. Scratched with abuse, the tyres were punctured the night he was killed. Know anything about that?" Grant raised his eyebrow.

"I know what you're implying. I damaged my ex-girlfriend's dad's car. Well, I know nothing about *my* dad's car; it wasn't me." Callum paused, "Do you think I killed him?"

"Did you?"

"I think you should leave now."

Grant dropped the two reports on the desk in front of Charlie One. "The long-delayed statements from Debbie and Callum Crisp to be input, please, Charlie." Grant's voice was light and cheerful.

"For fucks sake!" Charlie One spun around in his chair. "Is there any chance at all I could have two minutes without being at everyone's beck and fucking call?" The HOLMES operator was almost shouting, taking Grant aback with the suddenness and ferocity of his reaction.

"I don't know what your problem is lately, Charlie, but you don't fucking talk to me like that. And as I recall, your job is to be available for eight hours a day to *do* your job." Grant jabbed a finger on his statements. "*Now fucking do it!*"

Grant span on his heels, determined to speak with Paul about the attitude and behaviour of Mr Charles Buller of late. The strength of the Task Force was its cohesion and teamwork; it took only one weak link to damage that efficiency, and Charlie One was turning into that weak link.

Chapter Twenty-Two

"Do you have to do that right now? It's way past eleven, it'll still be there in the morning." Maud was swooping around the dining room table and chairs, collecting an empty coffee mug and a side plate littered with crumbs from a late-night ham sandwich. "And you shouldn't be eating at this hour, and coffee will keep you wide awake all night." Maud collected the items from the table and paused. "Are you listening to me? Am I talking to myself?" The object of her ire was sitting at the table, hunched over a laptop, the glowing screen casting a light over a face deep in concentration.

"Do I have any choice but to listen to you. I've a bit more to do, I need to look at these expenditure figures and try to make sense out of bloody Excel spreadsheets, and your interrupting isn't helping any."

"Bernard, you're supposed to be retired, you're supposed to be enjoying a well-earned rest, you're supposed to be enjoying time with me! For thirty-eight years, I put up with the long hours, the evenings and weekends of marking and lesson preparation, that school owned you, but that's over, finished these six years now." Maud replaced the mug and plate on the table, she needed both hands for emphasis. "I practically brought up our daughter on my own, why do you have to do all this council work now? I never see you, it's precious time, Bernard, and it's time that won't come back, it's gone."

Bernard looked up from the computer. "For God's sake, Maud, this is a busy time of year, the run up to Christmas, and don't pretend you don't enjoy being a councillor's wife, the functions and posh social stuff." He paused for effect. "Besides, I've heard a rumour." Bernard Huxton tapped the side of his nose and looked left and right conspiratorially, guaranteeing his wife of forty-two years full attention. "A little bird whispered in my ear, maybe next year I'll be Mayor. Imagine, Maud, you'd be The Lady Mayoress. How does that sound? Chauffeured in the Council's black Jag, opening care homes and supermarkets, planting trees, cutting ribbons, nibbling cake, sipping bubbly, and having your picture in the local paper. How does that sound?"

Maud Huxton crumbled as he knew she would. "Well, don't be too long, and no more coffee. Be quiet when you come up, don't disturb me, *I'm* tired even if you're not." Councillor Huxton had already reburied his face in the laptop, running his eyes up and down rows of figures, dates, and expenditures. Within twenty minutes, Maud turned off the light and settled down to sleep.

Theirs was a quiet but congested road of post-war semi-detached bay-windowed buildings. Few houses at the time of construction could boast ownership of a car; now, few houses had less than two as husbands, wives, and stay-at-home adult children crowded the street with their vehicles. Consequently, as midnight passed, no one, even if they'd looked, would have batted an eyelid as the car, a stranger to the street, slowly drove between the parked Fords and Vauxhalls. The interloper slowed almost to a standstill outside Bernard Huxton's residence, where the low lights of the front room telegraphed to an observer that there was still human activity. The car increased speed, turned into the wide mouth of a junction, and passed the house once more, the occupant this time paying attention to the dark, unlit windows of nearby buildings. Twice more the car drove by before parking in a space two doors away from the bay window behind which Bernard pressed on with his labours, determined to do more and do it better than any rivals to the Gold Chain of Office.

The grey-haired man was unaware he was being observed by the black clad figure standing a few feet back from the glass of the window, that his solitariness at that hour, in that room, was being verified once again, the latest and last of many such reconnaissance.

The house had a functioning doorbell, so why a caller at such a late hour would decide to lightly knock on the door rather than use the bell, which would ring out a loud and tuneful Westminster Chime, was a mystery to Bernard. He rose from his chair, muttering to himself at the interruption, speculating on the reason and concluding it was likely to be the nineteen-year-old son of the next-door neighbour complaining that Maud's car was once again in 'his' space, outside his parents' house. This knock at the door was probably an escalation of the dispute, made at an unsocial hour to create inconvenience and to intimidate.

By the time Bernard had reached the front door, he'd worked himself into a state of righteous indignation. He'd spent thirty-eight years dealing with obnoxious teenagers; there was nothing they could say or do he didn't have an answer to, and the next-door yob would be no exception.

Bernard turned on the hall light, seeing the shape of a dark figure through the glass of the top half of the door. Reaching for the latch, he took a deep breath, puffing himself up in height and size, and set a look of grim determination on his face. He turned the latch and opened the door.

"Hello, Mr Huxton." The voice was calm and measured but not familiar. Bernard was unable to connect the features of a face to the voice; all he could see was the muzzle of a gun a few inches away. Councillor Huxton opened his mouth in surprise, an act which saved his dentition but not his life. The 9mm bullet cut a furrow through his tongue in a rising trajectory, passing through the back of his throat and ripping a course which smashed his medulla, the brainstem which controlled the most basic functions of life, respiration, and heartbeat, and onwards through the cerebellum, before exiting to continue its journey. The bullet came to rest in the wood of the kitchen door several yards behind the crumpling body. The dark figure resisted the urge to spit on the corpse lying before him. He wouldn't gift his hunters such an easy sample of his DNA; instead, he pushed the Glock 17 deep into his pocket, turned, and unhurriedly returned to his car.

Barefoot and her senses still dulled from sleep, Maud carefully descended the stairs to investigate the unknown noise that had pierced her deep sleep. By the time her screams were echoing from the hallway into the neighbourhood, the killer's car had pulled away and was turning onto the main road at the end of the street.

Chapter Twenty-Three

Grant and Amber exited the headquarters of the Royal Parks Police and stood on the long veranda at the front of the hundred-year-old red brick building, surveying Hyde Park.

"Slightly different view of London than you get when you walk out the front door of most nicks, isn't it, skip?" Amber shook her head slowly from side to side, taking in the expansive area of trees, paths, lakes, and parkland that surrounded the cluster of buildings. "It's hard to believe we're only two miles from Buckingham Palace."

"Looking to transfer, are we?" Grant teased.

"I don't think so, I'll stick with what I've got, thank you. We should get this back. I don't hold out much hope, but you never know, our man may have made a mistake." Amber shook the brown paper property bag with its cellophane window, which revealed the black Berghaus rucksack sealed within.

"I doubt the copious amounts of dog piss dripping off it will assist forensics in their task, it bloody reeks." Grant chuckled as he stepped off the veranda and turned right towards their CID pool car, glowing in its bay. The visually offensive, fluorescent green Ford Focus was a running joke perpetuated by Amber on her sergeant; somehow, she *always* managed to be allocated this particular vehicle, which Grant had christened the radioactive bogey, when the pair required official 'Job-Wheels'.

"Dripping in piss or not, it's a good find. The dog walker could've just as easily ignored it; the guvnor's TV appeal struck a chord, and he dragged it out of the bush. He didn't have to."

"*After* letting his dog cock its leg on it!" Grant laughed again. "I suppose it *could* have been worse."

Amber dropped the evidence bag in the car's boot and slammed it shut. As she slipped into the driver's seat, she heard Grant concluding a radio transmission on the main set radio.

"Yes, that's all received, we'll make our way."

"What's that skip?" Amber enquired, "The only place I want to go to is the canteen for breakfast and coffee, it's not even half past seven."

"There's another one." Grant let the words hang.

"Shit!"

"Shit indeed," answered Grant, stretching for the London Atlas resting on the back seat. "Where the bloody hell is Norbiton?"

* * *

The scene was depressingly familiar, plastic cordon tape flapped in the breeze, and an obviously brand-new, fresh out of the box, shiny probationer stood nervous and wide-eyed with an incident log book in hand, recording names and times of persons crossing into the sterile area. The two detectives stepped self-consciously from the radioactive bogy and, with Warrant Cards open, walked towards the waiting officer with eyes on the forensic tent set up on the doorstep of Bernard Huxton's modest home.

As Amber booked them in, Grant looked for the senior officer in attendance and was surprised to see the familiar face of DS Panos standing back and observing the work of the white suit clad scenes of crime officers.

"Panos!" Grant called.

The spherical detective spun around at the sound of his name, his face breaking into a smile.

"Grant. Get ready for an attack of déjà vu." The Greek Cypriot stood aside to allow Grant a view of the scene. The body of Bernard Huxton was lying as it had fallen, on its back, arms held up as if in a posture of surrender, the left leg folded unnaturally under the buttocks.

"How did you end up here? Amber and I were assigned by the DCI via the main set." Grant couldn't hide the confusion in his voice. "It's not like Paul Winter to double-book."

"No, I know. I was on the way in, early start. I live down the road in New Malden, the shooting was on Capital Radio news, so I drove to Norbiton, found a local uniformed PC, and got directions, I thought it would be good to have a Task Force rep here. Not a problem, is it?"

"Errr, no okay," Grant shrugged, but an uneasy feeling swept over him, "so what've we got?" he asked as Amber joined the two DSs.

"Sarge, what you doing here?" she asked, as puzzled as Grant had been moments earlier.

"We're past that." Grant waved a hand dismissively, "Panos, carry on." There was an edge of prickly irritation in his voice, he felt his toes were being stood on by this unasked-for presence.

Panos scanned his notes. "The victim is Bernard Law Montgomery Huxton, aged sixty-seven, the parents were presumably fans of old Monty, maybe his dad was a desert rat."

"*Who?*" queried Amber. "A *what?*" Her bemusement unhidden.

Panos smiled indulgently. "You are *so* young. His wife, Maud, ID'd the body; she found him, as he is now, at 1 am, the emergency call was logged at 1.10 am, made by the next-door neighbour who was woken by her screaming. The apparent cause of death, there are no other injuries present, is a gunshot wound which entered the victim's open mouth and exited the back of his head." For emphasis, Panos formed a gun with his hand, pulling the 'trigger' with his index finger. "POW!"

"I hope that the new widow Huxton or a neighbour didn't see that." Grant's eyebrows furrowed, "Not really appropriate, Panos, not here, in public." Grant was definitely prickly.

Deflated, the DS continued. "Yeh, sorry, you're right. Well, a single gunshot through the mouth, like the others, he was shot at close range, there's evidence of powder burns on the face, and the clincher is a single 9mm casing about six feet to the right of the body. That's bagged up for firing pin scrape examination. The bullet itself is lodged in the kitchen door behind the victim. It's on the techie's list to recover intact for ballistic comparison to Sean and Bill Buckle's bullets." Having recovered his poise, Panos ended his summing up QC style. "I rest."

"Okay, thanks Panos, have the locals started door-to-door enquiries, hopefully we can catch a lot before they set off for work, school run or shops."

"Yep, already on it, the local uniform Inspector is on the ball, she's with the wife at the neighbour's, there." Panos pointed to the house. "I'll go and see how the door-to-door is doing."

"Good idea." Grant, still irritated, found himself wanting the fat DS to be somewhere else.

Grant shook his head, contemplating this new turn of events. He was sure ballistics would confirm the three bullets at three scenes were fired from the same gun, Sean Crisp's stolen Glock 17. The Task Force would have three apparently unconnected murders on its hands, all committed within five days. There *must* be something that linked the victims, something other than the 9mm hole that united them in death.

"You go on," Grant pointed to the neighbour's house in which the newly widowed Maud Huxton was being interviewed, "I'm going to take a look at our victim."

Chapter Twenty-Four

The Task Force office was packed for the evening briefing, the detectives and support staff waiting in eager expectation. Some had garnered another small piece of the jigsaw to insert into the puzzle, adding to the picture, while the majority, drawing a blank, waited to hear an overview of the investigation. Grant Maddox's face was taut and grim. The picture so far was discouragingly sketchy, with the growing number of victims, accompanying CCTV, physical, forensic, and ballistic evidence, *much* more should have been known at this point, but other than collecting victim biographies, nothing significant was driving the case forward.

Grant rubbed his chin hard, screwing his eyes tight shut. What was he missing?

"Penny for them, Sarge."

"What?" Grant opened his eyes and turned to the questioner sitting at the desk to his right.

"Penny for your thoughts. You go like this when you're working something out. What've you got?" Amber smiled sympathetically.

"What have I got? Too many questions and not enough answers. I've this horrible feeling that the key to this is already in front of us, something we've missed, and I keep going over and over trying to work out what it is."

"I know, three victims, what's the link? What's getting me is if we should include Sean as a proper victim at all. If you understand?" Grant knew what she was getting at. Amber continued, thinking aloud, "Was he killed purely as a means to obtain the gun? It's alright for the criminal fraternity or you and me, if we really wanted to get our hands on a gun, we know which pub to go to, which person to ask a question of, which street corner to hang around at. It's not like going to Tesco, but we *could* get a gun if we wanted to. But what if you've no knowledge or links to society's darker side? What would you do to get a gun then? Would killing an armed copper be the obvious answer? Would that make Sean disconnected from the other victims, in terms of motive to kill, I mean?"

It was a question Grant had asked himself in different forms since the discovery of the theft of Sean's weapon, and he didn't have an answer yet. Paul Winter emerged from the glass box office, followed by DI Heidi Yorke, clapped his hands for attention, and addressed the assembled.

"Good evening, team. Firstly, as usual, a big thank you for your continuing efforts. I know you're putting in one hundred percent, and I'll say this to you: at the moment, it feels like we're getting nowhere, but that's not true. There's often a pattern to major investigations like this. If we don't hit paydirt in the 'Golden Hour', if we can't point to a suspect or even a strong line of enquiry early on, there's a temptation to let our heads fall, to let despondency take a peek in. That hasn't happened, and I want you to make sure it doesn't. We *will* get a break, we always do, and when that break happens, everything that we've done so far will prove to be invaluable; it will be the foundation, the groundwork of our case. Remember, *everything* is important, even the negatives. Right! Pep talk over. We've a lot to discuss, Heidi, over to you please."

"Thanks, Guv." Heidi's face was all business. "The guvnor and I thought an overview of where we are would be in order, with the details of my visit to our Surrey colleagues and the additional case from Norbiton." Heidi took a few steps to the expansive whiteboard fixed to the wall, which was dominated by the pictures of three male faces and copious lists of details written beneath each one. She swept a hand past the panel.

"Firstly, I can confirm we have three linked victims. We've seen the shocking film of PC Sean Crisp's murder with his own handgun, and the shell casing and bullet from that killing were recovered for forensic comparison. Ballistics have pulled out all the stops for us and confirmed the firing pin scrape marks on the shell casings from Bill Buckle's shooting and the shooting of Bernard Huxton in the early hours of this morning match the mark on the casing from Sean's murder. The striation marks caused by the rifling in the gun's barrel have been matched to Sean's Glock 17 in Bill Buckles' murder, and we await the result from this morning's shooting, but I'm confident they'll only confirm what the firing pin scrapes have already told us. So, one gun, a Met Police issue Glock 17, 9mm calibre, semi-automatic pistol, killed our three victims."

There were no surprised faces in her audience, merely the acknowledgement of what everyone already suspected. "Each victim," continued Heidi, "was shot at very close range, powder burns to the face and gunshot residue on clothing prove that. Two victims were shot through the right eye, the most recent, Huxton, through the mouth. Let's not yet lay too much store in this, it could be coincidence or chance or deliberate, but it's noted. Each victim was killed in the early hours, and with the exception of the first murder, there are no witnesses or physical evidence other than the bullets left at the scene. In the case of Sean Crisp, along with the CCTV of the killing and the decamp, we have the shoeprint which has been identified, the mountain bike used to flee the scene, and now also the black Berghaus rucksack the suspect carried. Initial examination of the rucksack shows blood residue inside, which I'm sure will be identified as from Sean and was transferred from the knife when it was put in there in Montrose Place, behind the embassy. The mountain bike was stolen from outside an underground station in Hounslow, a full week before Sean's murder, and the CCTV which monitored that area was smashed the day before it was stolen. I suspect not a coincidence. The DCI and I think this could be a chink in our suspects' forensically aware armour so, DC's Nagur Padda and Craig Lines, we want you to concentrate on this please. Investigate the criminal damage to the camera, find witnesses, check other CCTV, and as for the bike itself, it must appear somewhere on film being ridden or wheeled away. Where was it kept? How did it get to Montrose Place? It may be our best chance to get a picture of our suspect. We want you two to concentrate on nothing else for now. Okay?"

Nagur and Craig sought each other out amongst the crowd, made eye contact, and nodded to each other before answering the Detective Inspector with one voice. "Yes, Guv."

"Thanks, gents," Heidi acknowledged. "Now for the story from Weybridge and the ex-Secretary General of the Confederation of London Underground Drivers, Bill Buckle. As you'd expect, the media is in a frenzy of speculation, and thanks to a leak from somewhere over the county line, the shooting of the 'Cluddite in Chief' has been publicly linked to PC Crisp's murder. Bill Buckle was shot on his doorstep at some time around half past midnight, but not found until the afternoon. As the papers have delighted in pointing out, there are about ten million suspects, namely every Londoner who ever had their day completely fucked up by Bill and one of his wildcat strikes dropping out of the blue. He was not a popular man, a raving Lefty who made the Labour Party blush at times with his extremism, but there *was* more to him than the public knew. The night before he was killed, he spent four hours at the local Samaritan centre where he manned the phones, taking calls from people in need of help. Something which was a regular practice"

There was a general murmur of surprise around the room. "*Bill Buckle*! A goody two-shoes at hand to help the suicidal? *Really?*" The incredulous voice belonged to DC 'Dirty' Don Chamberlain. "A few years back, I was on route to West Brompton for an interview at the Empress State Building and my train rolled to a halt in bloody Pinner. Pinner! No warning, no reason, and nowhere near where I needed to be. Just another one of Buckle's muscle-flexing demonstrations of union power. The train came to a stop, like every other train on the tube, and the driver walked away. If Bill bloody Buckle had been there, he'd have been lynched by a mob. I missed the interview and missed getting into the CID for a year."

"Buckle wasn't all bad then, if he saved us from you for twelve months." The room burst into laughter at Pat Kerrigan's jibe.

"Thank you all very much." Heidi took control again, but Grant could see Paul Winter behind his DI, trying to hide a broad grin with his hand. "If we could continue. I'm sure most of us have a story about how we've suffered because of Bill Buckle. The point is that we need to view him as a murder victim first and a public figure second; the two may or may not be connected. Keep open minds on this. Surrey and the Met are sharing the investigation into this one with myself acting as a liaison between us, I'm happy with that; we'll have our hands full after the events this morning."

Heidi took a step along the whiteboard and pointed to an A4 photo taped to it. "Victim three is Bernard Huxton, shot through the mouth in the early hours today. He was a local Councillor for the Conservative Party, having retired from teaching some years ago. He was married and had a grown-up daughter who lives in Australia. Charlie Two will be giving you all a handout with his details." The HOLMES analyst waved and smiled cheerily at the mention of her name, but Grant was looking at her colleague, Charles Buller, Charlie One. He seemed to be slumping in his chair, his head falling slowly backwards, as Grant watched, his eyes rolled up into their sockets, the irises disappearing, leaving only the ghastly sight of the whites visible. The fit started a few seconds later.

Chapter Twenty-Five

"Well, no one could accuse you of giving a briefing that lacked a dramatic climax. Even I didn't expect our chief analyst to round up proceedings prematurely by falling off his chair and thrashing about on the floor, foaming at the mouth. How did you arrange that?" Grant's voice dripped sarcasm and the unresolved rancour he was feeling for Charlie One.

It was the morning following Charlie One's collapse, and Grant was expressing his views to DCI Paul Winter and DI Heidi Yorke in the glass box office. Heidi shook her head, "I know he bit your head off, and he's been more than a bit cranky for a while now. Could it be what happened last night is linked to that behaviour?"

Grant considered his friend's words and implied admonition. By nature, genial and considerate, Grant Maddox recognised the possibility of Heidi's theory and was big enough to admit it. "Well, okay," Grant held his hands up in mock surrender, "but he'd really pissed me off, I was going to speak to you about him last night Paul, after the briefing. How is he? Do we know?"

Paul leant over and tapped a sheet of A4 on his desk. "He called last night from hospital, and spoke to the night duty inspector who left me a note. He apologised for last night's disruption and said the doctors diagnosed tiredness from overwork, plus dehydration, but most of all a dodgy prawn sandwich from the canteen. The combination induced his collapse; he's in hospital for twenty-four hours of observation, at home for a couple of days rest, and then he'll be back. Sounds like it looked more dramatic than it was."

"Well, that's good news. Have you spoken to Charlie Two? Is she happy to manage on her own for a few days?" Heidi asked.

"I spoke with her last night as her oppo was being carted off in an ambulance. She's competent and confident. She'll manage." Paul reassured.

Keen to re-establish his kind and caring credentials, Grant enquired, "Does he have anyone at home? Is he married or with anyone to look after him?"

Paul nodded. "I asked Charlie Two that last night. She said he lives alone and has done for years. He admitted to her when he was drunk at an end of case party, that he'd been engaged once, but it ended unhappily. He's been alone ever since."

"That's sad. To be that age, what is he, mid-fifties? and be alone." Heidi offered. "If it's okay with you, Paul, I'll leave it a day, then do the welfare home visit myself. Maybe we could have a whip-round and get him something, some fruit or chocolates?"

"Or a better mood and some fucking manners?" Grant butted in, unable to resist it.

Heidi lowered her eyebrows and grimaced whilst Paul, in a well-practised manoeuvre, hid a smile behind his hand.

* * *

Amber and Grant sipped at the exquisite tasting but extortionately priced coffee in the Migliorè Coffee House. Amber chuckled to herself.

"What?" Grant enquired. "What's so funny?"

"Just thinking back to the last time we were in here, when you dragged the manager over the counter and shook him like a rag doll. Hilarious."

Grant looked over his shoulder to the counter, the scene of one of his very rare losses of temper. The fabulously fashionable but utterly pretentious coffee house's previous 'Capo Del Barista Supremo', Derek Trubshaw, self-styled as Del'roi, who'd been the recipient of Grant's ire, was now long gone. "Irritating twat," was the Detective Sergeant's concluding observation of the event. "How's your il fantastico capo del magro frappuccino al cioccolato moka?"

Amber smacked her lips together, "Lovely."

"It should be, it cost more than my first car." The words were grouchy, but the facial expression which accompanied them was smiling. The over-priced coffee was Grant's treat after attending the post-mortem of Bernard Huxton; the fact he shared the event in the company of Amber Bennett had eased its unpleasantness. He liked Amber immensely, *and* they worked well together.

Amber laughed, "That name is etched into your memory, isn't it?"

"Yep! I'll be able to say il fantastico capo del magro frappuccino al cioccolato moka at the drop of a hat until my dying day. See, I did it again. And it's true, it did cost more than my first car, a little grey mini I bought for five quid off a mate in my squad. God, I loved that car." Grant said dreamily.

"Back when you were in the Royal Marines?" Amber asked. Grant nodded.

"Maybe one day you could tell me about that," she continued. "I know you were in Northern Ireland and served in the Falklands War. I'd be interested to hear."

"Maybe, one day." The image of a grimy face above his rifle sight trespassed into his mind's eye. The Argentinian soldier, standing in the trench next to his dead comrade, hands above his head, the inky darkness breached by abrupt bursts of illumination from muzzle flashes, parachute flares, and the impact of artillery shells, the chaos of war all around. *'No dispares. No dispares,'* he'd said. *'Don't shoot. Don't shoot.* Grant shook his head, dispatching the image and torturous memory to where it was safely hidden away. "Maybe, one day," he repeated, "but for now we have Bernard Huxton to consider. Tell me, Detective Constable, what have we got?"

Amber consulted her notes, written as she'd interviewed Maud Huxton a day earlier. "Bernard Law Montgomery Huxton, sixty-seven years old, no criminal record, married to Maud for forty-two years, one daughter, Claire, aged forty-two, resident in Canberra, New South Wales. He was a teacher at two West London secondary schools for thirty-eight years, the last one in Putney for thirty-five years, retiring six years ago. After a year of kicking his heels, he became a Tory Councillor where he was well enough thought of to be in with a shot as Mayor next year. He enjoyed gardening and Strictly

Come Dancing, although he couldn't stand Bruce Forsyth, to quote Maud, he thought 'men with wigs have something wrong with them'. That's it in a nutshell, skip."

Grant nodded, "What subject did he teach? Did he ever get any complaints as a teacher, any scandals? Why did he leave his first school after three years? Any hint of discord with Maud or neighbours, any issues in the Council Chamber? Did he have *any* enemies, anywhere?"

"A full statement needs taking, Mrs Huxton was understandably shaken to the core, but he taught maths and woodwork, he moved schools because he moved house, according to his wife anyway, she didn't mention scandal or problems, but she wouldn't, would she? I'll liaise with the local education authority for his record and can speak to the school he left six years ago."

"Good." Grant sipped his much cheaper Americano, "and the rest?"

"Maud says they were happily married, the only sadness in their life was their daughter Claire deciding to emigrate to Australia when she was twenty-five. She was a nurse; the Aussies snapped her up. Apparently, it broke Bernard's heart when she left; he cried for a week. They save up and visit her once a year. Claire's married with twin boys. I didn't pick up on any issues there."

"And his Council career?"

"Not especially controversial, he had an interest in the housing side of things, got into some heated debates about social housing stock, right-to-buy and stuff like that, but it's hardly earth-shaking stuff, it's just the local bloody council."

"Grant nodded once more. "Local or national, blood can reach the boil, maybe someone denied a council house, or wanted to buy theirs and got knocked back. We need to see if he made any enemies or if there was any personal animosity towards him."

"He did have a beef with one of the neighbours, especially their son, about parking in the street, Maud says it was an irritant more than anything and didn't come to blows or anywhere near."

"Okay, good stuff, we'll need someone to speak with him anyway, and also get a full statement off Maud Huxton when she's up to it. I'll get one of the lads to do that, you get what you can about Huxton's employment history, see what it throws up."

"Will do skip."

"You okay after this morning?" Grant asked, referring to the post-mortem on Huxton.

"God yes!" Amber replied perkily. "I'm well used to all that by now, neat, tidy, and not decomposed. Piece of piss!"

Grant laughed. "You've become hardened to the dark side, then?"

"No, not exactly." Amber shrugged, deciding to put aside the police officer's customary display of bravado. "I think I'm able to deal with the physical horrors of The Job, it's the emotional element which is tougher." Amber reflected for a moment. "I would've had trouble at Sean's autopsy," she declared honestly. "Because I knew him. It's having an emotional connection. I know it would've been just the Doc slicing and dicing as usual, cutting flesh which had already been desecrated by the killer, but it's *just* flesh, I know that. But I don't know if I can ever become hardened to the emotional side of *any* victim, for that matter, not just Sean. It may just be a body now, but the association, the memories." Amber lingered, gathering her thoughts. "Sean was so funny, outgoing, kind and helpful, outrageous sometimes, all the things which made him, him. Knowing it's over, everything he was ever going to see and do, every experience and contact he was ever going to have... gone. Forever. That's what's difficult." Amber paused again, collecting her thoughts, wanting to say something which was important to her, to her motivation and purpose as a Police Officer and a Detective. "Killing someone is a theft, the *worst* kind of theft, the theft of an individual's future. Is there *anything* worse than stealing someone's future?"

It was an excellent question. Grant made no reply but thought deeply on the words which Amber had sincerely uttered in an attempt to explain her feelings. His colleague was right, Grant concluded, but there was more than one way to take away someone's future. If stealing a future, in whatever form that may take, was the worst thing a person could do, didn't it stand to reason that the victim of such a 'theft' would have ample motive to seek retribution, even to the point of murder?

Chapter Twenty-Six

He felt sick. He was used to feeling sick, but familiarity brought no relief; it merely reinforced the paucity of time available to complete his tasks. Regrettably, this was a familiar journey on the underground train, but unusually, this occasion was at the height of rush hour and was pure hell. The hundreds crowding through the electric gates, up and down escalators, and cramming the stairways had brought him to the brink of a panic attack. He could feel the pressure building up inside. The train doors slid open, and he was forced to shuffle sideways to enter, as a dark-suited businessman forcefully shoved him aside to guarantee *his* place on *this* train, although the next one was only three minutes from arriving at the platform. Shoulders bumped into him, faces crowding his own, ugly faces, so many people were ugly, he'd never really noticed before how unattractive most people really were. He was sweating and nauseous, the heat from the bodies felt crushingly heavy on his chest, his knees buckled for a moment, but he caught himself, gripping more tightly on the chrome pole, which served as passenger handrails as the train accelerated, rocking and shaking its payload of humanity.

He released his hold on the steadying metal for a second to run his hand across the beads of sweat on his forehead, which were threatening to run down into his eyes. In that moment, the dark-suited man stretched out his hand and seized the space he'd vacated. Close to a dozen other hands gripped the metal support, leaving him with no place to hold on. He stared malevolently at the dark-suited man, who, after a few seconds, aware he was being looked at, returned the stare. His lips formed the slightest of smiles, he raised his chin a fraction, the barest leak of body language hinting at his superiority, his success in the game of commuter one-upmanship.

As the train lurched, his unsteadied body fell against the back of a fat woman who turned her bloated face towards him, uttering the exasperated condemnation '*well, really!*' Deliberately loud enough to cause faces to turn and look at him, assuming the perverted worst. His right hand was in his pocket, grasping the handgun; the dark-suited man, the bloated woman were potentially moments from death, *if* he chose to use the power he possessed. He recognised the recent, barely controlled fury, bubbling beneath the surface, becoming less resistible, the seductive urge to act on the spur of the moment when crossed, offended, or dismissed. As tempting as it was to yield to impulse, to do so at that moment meant his ultimate goal would remain unachieved. The gun stayed in his pocket. However, he took *huge* satisfaction, ninety seconds later, to ensure the vast majority of vomit which spewed copiously from his mouth showered over the dark-suited man and the vile, fat woman.

* * *

The journey home and the pleasure he'd derived were behind him now. Time was so valuable he'd practised mentally to move on quickly, to live the moments which were immediately before him. He'd rested during that evening, sleeping fitfully, the knowledge of the set alarm intruding on his ability to truly relax. When it beeped into life, he jumped with surprise. With an effort, he swung his legs over the side of the bed and rubbed his face, pushing the palms of his hands into his eyes, the green and red shapes dancing across his inner vision. It would have been so easy to slump back onto the soft mattress, to let the enveloping comfort of the pillow swathe his head and the body warmed duvet slide back over his aching frame. But he had a mission which needed to be fulfilled, time was short, and he had eternity to rest.

The shower revived him, the hot water spilling over his pain-wracked body giving him the strength and willpower to dress, prepare, and make the journey into central London. Now he stood in the shadow of a doorway opposite the brightly lit entrance to the underground car park. About twenty feet down the steep ramp, red barriers projected left and right across the entrance and exits to the car park, blocking the two lanes to all but authorised users. Only guests at the eye-wateringly expensive Park Lane London View Hotel and privileged members of the hotel staff were permitted access to that most prized of London possessions, a city centre parking space.

At this hour, the street was quiet, no vehicles or pedestrians trespassed to disturb the stillness. The hum of traffic on Park Lane, on the other side of the hotel, sounded distant and alien to the calm of the street, which held the back entrance to the huge building. He examined his watch, it was nearly time. He waited ninety seconds, *now*! He took a deep breath, pulled his hood forward and down, before plunging his rubber-gloved hands deep into his pockets. Hunching over, he stepped out into the light and walked across the road, skirting the barriers, and made his way down the ramp beneath the hotel.

He moved silently between the BMW's Mercedes, and Bentleys. He knew where the black Audi Q7 would be parked, in the extra-wide bay with a name plaque attached to the wall above it. He sighed with relief, although he was confident that the driver was in the hotel; he'd phoned to check earlier, there was always the possibility that plans could change. Now he just needed to secrete himself, avoid the random patrols of security guards, and wait.

It was nearing one-thirty in the morning, and after two and a half hours, the cold was creeping into his bones. He worried the white clouds of condensation escaping his mouth with each breath would betray his presence, but common sense prevailed; his fear was mere paranoia. In the far corner of the car park, he heard the familiar sound from the cables of the lift operating, followed moments later by the swoosh of the doors sliding open. His body tensed, six times he'd heard those sounds followed by footsteps, and readied himself, only to see the intruder wasn't his target. Perhaps this time?

The blonde hair tied in its distinctive pony-tail, the familiar swagger, and the dark coat pretentiously draped across the shoulders, cape-like, confirmed the identity of the figure. *Him!*

The lights of the Audi flashed as the remote control button was pressed, the doors unlocking with a chunky clunk. The man, oblivious to his danger, gripped the door handle but had no time to pull it when the voice intruded into his thoughts. "Hello, Konstanz." The pony-tale swished as its owner swivelled around in surprise. Konstanz Bassa's view of the speaker was obstructed by the muzzle of a gun.

The concussive sound of the gunshot echoed through the subterranean space, he thought it would wake the whole city. He'd expected to see the figure slump at his feet, instead he was showered in fragments of glass as the 9mm bullet smashed through the driver's door window of the Audi and exited on the opposite side, slamming into a concrete pillar beyond. Konstanz Bassa, the bad-boy, wild-child of 21st Century cuisine, holder of two Michelin stars and resident head chef at the London View Hotel, had dropped to the floor the instant he saw the gaping, lethal maw of the Glock. His lightning reaction saved him from the 9mm round, which ploughed a furrow through his scalp, grazing the bone of his skull, but inflicted no other harm. Now he knew he was fighting for his life. He launched himself from his crouching position, like a sprinter from the blocks, heading towards the brighter light, the doors of the lift, towards the best chance to escape. The best chance to live.

He shook his head, small, shiny cubes of shattered safety glass fell like raindrops from his hood and shoulders, he'd reacted more slowly than his victim, overconfidence and complacency playing their part, as did his physical deterioration. He recovered quickly, determination and resolve becoming his driving force. Bassa was already passing from his view, swerving to the left, the adjacent parked car blocking him from view, the draped overcoat falling to the ground as he accelerated away. He rushed to the rear of the Audi, instantly making the assessment he'd never close the expanding distance to his quarry in a foot pursuit. He was too weak and too slow, but the man who could outrun a projectile travelling at 850mph had yet to be born. He brought the pistol up and aimed at the fleeing figure, and pulled the trigger twice.

The second shot wasn't required, the first striking the celebrity chef in the centre of his left buttock, the next concluded its journey embedded, much to its owner's subsequent distress, in the bodywork of a Bentley Continental GT. The bullet's physical impact on Konstanz Bassa was of much greater consequence than the medical one, its blow propelling him forward, beyond the pace his frantic legs could carry him. He sprawled face down, arms outstretched, on the cold, unforgiving concrete. He heard the footsteps and panting breath of his assailant rushing towards him. He felt no pain from his backside, panic and terror blotted out every other feeling and consideration. He attempted to stand, but the effect of the next shot, to the small of his back, was monumental; it stilled him instantly.

The shooter wasn't aware that his bullet had shattered the chef's spine at the fifth lumbar vertebrae, but he *was* aware that the body before him was unable to move.

The plan had gone horribly wrong. The noise of so many gunshots, the presence of CCTV cameras all over the car park area, and the length of time the attack had taken, all added to the risk of capture. He wanted to turn his victim over, wanted to see his face as the end arrived, but self-preservation won out over personal satisfaction. It needed to be over. He pointed the barrel of the gun at the preposterous pony-tail and fired, the bullet crashing through Chef Bassa's brain, killing him instantly.

Chapter Twenty-Seven

As was often the case in the late evening, the scotch bottle was out on Paul Winter's desk, and two plastic cups, each with a measure of the golden liquid, were pushed towards the waiting detectives.

"Cheers." Paul raised his cup, tipping it slightly in the direction of DI Heidi Yorke and DS Grant Maddox, each mirroring the actions of their guvnor.

"Don't get me wrong, this is all very nice, but are we celebrating something?" Grant asked.

Paul shook his head. "I don't think we have anything to celebrate, not with another dead body with three holes in it, but I have had at least one weight lifted from my shoulders. It seems apparent that whatever it is, we *have* got it's not politically motivated or a terrorist linked act. I had my latest meeting with the Security Service at Thames House today, and pending any further questionable acts by our suspect, I convinced them that the murders don't fall under their domestic security remit."

"I should think so." Heidi placed her barely touched drink back on the desktop. "It was fanciful to think so in the first place. Although Sean was outside the Turkish embassy, nothing was directed at the integrity of the building. As for Bill Buckle, he'd retired from the driver's union and so was out of active politics. Huxton was a minor official in a local council, politically meaningless, and Konstanz Bassa was a celebrity bloody chef. These aren't attacks on the foundations of British democracy. It's a nutter with a gun."

Paul nodded his agreement. "In fairness, the government was under pressure from Turkish interests, so had to involve MI5, then the Loony

Left felt compelled to pitch in when their favourite son was killed too."

"Add a retired teacher who's a Tory councillor and a Michelin-starred celebrity chef to the pot and what have we got?" Asked Grant. "A mixed vegetable soup, to carry on the metaphor."

"I'm not having that! You can't call our victims vegetables." Paul laughed.

"Alright…" continued Grant, "*not* vegetables then. But what do we have?"

"A press corps who're baying like wolves."

"Thankfully, that's your area of responsibility, Guv, but we've such a wide range of victims, *what* connects them. We must be missing something." Grant banged his forehead with the palm of his hand in frustration. "This Bassa bloke who was killed in the early hours of this morning. Born in Austria, trained as a chef in France, and then set up a restaurant in London, won his first Michelin star before he was thirty, poached by the Park Lane London View to run their restaurant, and won a second Michelin star in the process. Right so far?"

"Spot on so far," encouraged Heidi.

"Okay," Grant was thinking out loud, "next he gets a chance to front TV cookery shows and competitions, and with his controversial opinions and wild reputation ends up rich and famous. He freely admits to a coke habit and screws some of the most famous and beautiful women in the world. His reputation was taking a hit, so he set up a training academy based at the hotel for up-and-coming chefs to give them a break into the big time. His benevolence rehabilitated him in the public eye, and he rode the wave ever since. That's Konstanz Bassa in a nutshell. Lots of friends and lots of enemies, lots of people who are indebted to him, lots who must feel the opposite. My guys will have their hands full just chasing down and interviewing all Bassa's contacts alone, never mind keeping on top of the other victims' cases." Grant drained his cup but held on to it, keeping it out of range of his boss, fearing a 'Paul Winter top-up session' was threatening.

"I've spoken with those upstairs, Grant. This is as high-profile as it's possible to get. Resources are not a problem, if we need more people, we get more people. Tell me about this morning's killing, our man didn't have it all his own way this time, did he?"

"No, he didn't. Amber and I attended the scene and had a preliminary view of the CCTV. Our suspect was dressed as before, at Belgrave Square, dark hoody, crouched over, so no view of his face. He had a bit of good luck, the outside camera covering the street showed him crossing the road and accessing the hotel car park via the down ramp. The internal cameras covering the entrance are monitored by security staff, but he entered bang on their changeover, at eleven o'clock, so although he was recorded, the screens weren't being physically watched; they missed him getting in."

"Good luck…or good planning?" Heidi speculated, "If it was planning, it may indicate inside knowledge. We need to look at anyone with a grudge against Bassa who works at the hotel or who did. Especially anyone dismissed by him."

"Not just employees, *any* association, maybe a supplier of food, ingredients, kitchen equipment, a person or company that was discontinued, disadvantaged, or suffered economically because of something Bassa said or did. That's a very wide net to cast." Grant held his arms out wide, conscious of the hours of work involved in trawling for a potential suspect.

"It's true, but this is good stuff." Paul seemed animated at the prospect of the hunt. "We'll start with the most obvious category, kitchen staff who've been dismissed recently, let's say in the last six months, remember Sean was stabbed with a chef's knife. Then we widen the search by time and association, check ex-employees for the previous twelve months, and include suppliers. Anyone who would know the security guards' duty rota, their way around that car park and was aware of Bassa's movements. If we input all that information and anything from Huxton's teaching and political careers onto HOLMES, surely some link with Sean Crisp and Bill Buckle will be thrown up." Paul slapped his hands down on the desktop. "Good! What with this line of enquiry and MI5 off my back, this is the first time in a week I've felt personally involved and excited."

"What a bugger we're down to just Charlie Two on HOLMES, can she cope? We're talking about a huge amount of data to input and then analyse. Should we get another operator until Charlie One is back?" Heidi asked.

"Well, hopefully Charlie One will be back soon, and she seemed confident enough when I asked her if she could cope. She's a really smart cookie, smarter than she sounds with her Brummie accent anyway." Paul laughed, slapping his hands on the desk once more. "Right you pair, what the fuck are you doing sitting on your fat arses drinking my scotch? Get home, it's late, I want you in good and early tomorrow. Let's attack this case." A wide smile decorated Paul Winter's face.

Grant smiled too, aware how much weight his friend had been carrying for the team and how much had been lifted from his shoulders with the exclusion of the Security Service's involvement. Paul seemed his old self once more. As for Detective Sergeant Grant Maddox, he had a plan of action too, one which had stood him in good stead time after time in the past. With an influx of more resources to dig and plough through the lines of enquiry, he felt free enough to follow his idea, first thing in the morning. He downed the dregs in his plastic cup, smacked his lips, and bade his colleagues a good night.

Chapter Twenty-Eight

There was a renewed buzz about the Task Force office in the morning, the team feeling the new impetus from their leader more by osmosis than by direct orders. Grant consumed his usual coffee, directed a couple of DCs to the Park Lane London View Hotel to compile a list of persons of interest from which a running order of interviews could be drawn. It was with some disappointment he learned that Amber Bennett had been assigned to visit Maud Huxton that morning to delve deeper into the life and background of her husband and was attempting to speak with the Local Education Authority for the same reason.

As he rose from his desk, he scanned the large room, noticing Charlotte Trent, universally known as Charlie Two, staring in his direction, plainly hoping to catch his eye. She confirmed the suspicion by gesturing for Grant to join her.

Grant lowered himself into the chair beside the HOLMES analyst.

"Can I help you, Charlie? Is everything alright?"

Charlie Two looked left and right in a time-honoured motion, signalling what she had to say was confidential. "Yes, Sarge." She leant conspiratorially towards Grant, uttering the words that *any* supervisor, in *any* role, learns to dread. "Can I have a quiet word?"

"Of course," Grant replied, intrigued. "What's up?"

"I don't want to speak ill, or criticise," Charlie hesitated, "or get anyone into trouble, but…"

Grant understood immediately. "You have a concern about Charlie Buller. If it's anything to do with the progress or integrity of the investigation,

Charlotte, you have the right and duty to bring it to a supervisor's attention. Okay?"

Charlie Two bit her lower lip but nodded. "Okay. The upgraded HOLMES system we use has a D.R.E. function, which has thrown up an interesting piece of data."

Grant held up his hand, "*Whoa!* D.R.E?"

"Sorry, Sarge. Dynamic Reasoning Engine, D.R.E., it's a sub-function of the system which automatically sifts input data and delivers suggestions or links which we weren't necessarily including manually in the search parameters." Charlie saw two blank eyes staring at her and sighed.

"I was with right up until, 'sorry, Sarge,'"

Charlie winced, not unsympathetically. "It looks for stuff."

"Got it. Carry on"

"We received Sean Crisp's mobile phone records three days ago, and obviously, that information was added to the database, the same day the D.R.E. function threw up a connection, a *really* interesting connection. When it does, that an operator must 'ack' it, that's 'acknowledge' the alert signal," Charlie pointed to a red key on the keyboard marked 'ack'. "The system automatically notes the operator ID, and the time and date of the 'ack'. The computer then sits back and relaxes, knowing it's done its bit and it's now down to someone else to do something with that information, and it has proof of the fact, set into the hard drive."

"I understand. Keep going."

Charlie lowered her voice. "Charlie 'acked' the alert three days ago and did nothing. *Nothing!*" She hissed. "After he went sick, I was going through the case updates on Charlie's side of the system, saw the alert and the ack, and realised that he'd ignored the D.R.E. update. There was no note made, no dissemination, no one told, no action, nothing, nothing at all."

"You said it was a *really* interesting connection, I take it from your concern that it's something which he couldn't possibly dismiss as unimportant?"

"No. Not at all."

"What was the connection?"

"For a couple of months, Sean Crisp was making numerous calls on his mobile to a land-line number, dozens and dozens of them, nearly always very short calls, but within a few seconds, he was phoned back on his mobile from another mobile number. We don't have that number on the system, but we do have the *land-line* number; it was input from the police contact list at Sean's Diplomatic Protection Group base."

"And whose land-line number was it?"

"It was Rory Caplan's home number." Charlie's voice was a whisper.

Grant shook his head in bewilderment. "Who the hell is Rory Caplan?"

"Police Constable *Rory Caplan*, he's the armourer at the DPG base, he issues the weapons. His nickname is 'Tiddles', the station cat, he never goes out. His leg got mangled in a motorbike accident."

Grant remembered the nickname now. "Yes, yes, Tiddles. He went sick the night Sean was killed."

"Yes, but this is the point, it may have been Rory Caplan's home number Sean was ringing, but, Sarge, it doesn't seem likely Sean was phoning Caplan? They worked together, Sean would know if Caplan wasn't at home, wouldn't he?"

"So you think that when Sean knew Caplan was at work, maybe he could even see him across the base-room, he was calling his *wife* at home, to get her to call him back on her mobile and arrange an affair?"

"Well…yes, that seems a good guess, doesn't it? The duty state would prove it. We've been looking for who Sean was seeing and split up with, about a week before he was murdered, *and* would you believe it, the last call his mobile made to that number was nine days before he was killed. It fits."

"Has Caplan been interviewed?" Grant suspected he knew the answer already

"No, Sarge, he's been off work since that night. It's not unusual, his sick record is atrocious, but he's been given a huge amount of slack, his injury was on duty, and The Job is looking after him."

Grant's mind was whirring, with question after question springing to the forefront of his mind. Was Sean Crisp having an affair with Rory Caplan's wife, and if so, did Rory find out about it? And if he *did* find out, what did he do about it? Was he capable of murder? He certainly wasn't seen at the base from the start of Sean's mid-post break at twenty minutes after midnight, and he hadn't been at work since. A time period in which a further three people had been killed. And what was happening with Charles Buller, 'Charlie One', a key member of the Task Force Team? Why had he failed to input and circulate such important information to the case? Especially when the fact was so easily proven, the data, the computer record couldn't lie. *Could it?* Grant would be speaking to Charles Buller very soon, and he suspected it would be in a small, windowless room with a member of the legal profession in attendance and a tape recorder running.

In the meantime, it had already been Grant's intention to attend Sean Crisp's central London Diplomatic Protection Group base that morning. His plan was to go back to the beginning, back to basics, to review the facts from the start, with fresh eyes and in light of developments in the case. He'd revisit any and all of the relevant locations and try to acquire a new interpretation or understanding. It was a procedure he'd employed before on other investigations, and usually it turned up new insights and fresh lines of enquiry. Now he was heading to the base with a suspect in his sights, now he was gunning for the Station Cat.

Chapter Twenty-Nine

The DPG base was near to deserted when Maddox arrived mid-morning, most officers out on post or on patrol. He was welcomed with a cup of 'hot splosh' prepared by a crusty old PC who promised it would "taste fuckin' 'orrible", but be "wet n' warm on a freezin' day." He was correct on both counts. The 'Old Sweat' PC solemnly offered Grant an open book. "We got a Book of Remembrance going, for Crispy's kid, we all writ summut in it, summut nice about old Crispy. You wanna put summut in? As you're investigating the case, huntin' the fucker wot did 'im." As he spoke, strangling the English language with a bare tongue, Grant noted his gravelly voice break slightly with emotion, and the lines in his face became overcast with sadness at the memory of his dead friend. "We're all 'urtin' Sarge, so you need to find that fucker, right?" Grant gave what reassurances he could and wrote a platitude to that effect in the book. He was guided to the sergeant's office and introduced to Chris Fallon, the supervisor who'd dropped off Sean Crisp the night of his murder.

Police Sergeant Christopher Fallon exhibited no anxiety at Grant's appearance or reticence to speak of his late friend and colleague, Sean Crisp. Nor did he display any reservations in discussing Sean's 'extra-curricular activities'. "He was a bit of a lad," Fallon offered, shrugging as he did so. "He was good good-looking bloke and very dapper, outside work he usually wore a suit and a shiny, brightly coloured waistcoat, black, patent leather, pointy shoes, he was a natty dresser. He was distinctive looking, the red hair, the dashing cavalier beard and moustache, he worked out in the gym so had a good physique for a man his age, he was very funny and personable, women *liked* him. He wasn't creepy or slimy, nothing like that, he came on to women with a cheeky smile on his face, he never made out he was anything other than what he was, he never led anyone up the garden path, made no promises he wasn't going to keep. He liked women, he liked sex, and he went for it."

Grant nodded, "From what I understand, he went for it quite a lot. It sounds like you knew him well?"

It was Fallon's turn to nod. "I did. We worked together as Constables, more years ago than I care to remember."

Grant decided to keep his powder dry for the moment and leave any questioning about Sean's possible involvement with a colleague's wife until later. "From Sean's perspective, he may have been doing no harm, just having fun, but I expect his behaviour must've upset some people. You knew him a long time, Chris. Did he make any enemies? Can you recall any that may have held a grudge?"

"Enough to want to kill him?"

"Anything?" Grant asked. "Go back as long as you like, sometimes hate and the desire for vengeance ferments for years before bubbling to the surface."

Fallon rubbed his chin, ordering his thoughts before answering. "Well, the first thing is that most of those who may have had cause for a grievance against Sean wouldn't have known anything about him. Sean wasn't the sort to crow about his conquests, he wasn't a bragger. He once said to me that he operated like the SAS, he'd get in and get out again without anyone noticing." The two sergeants laughed.

"I understand," said Grant. "And it may be true at the time, but as the years pass, a duped husband or boyfriend who learned of Sean's antics with his woman could be really angry about it. Who knows, even end up questioning the parentage of any children. That's enough motive for some people to kill."

"True," Fallon conceded, "but I can only tell you a few instances I know about. The most obvious one is the split from his wife, Debbie. I knew her, and I admit she was a wronged woman, but my Godfathers, what a venomous harpy she was, and as far as I know, still is. Her righteous indignation about

Sean's antics should be taken with a pinch of salt, too. When she started seeing Sean, she was engaged to another guy, so she was unfaithful herself. She was spiteful, bitter, and did her best to ruin Sean's life when he left her. She made allegations of mental and physical abuse against him, all *proven* to be false. She made allegations of theft and burglary against him, *all* false. She tried to prevent Sean's access to Callum with a host of fabrications. One example, when Callum was five or six, Sean took him to a shopping mall, and when Sean turned his back, Callum wandered off like kids do, for two minutes. *Two minutes!* The worst two minutes of his life, he told me, Sean made the mistake of informing a security guard about ten seconds before Callum wandered back. When Debbie found out from Callum, she put that incident in her back pocket until years later. After the split, she took it out again and alleged neglect and abandonment against Sean. She even traced the security guard as a witness and raised hell. It was all bollocks. But by using things like that and more, she turned Callum against his father. You know Callum punched Sean's lights out, right here, outside the base?"

"Yes, I heard about that," Grant said.

"And you know she stands to make a fortune out of Sean's death?"

"Yes."

"Okay. Well, you can tell, I don't think much of Debbie, and bloody Callum was far too ready to believe his mother rather than his own eyes and common sense.

"I'm aware of the bad blood with Callum and Debbie. Anything else?"

"Yes, I guess. When Sean and I worked at Hounslow, he was screwing a girl from admin who was engaged to another civvy in her office, buggered if I can remember his name now. This guy was nice enough, older than her and really dull and boring, so when Sean started to turn it on to her, she went for it, and they had a thing for a while. The boring admin guy found out, he was pretty humiliated and called off the engagement. He had a huge stand-up row with Sean in the public area of the front office! He promised Sean he'd regret ruining his life. I was there, he accused Sean of stealing his future. It was horrible."

Grant's pen was a blur as he rushed his notes. "What happened?"

"Hmmm, depends who you believe. Sean had reported a couple of burglaries on lone elderly victims, just two of a whole series that hit the area. Sean dug and asked around and identified three brothers as responsible. He set up a collection plan to tackle them, organised observations, applied for a warrant, sorted a drugs dog and ghostbusters to force entry at their house. He and his relief did the lot, a great job, three arrests, lots of stolen property recovered, and drugs found. Plenty on CID and Burglary Squads had their noses put out of joint, made to look lazy or incompetent, that a uniformed PC and his mates had put this whole operation together when they hadn't."

"As a CID sergeant, I can see how that might feel." Grant encouraged.

"When it came to trial, some of the case papers were found to be missing from the file. One of the main victims had passed away, and her original statement couldn't be produced or re-taken; some other bits were gone as well, identification of stolen property, stuff like that. Enough for the case to be dropped and for Sean to look incompetent, like an out-of-his-depth uniformed mug."

"Who do you think took the papers?" Grant had stopped writing, concentrating intently.

"The finger was pointed at one of the CID officers who'd got special criticism for prematurely closing the initial investigation into the spate of burglaries in the first place. There was a *lot* of bitterness. Sean searched the sealed confidential waste sacks that were piling up under lock and key, ready to be sent for incineration. He found the missing papers. Guess who was responsible for disposal of confidential waste?"

"Don't tell me, was it dull and boring admin guy whose ex-fiancée was porking Sean Crisp by any chance?" Offered Grant.

"Got it in one. He denied involvement, but Sean caused enough of a stink that the guy had to be posted elsewhere, and a promotion he was in line for went West with it. No one won."

Grant closed his notebook, mentally resolving to find out who 'Mr Dull and Boring' was. "May I see the duty state for the last month or so?"

Chapter Thirty

A station duty state lists its patrol and post commitments for a twenty-four-hour period, each day a new sheet is started and the old sheet filed. Every officer assigned to that station appears on the state in the form of their shoulder number, noted in the relevant small box in a large, complex grid. Those on duty are recorded, showing when their shift began and ended, and their role, also whether overtime had been incurred or not. Those on a rest day are included, as are those off work through sickness or injury, or away on courses, attending court, or posted on aid to another station or assignment. The duty state is the Holy of Holies, written in an immaculate script, only by a sergeant's hand, and is a definitive record of the location and movements of the whole of a station's complement.

***

Sergeant Fallon waved a hand across the pile of papers. "That's two months' worth; there are more if you want to go further back. What exactly are you looking for? Maybe I can help?"

Grant beheld the pile of paperwork and exhaled slowly, slightly daunted at the task he'd set himself. "I find, when a case has reached a certain point, it really helps to go back to basics, to re-visit the case with fresh eyes, literally, physically re-visit the crime scenes, the background, the associates. It's surprising how often it can help, to give a new idea or path to follow."

"You're the officer from the Dissection Murder case, aren't you?"

"That's what the media called it," Grant replied cautiously.

"Is that what you did with that one, go back to basics?" Fallon asked.

"Yes. It's what I did."

"It worked, you did a good job." Fallon paused. "Tell me what you're looking for. I'll help you. It'll take you all day to go through this lot on your own."

Grant smiled; he'd feared a prying series of questions into his role in the case, which had held headlines for weeks, a case in which he'd been centre stage. Instead, he'd received an understated compliment and an outstretched helping hand. It was ideal. If Fallon combed the records and compiled a full list of Sean Crisp's activities, it would free him to covertly search the same records to see what Rory Caplan had been up to during the same period. "You're right, it'd be a great help. Thank you."

An hour later, Grant folded a sheet of A4 paper covered in his notes, which showed the dates and times of PC Rory Caplan's work schedule, and pushed it into his pocket. On his return to the Task Force office, it could be compared with the times and dates of the killings. The scribblings would rule Caplan out completely, or leave a question mark hanging above him. Christopher Fallon, more familiar with the documents than Grant, had finished his examination fifteen minutes earlier, handing the completed notes relating to Sean Crisp towards the Detective Sergeant, making no enquiry of their purpose, and leaving to catch up with his own responsibilities at the DPG base.

Satisfied, Grant left the small records office and found Fallon in the base room.

"May I see the contact list?" Grant enquired.

Sergeant Fallon opened the desk drawer and passed a red ring binder to Grant. "It's all in there. I don't need to remind you of its confidentiality; it's sensitive information."

"I understand. I just want to check something." The contact list catalogued every officer's name, home address, home telephone number, and next of kin details. Such a record was jealously guarded for obvious reasons. Grant turned the pages to find Rory Caplan's record, holding open his notebook on the opposing page. He found the home number that Sean Crisp's phone records had shown him calling dozens of times, below was the name of Rory Caplan's wife, Heather, and her mobile phone number. Grant looked from the contact list record to the number written in his notebook and back again. There was no mistake, the numbers were identical. Heather *was* returning Sean's calls as Charlie Two had surmised. Heather Caplan was Sean Crisp's missing lover.

As casually as he could, Grant asked, "PC Rory Caplan, the armourer the night Sean was killed, is off sick, I understand. Has he given any indication of when he'll be back?"

Fallon shrugged. "How long is a piece of string? He pretty well comes and goes as he wishes, bit of a piss-taker actually. I know he got all mangled on an emergency call whilst a Job motorcyclist, but he's a constant duties abstraction, and trying to work around him all the while gets on your tits in the end."

"I need to speak to him, that's all, he's the only one on duty that night still outstanding, I've got his details from the list here, I'll sort something out."

"Okay, maybe you could give him a shove in our direction when you're done with him, remind him where he works."

Grant laughed. "I will, and can I ask a favour?"

"Sure."

"If you do happen to speak, don't tell him I'm coming to see him."

Fallon raised a quizzical eyebrow. "Okay. Whatever you say."

"One more thing, could you arrange a lift down to Belgrave Square for me? I want to have another walk around the scene and the suspect's escape route."

Fallon lifted a personal radio and transmitted the request to a patrolling car. "Sorted, outside for you in five minutes. Okay?"

"Lovely. I see from the list of duties for Sean that he was posted for ten successive day shifts to a post called 'Aid 101'. What's that?"

"Ah! 'Aid 101'. You know of the MP, Marlon Tredegor?"

"Yes, Labour Party bloke, shocked everyone in the House of Commons when he first appeared with three-foot-long dreadlocks! He hit the papers a month or so ago, too, what was it?" Grant searched his memory. "Didn't he go public with the intimidation and violence directed at youngsters in his constituency by gang members? That's it! They were forcing kids into drug dealing and worse. There were shootings and stabbings and a flat got burnt out too, nasty stuff."

"That's right," confirmed Fallon, "he went further, he identified the gang members himself, on the floor of the House of Commons, using Parliamentary Privilege. The victims were too afraid and intimidated to name names, but old Marlon wasn't. He kick-started a dozen investigations and arrests. He put himself right out there to re-house the youths who'd been dragged in against their will and to get the gangs prosecuted. A brave bloke, walking the walk, not just talking the talk."

Grant nodded in agreement. "Definitely, but what's that to do with Sean Crisp?"

"Marlon Tredegor is subject to more death threats than Salman Rushdie. All the assessments say there's a credible threat to his life, so he's been given full armed police protection, 24/7. His home address is just off Borough High Street, we provide the fixed post. The post call-sign is Aid 101."

"And Sean was there for ten-day shifts?"

"You bet. It's an overtime post, so he asked to work all his rest days there. The duties office cut him a deal because it's not a popular post, miles away from our usual beat, and gutty as hell. They gave him all the rest days as long as he also worked his day-shift rostered days there too. He jumped at it. Sean was a serious overtime bandit!"

"So I heard. Give me the address, would you? I'll make it part of my Sean Crisp tour."

As Fallon wrote down the details, the radio chirped into life, his transport was outside and waiting.

As Grant stepped out the door to the base room, he turned on his heel, "If you remember the name of 'Mr Dull and Boring', I'd really appreciate a call. Thanks for all your help."

Fallon smiled tightly. "You're welcome. Just get the bastard."

Grant nodded, his smile as grim and tight as Fallon's.

Chapter Thirty-One

The powerful engine of the area car roared as it sped away, leaving Grant staring at the front of the Turkish embassy. It was a Regency-style, white stucco building, dominated by the wide portico which covered the three steps up to the black front door, above which a red oval shield bearing a star and a crescent moon was fixed. At the door, watching the suited man who'd just exited the police car with interest, stood a shivering police officer. For now, Grant ignored him, taking a few moments to scan the area, cleared now of the incident tape, which had formed the cordons. Gone was the forensic tent and the white suited evidence gatherers, the crowd of curious public, the media mob, and of course, the body and blood of Sean Crisp. Only the makeshift 'shrine' of tributes nearby provided evidence of the recent horror that had taken place on this street.

"DS Grant Maddox, Major Investigation Task Force." Grant introduced himself and held up his warrant card to the officer, who slowly descended the steps. Grant saw he was equipped identically to Sean Crisp, with a Glock 17 pistol and X-26 Taser.

"You here to see someone at the embassy?" The officer jerked his head back, indicating the door behind him. "They've been good as gold, bringing out hot coffee and such, I think they've a bit of a guilt complex going on, because of what happened here." His head nodded down to the exact spot where Sean had fallen. "I'll buzz in and tell them you're here."

"No thanks." Grant smiled his appreciation. "Just having a fresh look, you know, now everything has been…" Grant paused, knowing how it sounded.

"Now everything's been *cleaned* up?" The officer offered.

It wasn't what Grant had meant. The inference that rubbish or litter is cleaned up from the street hung in the air. "No. Not at all. After everything has returned to normal, like before Sean was killed." The officer nodded, satisfied. "It might help me picture what happened." The officer nodded again. "You knew Sean?" Grant asked.

"Sure. We all knew Sean Crisp. Funny bloke, knew his stuff, dependable too. A good lad." Grant recognised the expression, the understated but universally understood, high praise, from one police officer to another, 'a good lad', it said a great deal.

"That's what I'd heard. A good lad. But did he have any enemies? I mean, someone was damaging his car, that happened several times, more than a coincidence. Two of his tyres were slashed the night he was killed, *and* he was getting threatening letters. He must've upset someone." Grant raised a quizzical eyebrow, It wouldn't hurt to ask; sometimes a fishing expedition caught fish.

The officer looked left and right to make sure he couldn't be overheard. "Fuck me, Sarge! You're kidding, right?" The officer laughed. "Sean *was* a good lad, but he totally caned the overtime, took more than his fair share, which pissed off some people, but most of all, he was a top shagger. He hit on every girl he ever saw, even if she was standing next to her husband, he'd chance his arm. Christmas do's, functions, sporting events, whatever, you hung onto your girl like a fucking limpet when Sean was around." The officer laughed again. "It was *Sean*! It's what he was like; nine out of ten just laughed, he never really meant anything by it, but a few got the hump. He wasn't popular with everyone."

Grant held the officer's eye. "*Who* wasn't he popular with?"

The officer hesitated, deciding he'd said too much. "No one in particular, just sometimes Sean pushed his luck, pissed a few off, but nothing serious, nothing that would lead to killing him. No way."

Grant recognised the impasse and decided not to press it; this wasn't the time or place. "Sure, okay, I understand. I didn't catch your name."

The officer cursed his big mouth; now he was on the investigation's radar and could expect to be called in for a full interview, a monumental ball-ache.

"Kelvin Twigg, Sarge."

"Thanks, Kelvin. Look, I'm going to wander around a bit, look at stuff, and probably spend a lot of time dreamily staring at things like some bewildered old man. Don't let me keep you from your job; you carry on and ignore me. Okay?"

"Yes, Sarge."

"Good lad." Grant winked.

Grant crossed the road and walked towards the junction with Wilton Crescent and halted at the northern corner of the square, next to the statue of José de San Martín, whoever he was. It was the point at which PC Gareth Took, who shared the Turkish embassy post with Sean Crisp on the fateful night, had said he'd seen a dark figure, shaded by the foliage which spilled over the fence of the square's garden. Grant backed up, pushing into the overhanging evergreen branches, seeking concealment, turning to face the embassy, trying to imagine the scene in the darkness of the night. He looked back to the statue, a dark bronze figure, high on a plinth, and realised that his silhouette would be lost at night to the larger, darker shape behind him, unless he moved, through discomfort, cramp, or intent, his position was unseen, giving a clear view across to the portico of the embassy.

As if on command, a DPG vehicle in its distinctive red livery drove past and halted outside the portico. Grant watched as Kelvin emerged from the recess, descended the steps to greet his relief, who clambered from the car. Grant stared. He looked up at the streetlights, described as 'poor' in all the statements, but could see at the point on the footway where the two officers exchanged words and handed over, one to the other, that they'd be bathed in a pool of light. A watcher from this shadowed corner would certainly recognise the features of the officers, especially one as distinctive as Sean Crisp, and remain unseen in the process.

Grant saw Kelvin point in his direction, and the new officer looked towards the Detective Sergeant hiding in the foliage. He could imagine the conversation. 'There's a DS who's investigating Sean's murder over there, can you see him, he's the one lurking in the bush. My money's on the suspect.' Grant shook off the thoughts and closed his eyes again. *If* the suspect was here, right here on this spot, watching the embassy, *if* his intended target was Sean Crisp, he'd have no problem identifying him as he arrived on post at 4.20 am.

Grant recalled the CCTV tape he'd watched with Amber Bennett in the depths of the embassy. He pictured the officer's movements and actions in those minutes leading up to the fatal confrontation. Sean had looked to his right, towards the corner, towards the statue, he'd shaken his head dismissively. A short while later, he'd looked again, but this time he *had* seen something; what he saw made him step down onto the pavement. Grant ran the film through his head, trying to freeze-frame the final moments of a fellow police officer's life. What was PC Sean Crisp telling DS Grant Maddox? How was Sean trying to help him catch his killer?

Sean Crisp had stood and faced the suspect; he'd taken up the standard, defensive, 'bladed stance', ready to deal with any eventuality, but his body language hadn't spoken of fear, alarm, or of a threat. What had happened next? Grant wracked his memory, something which he'd noted at the time, something that wasn't right, but he couldn't put his finger on and interpret.

It came to him in a flash of understanding. As the suspect had raised his head, Sean Crisp had relaxed momentarily; he'd lowered his arms from their defensive position, his body had responded in surprise to something he'd seen. Grant remembered when he'd viewed this moment of the film, his own reaction, and his thoughts. *'Whatever had surprised Sean Crisp, it* **still** *wasn't something which he perceived as a threat. '* Now Grant understood, there could be only one rational explanation. Sean Crisp's reaction had been because he'd *recognised* the hooded figure standing before him; Sean Crisp *knew* his killer.

Chapter Thirty-Two

Grant ran through his reasoning once more, checking himself, challenging his thoughts and assertions, looking for inaccuracies. But it made sense. It had to be true, and further, it answered the little voice in his head who'd been saying all along that the answer was looking them in the face. The realisation turned everything on its head, and the possible motivation to kill the subsequent victims in the process. What that motivation was had yet to be addressed, but for now, one thing at a time. Grant struggled to contain his excitement. His plan, to revisit the scene, to look with fresh eyes, was not yet complete; perhaps more revelations would present themselves to him.

The Detective Sergeant nodded an acknowledgement to the replacement officer who'd taken Kelvin Twigg's place in the portico, but made no further attempt at contact or conversation, his mind was elsewhere. Grant stood on the spot where Sean Crisp had lain, looking up into the muzzle of his own weapon a split second before his life's story ended. He took a few moments to stare at the corner of the square, at the suspect's point of observation and concealment, before nodding decisively to himself. He walked East to the junction with Chapel Street, where he turned left and left once more into Montrose Place.

He noted the high-definition camera set in an elevated position on a wall, which was recording his presence at that moment, as it had recorded the flight of the suspect. Was it really only eight days ago? Montrose Place was a long, straight, and narrow road, a hidden oasis of calm in the heart of the bustling Capital. Within a minute, he was at the alcove, which had hidden the mountain bike upon which the suspect had escaped. Examination of earlier recordings had shown the cycle being locked and stowed there at 2.14 am, a few minutes before the end of Sean's first two-hour stint at the embassy door. Efforts to backtrack the suspect's route *into* Montrose Place had fizzled out at Hyde Park Corner, and as with his escape route, no image of his face had been found.

Grant re-traced the route of the suspect to the end of Montrose Place and turned right into Halkin Street, making his way to Hyde Park Corner. Even though rush hour had long since ended, the traffic was backed up, congesting three lanes; only the bus lane was devoid of vehicles. On the night of the killing, the CCTV had shown the suspect pedalling like fury through a much quieter street than this, up to Park Lane and the entrance to Hyde Park itself, through the recently opened Queen Mother Gates to ditch the stolen bike and the bloodstained rucksack. Grant put himself into the organised mind of his quarry. What would *he* do? It was only a small step to realise the killer must have stashed clean clothes, shoes, and probably another rucksack at that hiding place, almost certainly disposing of the incriminating evidence on his journey to wherever he called home. The forensic awareness of the suspect had been admired before, Grant added his own.

The detective looked at his watch. He wanted to do much more before he returned to the office; he'd another venue he was keen to examine. Sean Crisp had spent the ten working days prior to his murder on a special posting, something out of the ordinary for the DPG officers at his base. Grant saw 'out of the ordinary' as a potential for evidence; he lengthened his stride and headed towards Hyde Park Underground Station.

* * *

A single change at Green Park onto the Jubilee Line took him to London Bridge Station, where Grant emerged into a chill wind and an already darkening sky. He stepped out onto Borough High Street opposite the entrance to the famous market and turned south, passing the war memorial around which lay numerous poppy-adorned wreaths, each in danger of being blown away in the growing gusts which now contained a sprinkling of rain. 'Brilliant', he thought, 'no umbrella and no raincoat'.

It had been years since he'd walked this street; it hadn't changed much. Traffic was heavy, running to and from London Bridge, just four hundred yards behind him. There was the inevitable Chicken Cottage takeaway, a couple of pubs, and hundreds of people of all races and religions crowding the footpaths. A few yards past the Café Nero outlet, he saw the sign he was looking for and turned left into Newcomen Street, a narrow road which, within a short distance, was blocked to vehicular traffic by metal bollards.

He spied the person he sought, standing as far into a shallow alcove as was possible, sheltering from the icy gusts which rushed down the narrow thoroughfare like a wind tunnel.

The uniformed figure in the doorway, spotting Grant's approach, eyed him cautiously. After serving eight years as an armed officer prior to his CID career, the detective recognised and empathised with the raised alert level in the officer's demeanour at the determined advance of an unknown person with their hands thrust deep into their pockets. When Grant was still twenty feet away, he slowly took out his right hand, which held the open wallet of his warrant card, and held it up; the protection officer's tension immediately eased, and a smile replaced the look of taut readiness that had been affixed to his face.

Chapter Thirty-Three

"Detective Sergeant Grant Maddox, on the Task Force investigating your colleague's murder in Belgrave Square," Grant introduced himself, plunging his rapidly chilling hand back into his pocket. "Sorry to alarm you," Grant looked around, "this is a bit serious, is it?"

"Too right, Sarge," the officer agreed. Stuck out here, miles from armed support, on your own, no ballistic cover, nowhere to retreat to, you feel more than a bit vulnerable. The threat to our man here," The officer jerked his head back, towards the door, "has been classified as 'credible', that's a bloody understatement. A load of *really* heavy-duty geezers are looking at doing years of slopping out time 'cos of Marlon Tredegor MP, he's viewed as a traitor to his community by a lot of the youth and a hero to a lot of the older ones. When he's out and about, you can relax a bit, but when he comes home with his Prot Team, it's high alert until that door shuts behind him. Then they bugger off, and it's just the lone silly sod here guarding the house. If the gangs get a chance to slot him, they will, and they won't mind killing a copper in the process, in fact, they'd love it, kudos and all that."

Grant noticed that even as the officer spoke, he was looking past the DS, observing the pedestrian traffic which flowed at a steady rate each way along the street. "I take it your man's in residence then?"

The officer grinned, "If I told you, I'd have to kill you." They both laughed. "I'm Vince, by the way, Vince Conisby, 'VC' to pretty well everyone. How's it going then? Sean's killer, I mean. We haven't heard much feedback except all the stuff on the news and the papers about the other victims who've been offed with Sean's Glock. Are you getting anywhere?"

Grant shrugged. "If I told you, I'd have to kill you." They both laughed again. "We're building a picture, that's why I'm here. Sean had this post for ten days straight, just before he was killed. That's unusual, something different from his normal routine. I wanted to see with my own eyes, see if there was a connection."

VC raised his eyebrows questioningly. "I don't see how. Are you sure you're making headway? Isn't this a bit…" he searched for a word, "desperate?"

"I'd rather call it thorough. Has anything happened? Anything been handed from officer to officer that would raise suspicion? Anything at all?" Grant knew he did sound a little desperate.

VC screwed his face up as he thought. "Well, last week, a group of guys who are associates of the main man who's been nicked because of Marlon, started hanging around at the junction there." VC pointed towards Borough High Street. They didn't do much more than look menacing and watch what we were doing. I'm sure that someone's been keeping a watch here, looking for weaknesses in our procedures, especially on pick-up and drop-off points."

"Hostile reconnaissance, that's to be expected," agreed Grant. "Anything else?"

"Nah. That's it." VC stared past Grant, grinned, and rubbed his hands. "Ah! Here we go, lovely."

"There you go, mate. Americano with hot milk. That'll warm you up inside." Grant started at the nearness of the voice and spun on his heels at the sudden interruption, to view a slim man of medium height and build in a dark puffer jacket and black woolly hat holding out a Café Nero cup. "Got to look after the boys in blue." The face was that of a man Grant estimated as being in his early thirties, but despite his broad grin, was pale, drawn, and tired-looking, making him seem older.

"Luke mate!" gasped VC, taking the cup, "what a lifesaver you are. That's just the ticket, how much do I owe you?"

"Have that on me, you're welcome." The man, obviously known to VC and identified as Luke, smiled questioningly at Grant and said, "You alright mate, how you doing? Bloody freezing isn't it, got to look after those who look after us." Luke held his gaze until VC took the hint.

"This is a detective on Sean's case, Sarge. This is Luke, he's up and down this road regular, he kindly picks up hot drinks from around the corner for us. Keeps body and soul together."

"Ah, right," Luke responded. "That's great, how's the case coming on? Sean was a lovely bloke, a funny guy, I can't tell you how upset I was when he…" He let the word hang, wincing as he spoke. "I couldn't believe it, not to someone you know." Luke shrugged helplessly, "I bet you hear that all the time."

"I do," Grant answered. "You knew Sean Crisp then?"

"Yes, briefly. I got him a coffee a few times, chatted with him, like I said, he was a funny man, I bet he was good company on a night out." Luke looked to VC.

VC nodded. "He was. The best. A laugh a minute old Sean was."

"Can I ask you, Luke, how is it that you take this route so often? Do you work along here?" Grant heard an intake of breath from his side, where the protection officer stood.

"S'okay," Luke reassured. "It's no secret, and our friend here is a detective after all. I'm an outpatient at the cancer centre, Guys Hospital, it's about two hundred yards down the road. I'm in and out several times a week for treatment on Cordelia."

Grant was bemused. "Cordelia? I'm sorry, I don't understand."

Luke laughed. "That's okay. Cordelia is my brain tumour, when I was first diagnosed, a counsellor advised me to give it a name, humanise it, personalise it, it's a method to deal with the situation and focus your emotions, to help you cope."

Grant hadn't felt so uncomfortable in a long while. "Oh, right, I'm really sorry to hear that. Why Cordelia? Isn't that from King Lear? Wasn't she the nice daughter?"

Luke shrugged. "It might be, but it's my ex-wife's name, and she *wasn't* nice. It seemed amusing and appropriate to name a brain tumour after her."

Grant could only manage, "Oh, I see."

"Unfortunately, Cordelia was declared inoperable a short while ago, so she's going to kill me, there's no other way to put it. They're lovely down the road, and doing their best, but the treatment is only prolonging the inevitable."

Grant now understood the cause of the pale and drawn features of Luke's face and guessed the woolly hat could hide a bald head, hair loss being a side effect of chemotherapy. He was overcome with several emotions, not least embarrassment at forcing into the open something so personal. That feeling was closely followed by sympathy and sadness, that such a young man should be so afflicted, was a travesty of natural law. "I'm really sorry to hear that. Truly. I'm not sure what to say."

"Do you know, I've heard everything from 'I'm sorry' to 'it's part of God's plan' to 'you must have done something evil in a previous life'. Seriously! So it's alright, Officer, I've got my head around it, after going through fury and denial and self-pity. It's okay."

"Hello, Mr Lancaster! See you in a bit, don't you be late." The three men turned to look at the slim, pretty woman on the opposite side of the street who waved and called out cheerily before wagging a finger in a mock threat. Luke smiled and gave a thumbs-up before turning his attention back to Grant.

"That's Maggie, one of the nurses who administers my chemo. A lovely girl. They all are. Where was I? Oh yes, acceptance. Once the truth finally sank in, once the inevitability was accepted, I decided to use what time I had productively."

"What did you do?" Grant was genuinely curious, to speak so frankly with a dying man.

"I thanked people. Such a simple thing, but I had the chance to show my gratitude to people who've touched my life. I had a teacher, a Home Economics teacher, Mrs Davis, she encouraged my ambition to be a chef. She was so lovely and supportive. She said I had a talent and even wrote a letter to my mum saying I had a gift. Well, I *did* become a chef. When I found out about..." Luke tapped his head. "...Cordelia, I visited Mrs Davis, bought her a big bouquet of flowers, and thanked her for what she'd done for me."

"That was thoughtful." Commented Grant.

"Not really, it's just letting a person know what they've done for you. I've bought little gifts for all my nurses, and one evening I invited the team who are looking after me to the restaurant where I work and cooked them all a special meal. It was one of the best evenings of my life, huge fun." He paused and thought for a moment. "Another example, I was in a supermarket a few weeks ago and had a funny turn, got a bit wobbly. There was a guy stacking shelves, a huge black guy, covered in muscles and tattoos. Honestly, if you met him in a dark alley, you'd soil yourself." The group laughed. "He saw I wasn't well and rushed to me and caught me before I hit the deck. He picked me up like I was a rag doll and carried me to the staff rest room, made sure an ambulance was called, and stayed with me, giving me sugary tea and patting my skinny arm with a huge hand. Such a kind man. When I'm gone, he's going to get such a surprise from my will. He'll need someone to catch *him* when *he* faints!" There was more laughter.

"It's also been liberating to tell a few people some home truths too, you know, the things you hold in, to keep the peace. I told a couple of relatives what I really thought of them, about their behaviour, things like that."

"'Liberating?' Yes, I can understand that." Grant smiled.

"Anyway. As you can see, being on the way out hasn't affected my ability to talk for England. I better be going, I don't want to be late and upset Maggie, you saw the wagging finger. I don't want to be the *'late* Luke Lancaster', get it? Not yet anyway." Again, there was laughter from the group.

Grant held out his hand, which Luke took. "I'm sorry this is happening to you, I admire your attitude. I wish you well." Grant said sincerely.

"Thank you, I'm nothing special, honest. Righto, I'm off then, will you be here later?" Luke directed the question to VC.

"Not long to go now, I get relieved at 7pm."

"Okay, I won't be out until after that. I'll catch you later in the week. Be good."

"You too." Responded VC, "and thanks again for the coffee, just the ticket."

The protection officer and the detective watched as the dying man walked away towards the hospital.

"Poor bastard," VC observed.

"Nobody said life was fair, and there's the proof," concluded Grant.

Chapter Thirty-Four

It was just after 10.30 pm when Grant, damp from the rain, with aching feet and a weary body, entered the near-empty Task Force office and saw the movement of figures in the DCI's office. He tapped the door and entered without waiting to be asked.

"Bloody hell, Granty, you look horrible," exclaimed the DCI, "horrible, old, knackered and wet. Where've you been all day?"

Grant slumped into the chair beside Heidi Yorke. "Well, you know how to make a guy feel good, thanks a bunch, Guv. I love you, too." He hadn't finished his sentence before a plastic cup half full of scotch was being pushed towards him. Paul Winter waggled the bottle in the direction of Heidi's near empty cup.

Heidi shook her head, putting her hand across the top of her receptacle. "Do you know the biggest danger we face on this unit is to our bloody livers. Honest to God, I didn't realise I'd be an alcoholic inside six months when I transferred from Surrey to the Met." Her comments were met with laughter.

Grant had much to say but took a long swig at the golden liquid first. Feeling its warming effects reviving his aging body. "I've spent the day digging around, and I think I've come up with some ideas." His colleagues moved visibly forward in expectation; anything Grant Maddox had to offer was worthy of consideration.

"I think the focus of the whole investigation should be Sean Crisp. I'm convinced he knew his killer. We find the link between them, and everything else will fall into place. The CCTV showed Sean lowering his guard as he saw the suspects face, *he lowered his guard.* It tells me he knew the suspect, *and* he felt no threat from him. *Sean is the key.*" Grant stressed before pausing.

"Keep going," was all the DCI said.

"I went to Borough High Street, there's a protection post there, right next to Guys hospital, for that MP who's under threat for breaking up the gangs."

"Marlon Tredegor?" Heidi put in.

"Yes, him," said Grant, his enthusiasm obvious. "I met a guy when I was talking to the protection officer. He was a young guy, thirty maybe, but really ill-looking, as well he might be, he's dying from a brain tumour." Heidi winced. "I know, bloody tragic. But this guy said some things which I've been pondering all the way back here. He said that once he'd got past the upset and denial of the diagnosis, he was able to use the time left to him. Now this guy, Luke, was a nice bloke, brought the officer a hot coffee on a cold, wet day, buys gifts for his nurses and cooks them meals, he even has something in his will for a supermarket shelf stacker who helped him when he fainted in a store."

"And?" asked Paul.

"When he said that he'd sought out a teacher who'd had a really positive effect on his life, and visited her to say thank you with a bouquet of flowers, that's when, as a bitter, twisted, cynical old copper, I turned what he did on its head. I was thinking about Bernard Huxton. We all keep thinking about him as being a Tory Councillor, shot at his doorstep as some sort of political act. But what if he was killed because of something he did as a teacher? What if he was a total shit, or a bully, or even a paedophile? What if someone decided to even the score?"

"Isn't Amber Bennett looking into his teaching background with the Local Authority? Has she come back with anything, Paul?" Heidi asked. "Likewise, the school, if there's anything official, I'm sure she'd have found it by now."

Grant shook his head, "Amber's unlikely to find anything officially, Huxton would've been vetted prior to getting a council seat, but it doesn't mean someone didn't have a serious beef with him, or indeed with the Michelin-starred chef Konstanz Bassa, who's famous for pissing people off. And if we're talking about pissing people off, who's annoyed more people in London than Bill Buckle?"

"But why?" asked the DCI, "why now?"

Grant hadn't the chance to speak of the identification of Heather Caplan as the elusive final lover of Sean Crisp, nor the perplexing procedural omission of Charlie One in failing to circulate the discovery in the dead officer's phone records. The office door burst open, and the face of a uniformed PC appeared around it. "Sir…" he gasped, evidence of the speed he'd run up the stairs to the Task Force office. "…the Duty Officer sends his compliments and asked me to tell you that there's been another one. It just happened, *minutes* ago."

Chapter Thirty-Five

DS Panayiotis Kalamatianos knew he should've been at home long ago, in a warm bed, curled around the ample form of his wife. Instead, he was driving aimlessly along the dark, damp roads of West London. He'd circumnavigated Hammersmith Broadway twice, travelled the length of Fulham Palace Road out to Craven Cottage and back, now he was on the Goldhawk Road, approaching Shepherd's Bush Green. The multi-channel police radio, which he'd unofficially acquired, rested on the passenger seat of his car, squawking intermittently, only a trained and practised ear could fully decipher the short bursts of distorted jargon, abbreviations, and call signs which it emitted, but Panos had that ear and listened intently.

* * *

When Panos had joined the Met Police over twenty-five years earlier, he'd high hopes for his career. Gifted as a linguist, he obviously spoke English and Greek but had studied French, Spanish, and German to near fluency. On completing his probationary period, he successfully applied to the Area Crime Squad, followed by a stint on the Burglary Squad before moving to the CID as a Detective Constable. All carefully considered stepping stones to achieve his ultimate ambition, to join Special Branch.

'SB', as it was known in police circles, was the shadowy department nestled between the Security Service of MI5 and the Counter Terrorism branch of the Metropolitan Police, responsible for intelligence relating to domestic subversive groups and extreme political activity. The SB officer was used to working hand in glove with MI5, often being the one to make the arrests, a power denied to Security Service operatives.

To Panos, SB spoke of status, understated glamour, and insider knowledge, he clamoured for the role. With his background and language skills, he was confident of success when Police Orders published applications for vacancies in the department. Perhaps he was too confident, or his language skills in the ever-changing political environment were the wrong language skills. Arabic, Urdu, Punjabi, Pashto, Russian, and Eastern European languages were what was sought. Perhaps he looked wrong, too fat, too swarthy, or his suit was ill-fitting and dated, or his tie not affiliated to the right school, club, or regiment. Whatever the reason, three attempts to join Special Branch resulted in three failures. It became obvious to Panos that the main cause of rejection on his third application, and so of any future endeavours, was his track record of failure in the previous two attempts. Failure breeds failure.

Panos fell back to routine main office CID work at a local level. He managed to swing an attachment to a single major incident enquiry, but he worked on the periphery, gained no reputation as a hotshot detective, and once the case was closed, resumed his regular work. In a fit of renewed enthusiasm, he succeeded in being promoted to Detective Sergeant, but the elevation in rank brought no elevation in the status and kudos of his detective role.

A week earlier, he'd received a phone call and found himself walking into the beating heart of the Major Investigation Task Force office. He was immediately charged with enthusiasm and determination to make the most of this opportunity, despite the use of the morale-sapping words, 'on attachment' being applied to him once more. Panos's avowed intent, no more, no less, was to forge a reputation that would ensure his *permanent* attachment to the Task Force.

Panos pored over the statements and analyses of the case. He'd studied the victims and suspects, but most of all, he'd scrutinised maps. Panos spent hours tracing his finger across the crime scenes and linked locations, and arrived at a conclusion.

The first victim, Sean Crisp, lived in Feltham with Lizzy; his estranged wife Debbie and eldest son Callum lived in Acton; his ex-partner Sienna and second son Casper lived in Brentford. Even the stolen mountain bike, used by the suspect, came from Hounslow underground station, all locations in *West* London.

The second victim, Trade Union leader Bill Buckle, had recently vacated his West London flat in Pimlico and retired to the scene of his murder in Weybridge, *West* of London. While the third victim, Bernard Huxton, had taught in Putney and lived in Norbiton, all in the West.

Panos had surreptitiously acquired the multi-channel police radio the day Bill Buckle's body was discovered, and it was whilst monitoring its broadcast, and *not* listening to London's Capital Radio, as he'd asserted to Grant Maddox, that he'd heard of the shooting of Councillor Huxton in Norbiton and hurried to the scene. His hope was to seize some grain of information, some significant item of evidence, *anything*, before anyone else, anything to make him stand out, to secure his position on the Task Force, *permanently*.

Panos had already formed his West-London-centric theory for the case when the multiple gunshots which had accompanied the murder of the world-famous chef, Konstanz Bassa, in the basement car park of the hotel in Park Lane were reported. That the murder scene was in the West End and Bassa lived in the exclusive West London district of Chiswick merely reinforced Panos's conjecture. Ill luck had placed the radio-monitoring detective too far from Park Lane to arrive before the full emergency response, but as a consequence, Panos now spent every moment he could keep his eyes open, outside of duty hours, patrolling West London, listening and waiting. Waiting for his chance.

* * *

It seemed as if the Angel of Destiny had answered his prayers as the radio on the seat next to him burst into life, relaying the message that only moments ago a man had been shot in the car park of the West London Ruffians Rugby Club, Scrubs Lane, Shepherds Bush. That same Angel had seen fit to place Panos on Shepherds Bush Green, driving north towards Scrubs Lane. Panos hit the accelerator pedal and sped north.

Chapter Thirty-Six

Eight nights earlier, some hooligan had vandalised the two inadequate lights which cast weak beams of illumination over the car park in front of the clubhouse. The secretary of the West London Ruffians Rugby Club cursed at the discovery, it looked from the small holes in the plastic covers as if pellets from an air gun had done the damage, smashing the bulbs within the casings. It wasn't an unknown event; four years earlier, the lamps had been vandalised to facilitate the break-in of several club members' cars, which had sat in the darkness for three nights until the lights were repaired. That incident had prompted the installation of a bargain basement CCTV camera, which sat atop a pole bracketed to the side of the clubhouse. After this latest damage, the car park was illuminated only by the ambient light from the clubhouse windows and the street lights from Scrubs Lane, at the end of the drive, fifty yards away.

* * *

The rough, uneven ground, pitted with potholes and an inconsistent scattering of gravel and stone chips, held about two dozen cars, some nose to nose along a central spine, others dotted about the perimeter of the area. It was there he waited.

Periodically, a light would pour out of the clubhouse as the front door was opened and an occupant exited, the night's drinking and socialising at an end. The brief burst of light momentarily cast angular, dancing, shadow shapes over the silhouettes of the cars, the door would close, and darkness returned. He'd listen as the crunching sound of footsteps, often unsteady through drink, traversed the car park towards a vehicle. At these moments, he prepared himself to either swiftly but silently move to a new hiding place should the figure heading in his direction not be the one he was waiting for, or be prepared to fulfil the night's mission if it was.

Unlike the night in the hotel's underground car park, he didn't have to wait two and a half hours for his quarry to appear. As the club door opened, he saw him clearly.

Sam Pendry was momentarily bathed in light and called out, "g'night Len, g'night Cliff, see you next week, take some pool lessons, losers!" The light vanished with the closing door, the noise of laughter and cat-calling from within was damped, the stillness only disturbed by the sound of Pendry's footsteps and the jingling of his car keys.

He knew Pendry's car and was ready as his target reached the driver's door. His heart was racing, his hands shook with excitement, he'd had to wait, but this was the one he really wanted, the one he'd really enjoy. He'd already decided he'd give himself a gift with this killing, he would let his victim see him properly this time, not by accident, as with the copper. He wanted to see the look on Pendry's face, to realise, to understand that for every action there was a consequence…except, of course, in his own case.

As he stood and took a pace forward, emerging from the murk, Sam Pendry jumped with fright, exclaiming, *"Jesus!"*

He withdrew his hand from his pocket and levelled the gun, pointing it directly at Pendry's face. "Hello Sam, had a good evening?"

Startled, Pendry took a stumbling step backwards, instinctively raising his hands in defence, not recognising the object held out before him for what it was. "Jesus! What the…?"

"Planning to go home now, are you? Planning to crawl into bed? Maybe enjoy a good, hard fuck? Is that the plan?"

Sam Pendry recognised the object as a handgun and the person pointing it at him in the same awful moment, terror overwhelmed him a split second later. "Oh Jesus, No! What's the matter with you? *No!*" As the clubhouse door swung open and the sound of those within intruded on the stillness outside,

Pendry turned his head away, towards the pool of spilling illumination. A wave of hope swept through him, the hope that comes with light in darkness and the presence of another human being when alone and afraid. He took a breath and screamed. *"HELP!"*

The bullet entered through his left ear, traversing the auditory canal, puncturing the eardrum, atomising the cochlea, and shattering his brain. Sam crumpled to his knees at the feet of his attacker. He was dead before he tipped forward, his bewildered face smashing into the gravel.

The only thing Gavin Cape saw as he opened the door to leave was his friend and fellow front row teammate, Sam Pendry, fall to the ground, the apparent victim of an attack by a dark-clothed assailant. Gavin assumed his friend had disturbed a thief in the darkness; the sound of the gunshot was lost amid the noise from the clubhouse and the desperate final scream for assistance from Sam.

He'd imagined the moment for years, never, ever thinking it would come to fruition. That he was prevented from relishing the moment longer was infuriating; instead of staring down appreciatively at his handiwork, he ran. His car was parked a short distance away, across the other side of Scrubs Lane in an industrial estate. He needed to get to it and get away, or his mission would end here and now.

The thief/assailant was already disappearing down the driveway towards Scrubs Lane. Gavin Cape hesitated, faced with several alternatives, temporarily overwhelmed by the choices; rush to his friend, chase the suspect, or alert the club members within. The dark figure, suddenly bathed in light from a main road streetlamp, turned left, heading up the hill. Gavin reached his decision, re-entered the clubhouse, and shouted at the top of his impressively loud voice that Sam had been attacked in the car park. Twenty blank faces stared at him, forcing the repetition of his message, content he'd done his duty on that score, Gavin followed his first instinct, ran outside, and began his pursuit.

Gavin Cape was a typical rugby prop, six feet tall, thickset and broad-shouldered; what he lacked in raw speed he made up for in stamina, so it was with steely determination he set off after the intruder. In the clubhouse, a call was made to police and ambulance services, whilst others rushed to assist Pendry. The first to reach the cooling body was an ex-soldier with tragically far too much experience of gunshot wounds. He announced that Sam Pendry had been shot and was dead. The news was quickly relayed via the open phone line to the police operator.

As Gavin neared the end of the clubhouse drive, he pulled his mobile phone from his pocket and dialled 999, swiftly being transferred to the police information room dispatcher. "I'm chasing a man who attacked my friend at the Ruffians Rugby Club", he gasped as he squinted his eyes and saw a dark shape break away off the road, turning right into the gloom of an industrial estate. "He's on foot on Scrubs Lane going towards Harlesden, I think he just ran into an industrial estate." Gavin Cape took a gulp of air, put his head down and ran, determined that the cowardly maggot who thought he could break into his team-mates' cars and deck his friend, would get some personal justice from his fists before he was handed over to The Law.

Chapter Thirty-Seven

Panos was driving like a madman, leaning to his left, towards the radio on the passenger seat, straining to hear the crackling voice above the high-pitched whine of the engine. The signal was poor, the transmission breaking up. He'd been unable to find a charger for the illicitly acquired radio, and the battery was choosing this moment to exhibit its final flickers of life. He'd discerned that someone was chasing the suspect on foot, up Scrubs Lane, perhaps into an industrial estate? This was the chance of a lifetime! If he could be there, somehow be the one to capture or just corner the killer who'd brought such fear to London, murdering two high-profile figures as well as a fellow officer and a councillor, Panos would be a hero. The chance to eclipse the years of mediocrity blinded him to the danger he was rushing into. The radio call had prompted a massive emergency response from patrolling officers and several Armed Response Vehicles, help was on the way; he *must* be involved, *must* get there first!

* * *

He felt weak, breathless, and in pain; he hadn't expected to have to run from the scene of his triumph with a pursuer. He regretted hiding his car so far away, this was not going as he'd intended. A second instance of a breaking down of his meticulous planning, after the near escape of Konstanz Bassa only forty-five hours previously. He was reduced to little more than a slow jog, the burning sensation in his chest and the wobbling of his legs relegated his flight to a snail's pace.

"*Oi! You!* Stay where you are, you shit."

He turned to see the huge, lumbering but relentless form of Gavin Cape in the centre of the road, closing down on him.

"Stay there, don't move, the police are on the way."

It wasn't part of the plan, and it wasn't something he wanted to do. He stopped, turned, and faced the oncoming figure, his hand gripping the pistol in his pocket.

Gavin saw a slim man, well under his own six feet, who seemed to be wheezing, out of breath, and apparently facing the inevitable. He reconsidered his intention of punching ten sorts of shit out of this scumbag, who seemed too feeble to survive what he had in mind, he looked pathetic.

"That's a sensible thing to do. Wait there," Gavin reached for his phone. As he glanced down at the illuminated screen, he was aware of movement and looked up to see the dark figure moving slowly and steadily closer, both arms stretched out before him. Gavin was incredulous, it looked like the pose of a man armed with a handgun. It was ridiculous.

The bullet struck Gavin in the centre of his chest and felt like the blunt impact from a sledgehammer. It was surreal. He reached his free hand across his torso and patted the impact point from which a searing, burning sensation was beginning to spread in waves, outwards, across his body. Confused and feeling groggy, he turned away from the man who still stood, only three yards away, in the same pose, awaiting a reaction to his shot.

The effort Gavin needed for each step mounted, the weight of his arms seemed to be growing; they fell to his side, he was vaguely aware that his mobile phone had fallen to the ground. The street lights of Scrubs Lane seemed alternatively sharp and blurred, near and far but he kept walking, staggering, like Frankenstein's monster, dragging each monumentally heavy foot, as if shod with divers lead boots, along the ground…until his right knee buckled and he fell rearwards onto his backside, leaving him seated on the ground, facing the lights, waiting for help.

* * *

Panos slowed when he saw the large sign on the side of the road indicating the home of the Ruffians Rugby Club. He saw a crowd gathered in the car park, others milled about near the open door to the clubhouse, while three men stood at the junction with the main road, anxiously looking left and right, perhaps for the ambulance or for some divine inspiration as to the direction the attacker had fled and what to do about it.

He reached across and lifted the radio, pressing the transmit button. He would deal with his possession of the equipment, his extra-curricular activities, and the questions they would prompt, later. For now, he needed to reveal his presence to the control room. As his car drifted past the rugby club, he transmitted, "MP, MP, this is DS Panos, on scene in Scrubs Lane, over." There was no reply, he tried again. Then he saw, the red light atop the radio was out, the battery was dead.

The detective's head swivelled left and right as he progressed north, spotting the industrial estate on his right, the unlit angular shapes of the squat, block units disappearing into the darkness off the main road, with numerous smaller side roads branching off it. The radio was silent, but he knew that support, much of it armed, was closing on the scene; this was his opportunity, and he allowed himself to be blind to the true risks involved. He turned the car into the industrial estate.

The headlights pierced the murky darkness, revealing a bulky shape on the roadside, he rotated the steering wheel slightly, turning the car, directing the headlight beams at the outline, gasping in surprise to see the slumped figure of a big man sitting on the ground, his legs spread out wide before him, his head and arms slumped down. As he closed, he could see the man was alive, his chest rose and fell with exaggerated slowness, each breath painfully laboured. Panos's reaction was automatic; he set the handbrake and exited the car, rushing to the casualty's side to help, reaching for his mobile phone as he did so.

***

He swore under his breath, *"shit! shit!"* It was unravelling, this wasn't what was supposed to be happening. His meticulous planning and preparation deserved better. He'd shot out the car park lights with a .177 air pistol over a week ago, plunging it into night-time darkness. He'd searched out and found a place to leave his car that was devoid of CCTV cameras, which would betray his presence. He'd even taken the precaution, using a throw-away, pay-as-you-go phone, to make at least two dozen bogus emergency calls to distant locations to tie up police resources and slow down any response to his activities. The action buying him extra minutes to execute his plan and escape. Sam Pendry was the one he wanted most of all, and he'd made the greatest effort to succeed in his task.

He'd visited the clubhouse night after night, seeking out Pendry's car. On a previous occasion, he'd lurked in the darkness, having spotted it, only to be thwarted when his quarry left the clubhouse in company with another man. Instead, that night, bitter and disappointed, he'd gone on to slaughter Bernard Huxton. Time was too precious to waste.

In the early hours of the previous day, he'd cornered Konstanz Bassa, only to use five of his precious 9mm bullets and remove him from the list. Now he'd been forced to shoot a man not even on that list. It was a line he'd crossed with reluctance, but without hesitation. There was a schedule to keep, he had the roll of names, and he had a shrinking window of opportunity to act. If someone got in the way, well...

He drove out of the side road onto the main thoroughfare of the industrial estate, knowing he must pass the crumpled body of his pursuer. Even with his precautions, the police response would be substantial and could arrive imminently; time was short.

He gasped with surprise and fury on seeing a car halted in the centre of the road, its headlights illuminating two figures next to the kerb, the fatally wounded pursuer slumped on the ground, the other bending over him, one hand reassuringly placed on his shoulder, the other to his ear, the illuminated screen revealing the presence of the mobile phone. There was only one way out of the estate, past the stationary vehicle and past the two figures. He and his car would be seen, and although he'd taken the precaution to fit false plates, he'd have no time to swap them again as the ring of police closed in.

It couldn't be allowed to happen. He accelerated.

* * *

Panos steadied the slumped man with his hand, seeking to reassure him. "You're okay. You're okay. I'm a police officer. Help's coming. You're safe now. Hold on." Panos could see the blood pouring freely from the chest wound, more with each rattling breath. He was shaking, steadying the casualty with one hand, trying to dial with the other. *What* was he doing here?

The full beam lights from his car, in whose blinding glow he stood, undid Panos's peripheral vision; it was the sound of the high-revving engine that alerted him. Looking up he saw the light coloured hatchback speed towards him, its lights turned off but the driver clearly visible in the shafts of brightness from his own stationary vehicle. 'there you are,' he thought, flexing his legs, preparing to jump aside, believing the car was being directed to strike him. Instead, it swerved to its left, halting side on, leaving Panos looking at the driver through the open window and a hand holding the pistol protruding from it. He understood instantly and was resigned. His stupid, blind, reckless ambition had brought him to this point. He had time to think of his beautiful, fat wife, whom he loved deeply, and his adoring daughters, whom he'd see no more. Instinctively, protectively, he stepped in front of the helpless figure of Gavin Cape.

The first bullet struck him in the stomach, the next punctured his heart. Panos fell, lifeless, across Gavin Cape's lap, who died three seconds after the police officer, a 9mm coup de grâce smashing through his forehead. The little beige car drove away, turning right and heading towards Harlesden, slipping through the closing net of police.

Chapter Thirty-Eight

While Grant and Heidi had rushed to the scene, DCI Winter remained in the office, phoning Task Force officers to 'get in now', arranging for support resources, forensics, photographers, POLSA search teams, tracker dogs, and the air support helicopter, the latter equipped with a million lumen, 'night-sun' spotlight. He called the force Press Bureau, warning them to expect the worst, another linked killing, never suspecting the true scale of the tragedy unfolding.

Arriving at the Rugby club, Grant and Heidi found a scene both chaotic and catastrophic. The darkness was lit with dozens of flashing blue lights from numerous police vehicles and ambulances. The car park of the clubhouse, the drive leading to it, Scrubs Lane, and the nearby industrial estate were teeming with police officers, paramedics, concerned rugby club members, and increasingly, curious members of the public. Grant knew it wouldn't be long before police-radio-scanning paparazzi would arrive to add to the disarray.

Heidi's voice was calm but decisive, "Grant, you see what's going on at the industrial estate and coordinate that scene, I'll see what's happening here, okay?"

"Yes, boss," Grant replied, staring towards the second crime scene above which the police helicopter, its powerful spotlight illuminating the narrow roads and dark corners of the estate, relentlessly circled. "One thing, Guv, this is Callum Crisp's rugby club, Sean's son. Can it be a coincidence that we've an incident here?"

Heidi nodded. "We'll find out shortly, I'm sure. Thanks, Grant." Heidi exited the car and strode into the mêlée, her warrant card held aloft, calling out, "I'm DI Yorke, who's the ranking officer here?"

Grant drove north a short distance and parked on Scrubs Lane behind a queue of police patrol cars, one, an Armed Response Vehicle. As he pulled his ID from his pocket and walked into the blue-strobed centre of attention near the entrance to the industrial estate, he saw the familiar shape of a huge police officer walking towards the ARV and leaning over to speak to its occupant.

"Bab's!" Grant called. ARV Sergeant Babatunde Okafor, Grant's close friend from his eight years as an armed officer, looked up, recognised Grant, and broke into a huge, beaming smile.

"Grant! What are you doing up so late, you old bastard? Shouldn't you be at home with Lyddy sipping Horlicks or something?" he teased.

Grant countered with the time-honoured standard police response to such banter, "fuck off," and tightly gripped his friend's outstretched hand. "I see you're still masquerading as a police officer."

"What've we got, Babs?" Grant asked, "All we heard was a shooting at the club and then a secondary incident at the estate here."

Babs walked towards the side road off Scrubs Lane with Grant at his side. "You're on the Sean Crisp, Bill Buckle job? All linked up?" Grant nodded. "I still have to deal with this as an active scene." Babs continued, "You know the score better than anyone. We've cordoned it off as best as we can, 'India 99' is providing the light," he waved a hand in the direction of the helicopter, "and the furry Exocets are leading the search with half a dozen of my guys providing armed support, I've got two carriers of TSG on the perimeter." As Babs spoke, he heard the sound of a search dog, a 'furry Exocet' barking furiously, deep in the heart of the sprawling area of small manufacturing units. "To be honest, I think we're wasting our time, our shooter is long gone. Our response time wasn't the greatest, our man prepared the ground."

"How so?"

"Before the shooting, Information Room was flooded with hoax calls, *all* 'I' Grade and so requiring an Immediate response and *all* total bollocks. I'd say our man was clearing the ground of us to free him up to do this." Babs halted and pointed, "I'm sorry mate, but we've got a blood bath here." Twenty feet away, two prostrate figures lay on the ground three feet apart, where medics had laid them, surrounded by the debris of the failed attempts to save their lives. Wound dressing wrappers lay discarded, as did several wet, glistening, rubber gloves, an unattended defibrillator, and several red-stained bandages and dressings gave testament to the paramedic's efforts.

"Best info we've got," explained the huge sergeant, "is the suspect was disturbed in the car park by a club member who he shot. He's deader than tank-tops, headshot. That guy there," Babs pointed to the nearest body, "is Gavin Cape. As he left the clubhouse, he saw the victim fall, alerted the other club members inside, and went off after the suspect, who legged it on foot. The thing is, Cape never mentioned a gunshot when he raised the alert. I don't think he was aware he'd witnessed a shooting. A minute later, he calls 999 from his mobile and gives this location for the escaping suspect."

"And the other guy, the fat one, is he the suspect? Did he get him?"

"No. No, he's not. We've no idea how he got here or what he was doing, but… he's a police officer."

Grant was thunderstruck. "*No!* Not again." He shook his head in disbelief, "Who is he? What's he doing here?"

"We found this in his pocket." Babs Okafor took a warrant card from his pocket and opened it for Grant to see.

The blue flashing lights, suffused with the dull glow of the street lamps, cast a spectral light, but there was no mistaking the face on the card or the name written underneath it. Grant walked closer and looked again at the body, tilting his head to the side to better see the features of the face. "Oh Jesus! What the fuck is going on?"

"You know him?"

"Yeh. That's Panos, he's on the Task Force investigating these murders." Grant held his hand to his balding head, rubbing the skin with confused exasperation and asked again, this time with despair in his voice. "What the fuck is going on?"

"I don't know Granty, but the car here," he pointed to the eight-year-old BMW 3 series, abandoned in the middle of the street, "is registered to your man, some sort of unpronounceable Greek name."

"It's Kalamatianos."

"Yeh that," Babs replied softly, "it's his private car, there's a police multi-channel PFX radio on the passenger seat with a flat battery. What was he up to Grant? 'Cos whatever it was, it got him killed."

Grant left Babs' side and approached the prostrate body of the man *he'd* brought into the investigation. Two blood-stained number one field dressings lay on his body, one on his rounded stomach, the other above the heart. Grant thought he understood what had happened. Many times, Panos had dropped huge hints about the prospect of permanent attachment to the Task Force. The radio, his private car, and his presence told the rest of the story and probably explained the Greek-Cypriot's sudden and early attendance at the scene of Bernard Huxton's murder, too. Panos was freelancing, looking for a little bit of glory, a small lever to prise open a door into the squad. It had led to this.

The scene was suddenly bathed in a pool of dazzling light as the night-sun of the helicopter, flying deafeningly low over the scene, passed across the two dead bodies. Grant shook his head, if only casting a revealing light on the case could be so easy.

Chapter Thirty-Nine

rant's stunning news of Panos's murder shocked Heidi as she took control of the crime scene at the clubhouse, where her priority wasn't the containment of a suspect still in the vicinity but the preservation of evidence, hanging on to witnesses, and finding out as much as possible about the victim.

This latter task was easily solved by the Club secretary, who'd identified the body of Sam Pendry. In order to render first aid, his clubmates had rolled his body over to reveal the expression of fear and surprise still frozen on his features. The entry point of the 9mm bullet in the left ear was clear to see, as were the powder burns from the muzzle flash of the weapon used. That this was the work of the same assailant seemed to be confirmed by the recovery of a single 9mm shell casing from the ground a few feet from the body. Other than the initial examination, the sad remains of Sam Pendry would have to await the arrival of forensic experts.

Heidi was delighted to learn of the existence of a CCTV camera which covered the car park, less delighted to see it was a cheap and low-grade model. Her viewing of the tape gave little information to the detective, neither showing the arrival of the suspect nor his point of origin. The top left corner of the screen depicted the murder as a series of blurred, furry-edged images of two men, one of whom materialised from behind a parked car to confront the victim, who was seen to fall. The suspect then ran out of the corner of the screen to never be seen again. It was infuriating.

The victim, Samuel Arthur Pendry, was forty-three, fit and healthy, a divorced independent estate agent who was planning to marry his girlfriend with whom he lived. Other than what Heidi considered to be the general antipathy the public held towards estate agents, at this early stage at least, Sam Pendry appeared to have no enemies.

During her establishment of scene control and enquiries, DI Yorke had kept the final words from Grant Maddox firmly in her mind. This was the Rugby Club to which Callum Crisp belonged, the sometimes errant son of the first victim. Could that fact just be a coincidence?

Two Detective Constables who hadn't left the Task Force office when the call came out had arrived a few minutes after the DI in support of the uniform local officers and night duty CID man, and began to collate details and pencil in very basic statements from the members who were at the club that evening. Heidi had pulled them aside, "Don't make it obvious, but ask everyone if Callum Crisp was here tonight, if so, what were his movements, and if he had any issues with Sam Pendry. Ask similar questions of other members so the interest in Callum doesn't stand out like a sore thumb. Got it?" She received a simultaneous response from each officer. "Yes, Guv!"

Heidi saved the longstanding bar manager, Dean Gunn, to herself, secure in the knowledge that if anyone knew of the comings and goings of the club members, it would be the barman. Confident that the support organised by the DCI was now in place and the forensic aspect of the scene preservation was in hand, Heidi approached the barman who sat, red-eyed, on a stool behind the counter. Now well into his seventies, Dean Gunn had once struck an impressive figure as a second row player in the club's original team over forty years earlier. A devoted 'Ruffian', he now served at the bar, knew everyone, and offered support, advice, and encouragement; he was part of the furniture. Informed Sam had been killed in the car park, he was beside himself in grief and shock, when a short while later the news filtered back that Gavin Cape was also dead, the news crushed him. He sat behind his bar and discreetly wept.

"Mr Gunn, may I speak with you?" Heidi asked quietly.

Dean looked up, disturbed from the dark, sad place his mind had travelled to. When he saw the six-feet-plus figure of the DI standing before him, he struggled to his feet as he'd spent a lifetime doing in the presence of a lady.

"Of course, Miss. How can I help?"

"The Club Secretary said we may use his office, away from this hubbub, so we can speak in private. Is that alright?" Dean nodded his consent, rubbed his eyes with a tissue he was holding, and led the way to the room, not much bigger than a broom cupboard, which served as the club office.

"Mr Gunn, I wanted to ask you something, a delicate matter and also an extremely confidential one. I'm asking you to keep this between us. Would you do that, please?" The barman looked bewildered but nodded his assent. "I want to speak to you about Callum Crisp, We know he's a member here. You'll be aware his father was Police Constable Sean Crisp, who was murdered in central London a little over a week ago."

"Sean Crisp, yes, I remember him, more interested in getting his end away than being a good dad, or husband for that matter, could've been a better than average player, but was too concerned about keeping his good looks than really getting stuck in." 'Good' and 'looking' were not words which could ever be joined together and applied to Dean Gunn. One glance at his face provided evidence aplenty of *his* willingness, in years gone by, to get 'stuck in'; his ears were cauliflowered, and his nose was crushed flat to his face.

"You knew Sean Crisp?" Heidi couldn't hide her surprise.

"He played here for a while, that's why he brought Callum to our youth team, but he did the dirty, if you know what I mean?"

"Perhaps you could explain for me., Heidi coaxed.

Dean winced. "He had an affair with the wife of one of the players. Caused a huge stink that did. It's not what a gentleman does, not with a teammate's lady. It's not on. So he left."

"Whose wife did he have the affair with?"

Dean looked uncomfortable. "It was a long while ago, Sean left the club, and the married couple concerned reconciled. Well, for a while anyway. I can't see that it's connected."

"Please, Mr Gunn."

Dean sighed deeply. "It was Sam Pendry's wife. Sean Crisp had an affair with Sam's wife."

Heidi was aghast, involuntarily turning her head towards the tiny, barred window which looked out to the car park, where Pendry's cooling body still lay. The complexities and connections in the case were mind-boggling, and everything seemed to lead back to Sean Crisp. It made Grant Maddox's theory seem all the more plausible, that the core of the case was wrapped up with its first victim, its strands radiating outwards from him.

"Did Callum know about this affair? Was it common knowledge?"

"Callum was only little when it happened, so you'd have to ask him, there may have been gossip and joshing in the club about it, he may have heard that. It *was* common knowledge at the time, they were spotted one evening, in the car park, she was…you know…to him." Dean Gunn was a typical old school, Rugby Club man, in the company of men, he had a mouth to make a monkey blush, hard drinking, hard playing, and super tough, but in the company of women he turned into a polite gentleman, unwilling to give offence or engage in profanity or discourtesy.

Heidi understood the implication and nodded her understanding. Not wishing to make her interviewee even more uncomfortable, she decided to put that information on the back burner for now. "Okay, let's get back to Callum. Was Callum here tonight, Mr Gunn?"

"Yes, earlier in the evening, he came in, drank four lagers, chatted with a couple of people, and then left."

"Did anything untoward occur, any trouble?"

The barman shrugged noncommittally, "Callum was a bit pissed and exchanged words with the guys at the pool table. He left soon after."

"Who did he have words with? Was one of them Sam Pendry?" Dean nodded.

"Do you know when Callum arrived and left?" Heidi opened her notebook.

"He arrived at nine-ish and left at ten-ish."

"Did he drive here? Was he alone?"

Dean thought for a few seconds. "He didn't say if he drove; he was certainly alone when he walked in. I know in the past his mother ran him around, dropped him off, picked him up, especially if he was having a drink. I assume that's what happened tonight. I mean, he shouldn't be driving after four drinks, should he?" He added quickly, defensively.

"Did Callum have any issues with Sam Pendry? Had they ever fallen out, argued, anything?"

"Good grief!" Dean put his hand to his mouth in a shock of realisation. "I'm sorry, but my goodness. You can't think Callum had anything to do with this… this massacre, this bloodbath. It's monstrous. I have two friends out there," he pointed a shaking finger towards the office door, his voice quaking with emotion, "two *good* friends, of many years standing, who are lying dead, and you think Callum is involved. It's impossible."

"Mr Dean, there's another dead man out there, ruthlessly gunned down, a police officer, and he was a friend of *mine*. I intend to examine *every* possibility, every scrap of evidence, and follow the trail to find who was responsible, and I can assure you, nothing, Mr Gunn, *nothing* is impossible."

Chapter Forty

Shell-shocked was not too strong an expression to describe the condition of the Task Force detectives when they were finally able to set aside the professional and methodical duties of the evening and early hours of the morning, and slump in the chairs of Paul Winters' office.

"How can this be?" Grant asked, his voice full of emotion. "How can this have happened? Two officers in just over a week, and five other victims, and what've we got? A tangle, a twisted, messed-up tangle." Grant had rarely felt so despondent. "I brought Panos onto the Task Force. I knew he wanted in, but who'd have thought he'd have gone to such lengths? *What* was he thinking?"

"*Grant!*" There was urgency in Paul Winter's voice. "Stop this. Stop now. You'll drive yourself crazy. As for Panos, I don't want to speak ill of the dead, but what he did was foolish, even if well motivated. He was an experienced officer; he made a mistake and paid a terrible price, but it wasn't the fault or responsibility of *anyone* here. There's a saying, 'Be careful if you go looking for tigers, you may find one'. Panos went looking and he found one. *If* only he'd stood back, he was right on top of our suspect, we *could* have had him."

"We should be asking what did he know that we didn't to get that close to the suspect? Had he worked something out we haven't, or was he just lucky?" Heidi realised what she's said and revised herself. "Unlucky."

"He had a wife and two daughters, and only a few years before retirement." Grant made the statement, thinking out loud.

"I spoke with the Chief Superintendent of his home station, they've sent someone from his office, someone he'd worked with for years to inform the family, it's better that way, we didn't really know him that well, it was a short time," Paul said. "We know they'll be looked after, the best support financially and emotionally, for all of them. It's something The Job does get right at least."

The three officers fell into silence.

"*Right!*" Paul slammed the desktop with his hand. "We're professional police officers, we've taken a huge knock, we're hurting but we do what we do, we solve this, we find the fucker who's terrorizing our city. So…Right! What have we got?"

Grant had been awake close to twenty hours. He was a balding, overweight man in his fifties, the days of his youth when he wore the green beret of the Royal Marines and had the stamina of a Duracell Bunny were long gone, but he dug deep; duty demanded it. "We've a problem in the team." He waited to let the importance of his statement sink in. "I spoke with Charlie Two about a thousand years ago, it feels that much anyway. She discovered a huge mistake that Charlie Buller had made. At least I hope it was a mistake. Cutting a long, technical story short, he was given information by the HOLMES system, which he sat on, overlooked, or failed to understand the significance of. Sean Crisp's newly entered mobile phone records and the data already input shows pretty conclusively that until a very short while before he was killed, he was seeing the wife of the DPG base armourer, Rory Caplan."

"He was screwing a colleague's wife!" Paul couldn't hide his disapproval.

"I found out tonight that ten or eleven years ago, he was screwing the wife of a fellow Rugby club member, getting blow jobs in the car park, no less. Guess whose wife it was playing the pink oboe?" The two men looked to Heidi open-mouthed. "The wife of Sam Pendry, who was undoubtedly our suspect's target tonight. Gavin Cape and Panos were incidental; they got in the way of his escape, so they had to go. But the target was Pendry."

"Sean Crisp was having an affair with the wife of tonight's victim?" The DCI was incredulous.

"A *decade* ago," Heidi stressed.

"But it's the wrong way around, if anything, it should be Pendry wanting to kill Sean bloody Crisp, and why now, ten years later? But Caplan, that's more current, doesn't he have a better motive to off Sean?" Paul was thinking aloud.

"Guv, we need to look again at everything, the whole investigation may've been compromised by Charlie One," Grant stressed, "if he missed this little nugget, what else has he missed?"

"Is Charlie Two on it? Is she looking through the system? She found this error, if it was an error." Heidi put in. "Maybe it's an aberration, he *did* collapse, maybe he's not well."

"Well or not, he needs to be spoken to." Paul clapped his hands together. "Grant, that's yours, go and see Charlie, don't take no for an answer, besides, he's off sick and we have a duty of care to fulfil, a welfare visit, use that if need be. Find out what the fuck is going on with him. Okay?"

"Yes, Guv."

"Can you do PC Caplan as well, Granty? Did he know Sean Crisp was pumping his wife's tyres up? He has to be questioned. Can you fit that in, too?"

"Yes, Guv."

"Heidi," Paul continued, "I know you *were* doing the welfare visit on Charlie but you're far more technically minded than us dinosaurs, I want you in the office please, go through the whole system with Charlotte, find out if there's anything, *anything* else we've missed, I need to know that this investigation is operating on a sound basis. Chase up Amber to see where we are on the background of Councillor Huxton, his personal records, from the school or local authority. I want to know about any complaints, anything from giving poor grades to paedophilia. Okay?"

"Yes, Guv."

"And Heidi, put Nagur and Craig onto the rugby club, they've drawn a blank with the stolen mountain bike, I want them digging into Pendry, I want to know everything about him. Why did our suspect want to put a bullet in his head? Get Dirty Don to find and interview Callum Crisp, too. I want to know where he was when last night's massacre took place. Can you do that, please?"

Heidi smiled, "Yes, Guv." It felt like momentum was gathering again.

"Good stuff. Now, it's been the longest day ever, get home, get some sleep, this has got to be nearing the end game, hang in there." Paul smiled an encouraging smile.

"Shouldn't you be getting off home, Guv?" Grant asked.

"I will, I will. I just need to put something together for a press release in the morning, and our Press Officer has arranged another TV witness and information appeal I have to front; the Big House is putting up a reward. When London wakes up in the morning, it'll be looking at the biggest story for years. Our very own St Valentine's Massacre. Now go on, get out of here."

Grant turned as he opened the door to leave the Task Force office. Paul was in the glass box, head down, writing furiously.

Chapter Forty-One

"Y ou do it on purpose. I know that. And I want you to know that I know that you do it on purpose."

"Sarge! Honestly, *it's all they had.*" DC Amber Bennett couldn't keep the amusement out of her voice; Grant's mock annoyance fuelled her hilarity even more.

"I've heard that before, 'it's all they had'." He mimicked her words in a whiny voice. "For God's sake, the worst car in the pool. The radioactive bogey!"

Grant was absolutely correct, there *were* newer and much better vehicles available in the car pool for CID officers' use, but Amber couldn't resist picking the ancient, luminously bright green Ford Focus, christened the radioactive bogey by her sergeant, for their use this day.

"Look on the bright side, we'll never lose it in a car park and we can be damn sure no-one will ever steal it." Amber tried but failed in her bid for self-control, the dam breaking when she looked sideways to see the pouting, false fury on her sergeant's face. She burst out laughing, to be joined by Grant. It was a rare moment of frivolity and fun in the darkest and most depressing period of her working life. The truth was, she'd ensured the two friends and colleagues would spend the day together in the green monstrosity for that very reason, to be a catalyst for the good-natured playfulness which marked the relationship between the two. The loss of Sean Crisp, a friend who'd guided and navigated her through the early part of her police career, was bad enough, for the same monster to then casually slaughter a new friend and colleague, DS Panos, was near to being unbearable. Amber wasn't alone amongst the members of the squad of investigators to force something approaching almost inappropriate hysteria to the surface rather than succumb to the crippling effects of grief and sorrow. Black humour hid and controlled true feelings and permitted the ongoing function of scrutinising minds with a job to do.

* * *

The block was a typical example of early 60s concrete, a low-rise, chunky slab of mediocrity which had probably won the architect a prize, but neither he nor the prize givers would ever have to live there. The two detectives stood on the path leading to the walkway, which accessed numerous identical red front doors on the ground floor, beneath a long row of identical blue doors on the level immediately above, and green doors above that. Two unfettered, unsupervised dogs ran happily around the grassy area in front of the grim, grey housing estate, halted long enough to sniff each other's rectums before one enthusiastically mounted the other.

"Nice," observed Grant. Tearing his eyes from the canine coitus taking place before him, he scanned the area, taking in the graffiti, litter, and general rundownedness of the bleak development in which Charles Buller, 'Charlie One', resided. The canine 'mounter' finished its business surprisingly quickly, alighted from the 'mountee' with a lolling tongue and a contented look on its face. To the detective's surprise, the recently mounted animal clambered aboard the other and, as enthusiastically as the first, went at it like a Spaniard on his wedding night.

"Gay dogs," offered Grant, "good to see they're embracing diversity."

Amber couldn't take her eyes off the spectacle. "Is that normal?"

"I hope you're not overlaying your biased preconceptions of what is or isn't 'normal' on a minority group, or attempting to oppress the inalienable rights of those dogs to express physical love in their own way."

"No, Sarge. I wouldn't do that."

"Good. Otherwise, I'd have no choice but to challenge your unacceptable behaviour." Grant nodded in finality. "Okay, let's find 11B."

"You've had your Diversity Training Course, then skip?"

"Yep. Two weeks ago."

"Thought so."

* * *

Both detectives were in shock. The apartment, which Charlie One called home, was in a state of filthy disorder, clothes littered every seat, newspapers and used crockery covered the surface of the coffee table, whilst the stained curtains were closed, necessitating an unshaded bulb to be turned on to illuminate the disarray.

"Sorry about the mess. If I'd known you were coming, I'd have tidied up and run a vacuum over the place. Tea or coffee?"

Both officers answered in unison, "No, thank you." Sharing the same repulsion at the thought of consuming anything prepared in such a place.

"You live here alone then, Charlie? I don't see the sign of a woman's touch." Grant asked.

"Yes, I've decided that's the best way, not responsible to anyone, do my own thing, my own way, in my own time. I'm fifty-four, too old to change now."

Both officers chuckled politely. "We wanted to come and see you, Charlie, make a welfare visit, see if you need anything, see how you are," offered Amber.

Grant was struggling to overcome his surprise and disgust, uncertain which feeling was taking priority, but managed to follow the DC's lead. "That's right, to see how you are. So, how are you?"

"I'm feeling better, much better. I apologise for what happened, the doctor said I was dehydrated and stressed, I blame the prawn sandwich."

"Well, you gave us all a fright, but I'm glad to see you looking better." Amber smiled encouragingly. Charlie One *was* looking better, better than a man lying on the floor having a fit, but no one with a standard interpretation of normal could say that Charlie was looking well. He hadn't shaved in days, his eyes were reddened, and dark shadows and bags nestled beneath, suggesting he had recently enjoyed little sleep or rest. His hair was greasy, and his manner belied his affable words of welcome.

"So, is it tea or coffee? I have some biscuits somewhere, too."

The detectives exchanged puzzled, covert glances as Grant answered. "No, thank you, Charlie, honestly, we stopped for a coffee and a bun on the way, didn't we, Amber?" Grant was glad to see his partner nod in agreement. "So, when do you think you'll be back to work? There's no rush, Charlie, Charlotte, is managing, you can take off as much time as you need."

"Well…" Charlie hesitated. "Obviously, I want to get back, but the doctor signed me off for a fortnight, so I can't be back before then, so I'm finding things to keep me busy."

"Of course." Amber smiled encouragingly.

Grant took a deep breath. There were issues that needed addressing, whether Charlie lived in lonely squalor or not. "Charlie, I need to ask you something about the case, something about the HOLMES system, an anomaly, perhaps you can put our minds at rest." The previous antipathy Grant had harboured to Charlie Buller had fast evaporated upon seeing his domestic situation, the man was clearly struggling.

"An anomaly? What sort of anomaly? Are you saying there's something wrong with my work?" Charlie's previous affability appeared to be dissolving into animosity at the suggestion of criticism. His tone more reminiscent of the unacceptable end of his mood swings. "I think you'd be hard pressed to find a more proficient operator of our system than me."

"Exactly, Charlie," Amber placated, falling seamlessly into good cop, bad cop. "That's why we need *you* to help us."

"Oh, right. Well, ask away."

"What it is, Charlie," continued Grant, "is that the system, the Dynamic Reasoning bit,"

"The D.R.E." interrupted Charlie, "what about it?" Irritable again.

"Yes, the D.R.E., it flagged up a link between two telephone numbers, one was Sean Crisp's, the other was the landline number of PC Rory Caplan, who was a colleague of Sean's. What it showed was that Sean was calling that number…often, and for the briefest moment, and then usually straight away, a mobile number called Sean's phone. We've found that the number returning the call belonged to Rory Caplan's wife. It seems likely they were having an affair."

"Right!" answered Charlie. "That's good news, then. We knew there was someone Sean had been seeing and split with, so that answers that. What's the anomaly?"

Grant glanced to Amber. "Well, Charlie, it seems that the system identified the numbers and sent an alert to the operator, which was then 'acked'."

"That's right, the red 'ack' button, to acknowledge the alert. It's like an electronic signature of receipt." Charlie nodded his understanding.

"Yes, exactly. The thing is, Charlie, the alert was sent to *you*, it was *you* who 'acked' the message. Charlie, it was really important information, and you didn't do anything with it. There's no record of its dissemination to the Task Force, its inclusion in the HOLMES database, or anything, anything at all. It seems you either sat on it deliberately for some reason, or you forgot about it. That's the anomaly, Charlie, and we both know that you're good, that you're the best, so the question is…how did that happen?"

Chapter Forty-Two

An 'Old Sweat' PC once told a probationary Constable Grant Maddox there was power in silence. He'd said, 'When you ask a question, *wait* for the answer. If the answer isn't immediately forthcoming,' he'd explained, 'resist the urge to fill the silence, keep still, hold the stare, keep quiet…and wait.' It was a technique or trick, whichever description you chose, which had often paid dividends for Grant.

The question hung in the air. 'How did that happen?' Grant had asked. He held Charlie's gaze; he didn't stare with aggression or menace, his facial expression, if anything, was nestled somewhere between open enquiry and benign confusion, but he held the gaze and waited. Amber fought the urge to squirm uncomfortably in the chair and make some comment which would break the tense, uneasy atmosphere. Instead, she sat still and in silence. Amber Bennett, too, had received the words of wisdom of a long-dead copper, passed down via Grant Maddox to her, as it would be passed down from Amber Bennett to coppers yet to come. So the officers waited. Waited as Charles Buller stared at Grant and felt the awful power of silence.

"How did that happen?" Charlie One echoed, finally. Grant nodded but said nothing. "I'm not sure I understand." Silence. Charlie broke the stare, looking away from Grant to Amber, looking for an ally, the 'good cop' of moments earlier. "There must've been a human error. *Charlotte*! It must have been an error by Charlotte; she's not so experienced, she makes mistakes *all* the time, mistakes I've had to cover up."

Grant raised a questioning eyebrow at the deflection of responsibility, expressing surprise and dismay at such a response. Now, the Detective

Sergeant furrowed his brow, lowered his head, ever so slightly, his expression communicating something quite different. Charlie read it as if reading text on a page, 'that's not good enough', it said, 'do you think I haven't checked thoroughly, do you think I haven't done *my* job?'

When the answer came, it was one that neither Grant nor Amber had expected.

"I'm ill, Grant. I'm very ill. I'm sorry." Charlie stuttered the words, heaving with emotion, and then, to the detective's utter astonishment, burst into convulsive tears.

Amber pulled a tissue from her pocket and passed it to Charlie, taking a seat on the arm of the chair, next to the weeping analyst, rubbing his back and saying "there, there", whilst shrugging to Grant with a look of bewilderment on her face. "Grant's going to go and make a cup of tea for you, do you take sugar?" Charlie nodded his head between wailing spasms. "There you go, nice cup of tea with sugar, Sarge." Amber jerked her head towards the kitchen, "he's going to do that right now." Grant took the hint and headed for the kitchen, dreading what he'd find there.

When Grant returned, holding a steaming mug, Amber had regained her seat and was smiling encouragingly at Charlie, who dabbed his eyes and blew his nose noisily. With the horrors of the kitchen behind him, Grant passed the tea to Charlie, who took it gratefully. "Thanks, Grant."

"You're welcome." Grant took his seat, leant forward, and in a voice he hoped was a combination of firmness, interest, and compassion said, "Okay, Charlie, tell me, I'm listening."

Charlie One took a deep breath. "It wasn't always like this." He looked around the detritus of his living space. "I used to have a handle on it all; my life was good. I had a decent job, I had promotion prospects, I even had a woman I loved and planned to marry. It all spiralled out of control." A catch of emotion cracked his voice. "I'm ashamed and embarrassed." Amber passed a second, much-needed tissue, and Charlie nodded his thanks.

"You said you were ill, Charlie." Grant encouraged.

"Yes. That's right, ill. Very ill. It's been horrible, terrible in every way, I knew what was happening to me, knew what was *going* to happen to me, I knew my future, I've been living with that and trying to keep it a secret. I should have informed work, but I knew I'd immediately lose my job. I've lost it now anyway, I'm finished." Charlie began to sob once more as Grant caught Amber's eye, communicating his impatience and growing irritation.

"I'm so sorry, Charlie. I can't imagine how it's been for you, but I can tell you that The Job excels in the welfare of its employees. I'm sure you'll be looked after, but we need to know what's wrong with you." Amber's voice was soft, feminine, and encouraging. Grant was grateful for her presence and intervention, his inclination was to slap Charlie around the face like a gangster with an hysterical moll, 1950s movie style.

Charlie took another deep breath and looked plaintively into Amber's eyes. "It's early-onset dementia."

Grant's irritation immediately evaporated on hearing the word dementia, a nightmare word and one which had touched him personally. His grandfather, whom he'd adored, had succumbed to the illness and, as his heartbroken mother described, had 'died a little death each day', as his personality, faculties, and dignity had dwindled.

"Charlie, I'm so sorry." Grant meant the words. So much was explained, the condition of the apartment and the state Charlie Buller was in personally, and of course, the inaction over the matching telephone numbers. "What can we do to help?"

"Help? What help is there? I'm alone, and I'm staying that way. Who'd be interested in me? I've no one to talk to, no one to confide in, no one who'll travel this road with me. I'm not so far gone that I can't picture the future. I'm tired, aching, and getting periodically confused. Sometimes I can see the mess around me, sometimes I can't, but *all* the time I don't care. The clutter, the grime, it's minuscule compared to the enormity of what's happening to me."

"The welfare department of The Job can arrange for a cleaner, for a carer to visit. As things…" Amber struggles to avoid saying 'get worse' instead finding, "…progress, then they can help you sort out other living arrangements, if that's what you want."

"You mean a nursing home. Propped up in a high back chair, stuck in front of a TV showing back-to-back *Cash in the Attic*, *Last of the Summer Wine*, and *Escape to the Country*, while the dribble runs down my face and I quietly piss myself. That's the reality."

"But Charlie, you're a long way from that." Amber's voice was full of feeling. "You're talking coherently, and apart from the mistake of the phone number data, you've been functioning. No one would've guessed you had a problem. It may be a long way off before you reach anything like you've described, and that's a pretty stereotypical picture you've painted and not one that's true nowadays."

"Have you heard of 'Sundown Syndrome?' No, of course not. It's a part of dementia, its symptoms appear during the late evenings or at night, symptoms of anger and agitation, short temper, aggression and abuse, confusion, and anxiety. Does that sound familiar?"

"Sundown Syndrome?" Grant's thoughts rushed to the changes in Charlie's demeanour, his brusqueness, and sudden outbursts of anger. "A few nights ago, the day Huxton was murdered? At the case review, it had been a long day, a late night. It was 'Sundown Syndrome?' When you collapsed?"

Charlie nodded. "That's what my doctor said, and I should've told you. I'm sorry, I'm sorry for everything, sorry to everyone. It's a clear sign the condition is accelerating. I'm no use anymore. I can remember the past, clear as day, but my short-term memory is screwed, Grant." Charlie shrugged. "I can remember the past, but my short-term memory is screwed, Grant."

The Detective Sergeant looked from Charlie to Amber and back again, unsure of what to say.

"That was a joke, by the way." Charlie laughed feebly. "Get it?"

Grant smiled awkwardly before returning to the matter at hand. "I have to report this to Paul Winter, and he'll formally inform The Job. I imagine you'll be suspended from the Task Force, and someone from Human Resources will be in touch to assess your needs and offer help."

"I understand."

"Charlie, can you think of anything else, anything at all that you may have done or not done on the HOLMES system, or tell us about anything else for that matter, which we should know about, anything which could hamper or aid the investigation. It's really important." Grant had to ask.

"In all honesty? No, I can't think of anything. I've been racking my brain to remember the incident you were just talking about, the details of which have already slipped away. Phone numbers, was it?" he offered.

Grant stood, followed by Amber. "If you do think of anything, let us know." Grant offered his hand. "Good luck, Charlie, I'm really sorry this is happening to you."

Charles Buller watched through his grimy window as the two detectives made their way down the path towards the ugliest vehicle in the car park, both oblivious they were passing his light coloured hatchback as they did so. He clenched his fists and, with a face twisted in fury, spat the words "stupid bastards", flecking the glass with his spittle.

Chapter Forty-Three

To conclude Amber's investigation into the teaching background of Bernard Huxton, the third victim of what the press had sensationally branded *'The 9mm Killer'*, Amber had made an appointment at the Offices of Wandsworth Council, which oversaw the Putney school at which Huxton had taught for over thirty years. The route from Charlie One's single bedroom hovel to Wandsworth was heavy with traffic, and the going was slow. For the first ten minutes, the two detectives sat in contemplative silence.

"Tragic." Amber broke the stillness. "You'd have to have a heart of stone not to pity him." Grant kept his counsel, sighing loudly, irritated by their slow progress.

Amber tried again. "I mean only in his mid-fifties and to face that prospect." Amber looked across to Grant, who was sitting tight-lipped. "Tragic. Don't you think?"

"Yes. It's tragic." Grant finally responded. "It's all around us, Amber. It can weigh you down. Sean Crisp was looking forward to marrying Lizzy and getting his life in order, but he got his throat ripped out and a bullet through the eye. Tragic. Gavin Cape was just a guy doing his civic duty, trying to catch what he thought was a thief, more holes. Tragic. And Panos was a little fat fella with unfulfilled ambitions who pushed too far and ended up with two 9mm slots in him. Tragic." The car jolted as Grant braked, the cars ahead backing up from a red light.

"Sarge?" Amber's voice betrayed her concern. "This doesn't sound like you."

Grant sighed once more. "I know, I'm sorry." He shook his head. "I'm so tired, I'm so angry and so guilty about Panos, and so frustrated." Grant forced a fake laugh. "Ignore me." The car behind sounded its horn. Grant looked ahead to see the traffic had moved on. "And I fucking hate traffic jams!"

"Look, skip, a café, pull over, I'll buy *you* a coffee and a bun."

"Deal."

* * *

"What sort of place is this that doesn't serve a fantastico capo del magro frappuccino al cioccolato moka? Poor show, I reckon." Grant shook his head slowly in simulated disappointment.

Amber laughed. "I don't think I've ever seen a human being look so bewildered and lost in my life as that barista, when you asked for that?"

"As I can say it at the drop of a hat, I feel compelled to never let an opportunity slip by." Grant shrugged as if that was explanation enough.

"Feeling a bit better now?" asked Amber as Grant pushed a huge piece of chocolate sponge into his grateful mouth. "Do you feel like telling me what's bothering you?"

Grant smiled broadly. "Just a sugar low, better now." Amber raised her eyebrows as a mother would to a child telling a fib. Grant caved. "Okay. I think the bottom line is I'm conflicted, mentally, that is. It doesn't happen too often, but it's a state I don't deal well with. I like to know where I'm going, what I'm doing. We're puzzle solvers, and I can cope with the conflict of not knowing an answer, for a while anyway, but the feeling of not fully understanding what's going on doesn't sit well with me. Add a healthy dose of guilt, a baby that cries all night, and you get a grumpy old Detective Sergeant."

"Conflicted? Amber pushed.

"*Everything* is conflicted. I was convinced that Sean knew his killer, from the film of his body language, and I was convinced *he* was the key to the whole case. Crack his part, and the rest would fall into place. Now, I'm not so sure. It's such a tangle of relationships, emotions, and evidence. Just look at the bloodbath yesterday at the Rugby Club, *Callum's* Rugby Club! And the first victim there, Sam Pendry, his ex-wife, was over the side with Sean Crisp, and what the bloody hell has Bill Buckle, union firebrand, got to do with anything? Or a Michelin-starred chef. We're being bounced from pillar to post. Just look at today for example, we're on the way to Charlie's, we were bantering, taking the piss out of each other, moaning about the radio-active bogey, you know?" Amber nodded. "And yesterday, a man I arranged to join us on the squad was murdered. A wife and two kids, fatherless, a life cut short, and we're fucking about making 'let's embrace diversity' jokes while two gay dogs bum each other. If a normal person, a person from 'outside' was listening, *judging*, what the hell would they think of us? What has The Job done to us? What sort of twisted, mutated humans have we become?"

"But they're not us; they can't judge. Walk in our shoes first, *then* judge."

"Then there's Charlie One. I've been *really* pissed off with him; he's been rude and unprofessional, and he made a huge cock-up. I went to see him today, looking forward to tearing him a new arsehole, and we find he's living in squalor and dying from dementia. And to use your word, yes, it's tragic, and it's sad and it's not fair, but…there's this."

"What skip?"

"I'm *still* really pissed off with him. I'm really unhappy with what he was saying. I didn't trust him, not totally. There's more Amber, I felt it. Wasn't he laying it on a bit thick, don't you think?"

"Hmmm, your famous Spider-Sense is tingling, is it?" Amber grinned from ear to ear.

Grant laughed. "You're a cheeky bugger. Come on, let's finish up and see what we can find out about Bernard Huxton. We've got Rory bloody Caplan to see this afternoon too."

* * *

"You do understand that these files are strictly confidential." The middle-aged lady with glasses perched on the end of her nose like a Victorian governess repeated the words for the umpteenth time since she'd guided Grant and Amber to the Education Authority records store room. "This is something we don't usually do."

Grant couldn't stop himself. "I see. Just out of curiosity, what do you *'usually do'* when one of your teachers is shot to death on his doorstep and the police try to solve his murder?" Amber smothered her laugh with a hand.

Bewildered, the woman returned to her default setting. "The files really are strictly confidential."

Grant gave up; administrative apparatchiks were the same wherever you went, procedural and humourless. He plumped for, "It's very kind of you to assist us, thank you." The school ma'am smiled an undertaker's smile.

"These are the Annual Assessment Reports relating to Mr Bernard Huxton, written by the relevant Head Teacher during his period of employment in Putney." She pushed the thirty years of files across the table and waited.

"We can't take the file?" Amber asked.

"Certainly not, these are…"

"Confidential?" Grant cut in.

"Strictly?" Added Amber, planting a helpful smile on her face.

"Quite so." The woman adjusted her glasses and looked from one detective to the other, not sure what was happening.

Amber began to examine the report sheets, held in date order, enclosed within the orange docket. "It's alright, Miss, you can leave us to it, I'm sure you have lots to do."

"Indeed, I have, Officer, but our protocols state that I can neither let the file leave the building nor my sight, they are…"

"Strictly Confidential!" Amber and Grant said in unison.

Amber took out her notebook and began to scribble.

* * *

"What do you make of that, then?" Grant asked as he manoeuvred the radioactive bogey out of the car park.

"It didn't really throw the case wide open, did it?" Amber admitted,

187

"Why such a load of repetitive, boring nonsense should be considered so confidential and secret, I don't understand."

"There were two entries which *were* interesting, the very vague references to what we have to assume were complaints of bad teaching at best or bullying at worst."

"Hmmm," pondered Amber. "Those reports were made in consecutive years, eighteen and nineteen years ago, by a woman who was an acting or temporary Head Teacher of the school for just two years, then moved on. There was nothing untoward in any report before her or after her, by other Head Teachers."

"Well, you can look at that two ways," speculated Grant, "either she had a bone to pick with Huxton, maybe she just didn't like him or the colour of his tie, or any of a hundred things which can sway an opinion.

"Or?"

"Or she was the only one who was honest enough, brave enough, or conscientious enough to actually record an issue that everyone else didn't have the wherewithal or balls to address or report. Remind me what she said." Grant asked. "I saw you copy the relevant bits down."

Amber examined her notebook. "Okay, here it is. She says that 'Mr Huxton is a competent teacher with a robust style which doesn't suit the temperament of every pupil he teaches'. That's quite telling and speaks volumes, I think, especially the word 'robust'. She goes on to say, 'Mr Huxton teaches woodwork exclusively to boys and mathematics to a mixed class but appears to apply the same spirited style of instruction to the two different groups of students. A little flexibility in this area would benefit everyone.' Ouch! This woman is good with words."

"She is," Grant agreed. "We have to remember that her report on Huxton is a permanent record and could affect his career prospects for all time, so she had to be circumspect and able to defend what she's committed to pen and paper, or the teachers union would be on her like a fucking leopard."

Amber laughed. "Nice image."

"What about the following year?" Grant asked.

"In this report, she's a bit more specific, more pissed off, maybe? She was promoted to be a permanent Head Teacher and transferred to another school right after writing this one, she may have felt more liberated by that prospect, to be a bit more 'robust' in her comments herself. After all, she wasn't going to be around to have to look at Huxton's angry face afterwards."

What did she say?"

Amber scanned her notes. "Okay, here's the relevant line. 'Mr Huxton seems more suited to handling students of a more robust temperament', there's that word again, robust, 'and seems reluctant to adapt his style and approach to meet the character and needs of all his pupils. This intransigence is evidenced by several missives from concerned parents and necessitated verbal guidance from myself at the end of summer term. I am glad to report that Mr Huxton has embraced this supportive intervention'. Whoa! What does that all hide, do you think?"

"I think," Grant pondered, "it means our man Huxton was a bully and had to be picked up by the Head because of it. It's a bugger the so-called 'missives' don't form part of the record. Maybe we could get one of the lads to re-visit the widow Huxton and put this to her, maybe there was just *one* boy who'd held a grudge all these years."

"Maybe there was. But it was heading towards *two decades* ago, skip."

"Do you know the thing about hate, Amber? It percolates."

Chapter Forty-Four

It was turning into a packed-full day, and part of Grant cursed his DCI, Paul Winter, for laying so much responsibility and so many tasks at his feet, whilst in the same breath he recognised the assignments as an expression of trust in his policing skills and thoroughness. If the truth were known, he was also grateful that his role was pursuing the main paths of the evidence trail. The humble DCs on the case were trawling through the dozens of potential grudge-holders accumulated by the controversial chef Konstanz Bassa or the firebrand union man Bill Buckle; others were making phone calls, taking statements, viewing CCTV tapes, wearing out shoe leather, and knocking door after door, enduring the grind and graft which the reality of detective work entailed. So it was with mixed feelings of fatigue and responsibility that Grant and Amber rang the bell at the New Malden home of PC Rory Caplan.

* * *

Grant and Amber settled onto a comfy sofa in a large sitting room as Rory's wife, Heather, disappeared into the kitchen to make tea. Rory was still looking as uncomfortable as the moment he'd opened the door and seen the IDs of the two detectives. He stood rather than sat, as if considering escape, a doomed endeavour if contemplated, Grant surmised. Rory Caplan's limp was pronounced, and he winced with every step, a little too much, the DS thought. Was he really so disabled? Was he disabled at all?

"Lovely house, Rory, a nice area too." Grant made small talk.

"Handy for the shopping in Kingston and good connections into London." Amber contributed.

Rory tapped his damaged leg, "I've got this to thank. Compensation payout bought this place; we were languishing in a two-bed maisonette before. The cost of living in London is crippling." He tapped his leg again. *"Crippling,"* he forced the joke. No one laughed.

"I know it's a platitude, but it could've been much worse," Grant tried to sound sympathetic. "Every copper's seen terrible sights as the result of motorbike accidents."

"Yeah, you're right," Rory replied, unconvinced. "Ah, here's Heather with the tea."

At the reappearance of Mrs Caplan, Amber rose in a prearranged plan, made en route. "Heather, let's talk in the kitchen while these two talk 'Job' in private. I bet it's as nice as the rest of the house. I'm so jealous."

"Sit down, Rory, nothing to worry about, just routine stuff." Grant gestured to an armchair opposite him, taking a sip of tea as he did so. "Ah! Lovely stuff, life without the hot splosh, unthinkable." Rory sat, dramatically wincing in pain as he did so. He *was* piling it on, and Grant could see where the irritation with 'Tiddles' he'd witnessed at the DPG base may have come from.

"Nothing more to be done with that, then? To make it less painful?" Grant enquired casually, sipping more tea.

"No. I've run out of specialists; this is as good as it gets. What's this visit about, then?"

Grant smiled. "No need to be concerned. A colleague of yours has been murdered, everyone is interviewed, unfortunately, because you were sick the night Sean died, you haven't been seen yet, that's all. I'm sure you've seen the news and the papers. We've had our hands full, so it took a while to get to you."

"Oh, right." Rory visibly relaxed. "How's it going? The investigation, any nearer to getting the bastard?"

Grant smiled, holding his stare. "Nearer but not there yet. Can you tell me about your evening the night Sean died? You were the armourer, issuing weapons and ammunition." Minute by minute, Grant led Rory through the night of the murder, requesting he expand on his actions, procedures, and his role at the Diplomatic Protection Group Base.

While Grant was taking as much time as possible to question Rory about very little, Amber confronted Heather Caplan in the kitchen.

"Mrs Caplan, I need to talk with you privately, about a delicate matter."

Heather looked mystified. "Me? Really? I'm not sure how I can help you."

"I think you can. Tell me about your relationship with Sean Crisp?"

Heather's hand flew to her mouth, and her eyes welled. "I don't know what you mean. I knew him, of course, from Rory's work functions, and I was heartbroken to hear what happened, but what relationship?"

"Heather, we have phone records, times, dates, duration. It all adds up. Please…please don't treat me as a fool. Whether you like it or not, you're bang in the middle of a murder investigation, which so far has seven victims. We know the relationship ended a week or so before Sean was shot, that it was over. That's right, isn't it?"

Heather slowly nodded her head, the tears running freely now. For the second time in a day, Amber pulled a tissue from her pocket and passed it over. "Did you love him, Heather?"

"I think I did, he was funny, charming, and exciting." Heather sobbed.

"I knew Sean too, we were friends," Amber empathised, "but what about Rory?"

Heather took a deep breath. "After the accident, Rory…Rory changed. He was bitter, short-tempered, sometimes aggressive, and…" she hesitated again. "He wasn't the same sexually. He'd been damaged. Understand?" Heather covered her face with her hand. "I'm so ashamed. But it matters, it's important. I'm still young, I've still got needs and desires…" Her voice faded to nothing, lost in the sobs.

"I'm sorry. I do understand." Amber reached out and squeezed her shoulder, "Heather, this is *really* important, does Rory know about your affair, did he find out about you and Sean?"

The real nature and significance of the question suddenly dawned on Heather Caplan. "*Oh my God!* No! That's not possible, he wouldn't, he couldn't!"

"Did he know Heather?"

"Yes. Yes, he knew, he found out."

The door to the kitchen quietly opened, revealing Amber's grim face to Grant. Slowly, deliberately, she nodded her head twice in a pre-arranged signal, then closed the door, unheard and unseen by Rory.

Earlier, as Grant and Amber had sat in the car outside the Caplan's home, the DS had run through the strategy for the interview once more, finally reiterating, "If Heather confirms the affair with Sean, nod once, if Rory knew about it, nod twice, if he didn't know, then nod once and shake your head once. Got it?" She'd got it, and now Grant had the information he needed to question Rory properly.

"Can I ask you about Sean now, Rory? How did you get on?"

"We got on fine. We didn't mix so much, my job was in the armoury or the base room, his on post. When he wasn't on post, he was in the canteen or gym."

"You didn't have any personal animosity towards him?"

"No."

Grant leant forward in his chair. "I want you to think about your answer carefully, Rory, *very* carefully. I'll ask again, was there any reason you may have felt animosity towards Sean Crisp?"

The detective could almost hear the cogs turning in Rory Caplan's head. His eyes flicked back and forth towards the kitchen door and back to Grant's penetrating gaze. "What do you mean?" Grant said nothing. "What are you getting at? What are you implying?" His words were riven with agitation bordering on panic.

The kitchen door opened, Heather Caplan re-entered the sitting room, closely followed by Amber, and uttered two words. "They know."

For the second time that day, Grant was presented with the sight of a grown man bursting into tears.

"I'm sorry. I don't know what I was thinking." Caplan stuttered between sobs. "I was full of anger, humiliation, and jealousy." Heather moved to his side, placing her hand on his shoulder. Rory Caplan looked up, holding

Grant's stare with his wet, reddened eyes, "It was me," he said, "it was me."

Chapter Forty-Five

"Well, Detective Sergeant Maddox, you've had a hell of a day, haven't you?" Paul Winter stretched back in his chair, hands behind his head. "We now have our chief HOLMES analyst permanently suspended because he could start talking to trees or licking windows any minute, and a crippled PC who could start coughing up fur-balls any minute, in a cell awaiting interview in the morning. Is that a reasonable assessment of your day's achievements?" Paul was grinning broadly.

It was nearing eight o'clock, and DI Heidi Yorke was in the main office preparing to give a case review to the Task Force. Grant mirrored his friend's posture in the chair opposite. "Don't forget that Amber has useful stuff on Bernard Huxton. It seems likely he was a bully to his pupils, some of them anyway; it may be a long shot, but we should look into his past, too."

"Do you know what my wife does?" asked Paul.

"You've told me some of the things she does, and I reckon that makes her a rare woman and you a lucky man."

Paul laughed, "Other than that."

Grant laughed too. "I don't know. Tell me."

"She makes lists of things to do, long bloody lists, and when she crosses something off the list, she writes something new at the bottom. Her lists *never* get shorter, and you're the same, we tick something off and *you* add something else."

Grant shrugged, "That's nothing, if Lydia does something which *isn't* on her list, she writes it in and crosses it out straightaway so it *looks* as if the list is getting done! Madness."

"Well, for God's sake, don't start that!" Paul pointed an accusatory finger at his DS. "But good work today, Granty, Rory Caplan is banged up on several counts of criminal damage to Sean Crisp's car and for offences under the Malicious Communications Act for the threatening letters he sent. What an idiot! Throwing everything away, job and pension gone. What's he going to do for work now? Who's going to employ him? A man who can barely walk *and* with a criminal record."

"I'm not excusing him, Guv, he was stupid, but I can sympathise. He's a man who had a responsible job, a bit of status, a good living, and in the twinkling of an eye it went, leaving him with a menial job handing out guns instead of carrying one, in almost constant pain, and to add insult to injury, Mr Floppy problems downstairs. If that's not bad enough, he finds out his wife is getting her tyres pumped up by someone he works with. He's humiliated; he doesn't feel like a man anymore. He had to hit out somehow, and he did…and now it's rebounded back. It's a tough deal."

Paul softened slightly at Grant's words. "Well, okay, he may have had a bad hand dealt, that's not our fault, what counts is he's off the list of potential suspects and we've cleared up one of Sean Crisp's mysteries."

"I never really had him near the top as a suspect. I know he could've been exaggerating his injury, but the killer didn't limp at all, and the clincher was the embassy CCTV showed the attacker struggled to remove the Glock from Sean's retention holster. Caplan wouldn't have had any difficulty doing that. He was proficient in using the issued equipment, and we've found no connection between him and the other victims."

Paul sighed, "We've found no connection between *anyone* and *any* of the victims."

"Except Sean Crisp keeps cropping up, and his son Callum."

"And if Callum crops up, then by default, his bitter and twisted mother, Debbie, pops up too. Whatever the link is, we'll know when we identify the one who's the 'Ground Zero' victim, if I can put it that way, we can't ignore the fact Debbie does have a strong motive to kill Sean."

"She does. Revenge for past humiliations and what she sees as her and

Callum's abandonment. The trigger could've been the news Sean was planning to finally divorce and remarry. The financial gains and losses, insurances, and pensions amount to big numbers. She and Callum can't be ruled out, but I can't see what the connection between Sam Pendry and Callum would be."

"It could be a coincidence. People can be members at the same club. It can happen," offered the DCI.

"The 'Ground Zero' victim," mused Grant. "I like that, boss. Which is the killing that prompted the series, and the *reason* for the killings? It isn't necessarily the first; Sean Crisp may only have been killed to steal the weapon, it may not even be the one after that, Bill Buckle. But one is the key, the link is hidden in there, somewhere."

Before Grant could expand further on his thoughts, Heidi opened the door. "If you two are ready, we have a case review to deliver."

"Sorry, Heidi, on our way." Paul pulled a face at Grant, "We're in trouble now."

Chapter Forty-Six

DI Heidi Yorke stood before the complex diagrams, victim photos, linking lines, and proposed investigative actions that plastered the whiteboard behind her. It had become necessary to affix a second board alongside the original to accommodate the scale of the case and the slaughter, which was challenging the Task Force. One joker had offered to obtain and attach a third board to the wall to 'get ahead of the game'. Another commented, 'I think we're going to need a bigger whiteboard', in an homage to the movie 'Jaws'.

"Okay, ladies and gents, *now* we're all here," Heidi gave a school-ma'am look at Paul and Grant. The first thing I want to talk about is Charlie Buller. As you know, he's been on sick leave since his collapse. I need to tell you his condition prevents him from continuing his role in the investigation, and he won't be returning. His illness necessitated a review of the data on the case thus far, a review that Charlotte and I undertook today and have just concluded. You'll all be pleased to know," Heidi directed her glance towards Paul and Grant, "we are satisfied with the integrity of the data on the system. It's all good." Heidi smiled as Paul gave a slow, exaggerated wink towards her and mouthed the words, 'well done.'

"The next news," Heidi continued, "solves a mystery and clears the decks a little for us. It was good work from DS Maddox and DC Bennett that established the woman Sean Crisp was seeing and finished with, just days before his murder, was Heather Caplan, the wife of PC Rory Caplan, the DPG base armourer. They obtained a verbal confession from PC Caplan for damaging Sean Crisp's car and sending him numerous threatening letters.

PC Caplan has been arrested and awaits interview. We've eliminated him as a suspect in the murders, dates, times, and alibis have been accounted for. He was just a pissed off husband trying to get back at the man screwing his wife, nothing more."

Grant scanned the room, several faces seemed to express the pity for Caplan he'd earlier articulated to Paul Winter, it was another tragic twist in the whole story, and of sorts, another police casualty.

Heidi continued her briefing. "Now, DC Padda and DC Lines have interviewed the partner of Sam Pendry, the first of last night's three victims at the Ruffians Rugby Club and nearby. We must assume Pendry was the intended, primary target." Grant rubbed his chin, the words thrown out so casually by the DCI, 'Ground Zero Victim', were making him look anew at each fatality. What had initiated this bout of violence? The number of shootings alone in such a compressed time frame spoke of a killer in a hurry. Grant shook his head with frustration, returning his concentration to Heidi.

"The evidence suggests the subsequent murders of DS Panos and Gavin Cape, a short distance away in the industrial estate, were committed to facilitate the escape of our killer. Before we hear from Nags and Craig, I have some info for you. A very poor, black and white CCTV camera on one of the units on the estate picked up a light coloured hatchback car leaving the murder scene. I haven't seen the film yet, but I'm told it is a fleeting glimpse in a corner of the frame which lasts for less than three seconds…but…it *is* the car of our man. A small white hatchback. The tech guys will have the original recording tomorrow, enhance the picture, and attempt to ID the make, model, even the year. Then we can start weeding the Police National Computer system for possibilities." The DI's news was met with smiles all round. "Okay, gents, can you tell us what you've found out, please?"

Craig Lines nodded to his colleague Nagur Padda, who nervously stood up to address the Task Force. "Okay, yeah." He consulted his notes as a voice full of humour called out from the back of the group, "Get on with it!"

Craig Lines stood up, calling out, "Oi! No heckling!" There was laughter again, Craig nodded to his friend encouragingly, "Go on, Nags."

"Okay. Sam Pendry, male, white, forty-three years old, divorced, an independent estate agent doing well financially, lived with his partner, Delia Lancaster, for five years; she states they were intending to marry; she's also divorced. There are no children from either of their previous marriages. Last night, Pendry drove to the Ruffians Rugby Club for a training session at about 7 pm, afterwards he settled in the clubhouse for a meal and a drink. He played a few games of pool with two friends and left the building at 11 pm. A few moments after Pendry exited the clubhouse, his friend Gavin Cape also left but shouted a warning from the doorway to other members that Pendry was being attacked. Pendry's body was found lying face down next to his car. Gavin Cape evidently saw the suspect and gave chase. He was found dead in the industrial estate after calling for police on the 999 system. DS Panos appears to have been monitoring police channels off-duty, attended the scene, and was found dead, collapsed across Gavin's body. These two murders will be covered later; our interview with the widow concentrated on Pendry. The cause of his death was a single gunshot to the head, the entry point was through his left ear, it seems likely he was turning away from his attacker. Perhaps he saw his friend at the door to the clubhouse? That would be the direction he was looking. A 9mm shell casing was recovered at the scene. Preliminary examination suggests it was fired from Sean Crisp's stolen Glock 17."

"When can that be confirmed?" The question from Paul Winter."

"The post-mortem was this afternoon, the bullet was sent…with the others… to ballistics straight away, we'll know definitively by 10 am tomorrow…about all three shootings." Paul nodded his approval. Nagur, although nervous at addressing a crowd of his peers, was showing himself to be a competent and efficient detective.

"Pendry was a keen sportsman," Nagur continued, "and super fit, he was still first choice in the ruffians front row at his age. He'd been a member for nearly fifteen years. Very popular, for an estate agent anyway," there was a ripple of laughter. "Apparently, he had no enemies, although there was a bit of a scandal some years back. Pendry's first wife, Gayle Pendry, was having a fling with another club member, none other than Sean Crisp! After she was caught giving Sean a blow job in the car park, Sean was asked to leave the club. Gayle and Sam reconciled but split up two years later anyway. Delia says that after splitting from Gayle, Sam had a few girlfriends with whom he seemed to have parted on good terms; we have details from an address book to check on. There's nothing to suggest anyone with an axe to grind. Also, Delia will happily allow access anytime to all Pendry's client files kept at his office. Considering what's happened, she's been great and is holding it together really well. I took the liberty to sort a Family Liaison Officer for her, I hope that's okay?" Nagur looked to the DCI, who nodded with approval. "The client list is extensive and will need trawling through. There may be a disgruntled customer, someone who was gazumped on a house purchase, someone who felt they'd lost money or an opportunity because of business dealings with Pendry. It could be a motive to kill him. But Delia was very confident that Pendry was a straight-up guy and well thought of. But those are the two lines of enquiry that came out of our interview, ex-girlfriends and ex-clients." Nagur gave a nod to the DI and retook his seat. Attention turned back to Heidi Yorke.

Chapter Forty-Seven

"Thank you, Nags, good work, as you've obviously built up a rapport with Delia, is it?" Nags nodded. "Would you and Craig stick with it, and between you, look into the client files and the ex-girlfriends. Tread carefully with that last one, I'm sure the last thing she'll want to be thinking about is her dead partner's ex-shags. Okay?"

"Yes, Guv, we'll liaise with the FLO, maybe she can get hold of the address book and any old diaries for us to sift through," Nagur answered.

"Yes, good, do it. Okay, next, DC Chamberlain could update us on Callum's movements last night."

Dirty Don rose, "Okay, Callum Crisp, eldest son of Sean Crisp, has been a member of the Ruffians Rugby Club since he was eleven. He's not a regular player but is a regular attendee at the bar. I spoke with Callum and his mum Debbie this afternoon." Don consulted his notes, "yesterday Callum slept late, got up at about noon, grabbed some lunch, then took the 207 bus from Acton Central to White City, and says he wandered around the Westfield Shopping Centre for a few hours, meeting some mates, just 'hanging' apparently. It shouldn't be hard to prove one way or another, the bus will be camera'ed up and Westfield has CCTV's coming out of its wazoo. So I don't doubt the truth of that; it'd be too easy to catch him in a lie. He admits that he went to the underground car park with two mates and smoked a bit of blow. I suspect that's the real reason he went there, to score, but that was an admission too far to get out of him."

"What was Debbie doing all this time?" Grant asked.

"Ah, the delightful 'Acton Harpy'," Don couldn't help but sneer, his dislike of Debbie Crisp obvious. "She was up before the sun and cleaning a suite of offices in central Acton from 6 am until 9.30 am, then she went to the Tesco supermarket to begin her shelf-stacking shift at 10 am, where she worked until 6 pm. She did her shopping at the store after her shift and got back to her flat a little after 7 pm, about half an hour before Callum got back from Westfields."

Grant recalled his interview with Debbie Crisp, her misery at the turn of events in her life, and her struggles to survive and put her son through university. She'd spoken of her punishing schedule of work; it appeared she wasn't exaggerating, and he felt a twang of sympathy. The feeling was accompanied with the recognition that the prospect of lump sums from insurance payouts and the security of a pension for life would transform her fortunes and so provide a reason to want Sean Crisp dead whilst *still* joined to her in marriage. The circumstance couldn't fail to turn a spotlight on her and her son.

"Callum and his mother ate dinner together. Debbie decided to play Bingo in Shepherd's Bush, and Callum asked to be dropped off at the Rugby club for a few beers. Debbie drove to Scrubs Lane, dropped him at the entrance, and continued on. This is where it gets interesting."

Ears pricked up around the room as Dirty Don raised the tension with his words. Had he found something significant?

"Callum was in the clubhouse and downed his first pint at about 9 pm. Sam Pendry was already in the bar after the training session, playing pool. Apparently, Callum wanted a game, but Pendry's group had an informal league table going and hogged it to themselves. Callum says he directed some abuse at the guys, which was reciprocated. Callum admits he was probably still a bit high from earlier in the day and a bit pissed after three or four beers in a short time. He stressed that the exchanged words didn't amount to anything more than banter. Whatever the truth of it, Callum decided to leave the club soon after the confrontation, at about 10 pm."

"An hour before Pendry was killed." Heidi put in.

"That's right."

"What were his movements when he left?" Heidi asked.

"He says he decided to walk down the hill, into Shepherd's Bush, to meet his mum and get a lift home."

"What did Debbie say?" The room was hushed as Heidi pressed for information.

"Well, that's the problem. She says she came out of the Bingo Hall at about 10.45 pm and Callum was leaning on her car in the car park, waiting for her. Fifteen minutes *before* the shooting. Callum's walk would be just over two miles, the times aren't far out, that's *if* he did walk to her. If he's telling the truth and left at about 10 pm and dawdled, it wouldn't be too long a wait for her to come out."

"But," pressed Heidi, "the only corroboration to all this is his *mother*?"

"The only thing we know for sure is that Callum left the Rugby club at 10 pm and his mother walked out the bingo hall at 10.45 pm. I called the place, they have CCTV, it'll be easy to prove."

"It's less than a five-minute drive back to the club from Shepherd's Bush, either with Callum in the car, or to be in place, ready to pick him up and get him away after he'd re-enacted the gunfight at the OK Corral." Heidi pointed her finger in a back-and-forward motion as she spoke.

"What if they're in this together," Amber pitched in. "If it's Callum, he could have dropped his mother at Bingo and parked the car in the industrial estate, crossed the road to the clubhouse at 9pm, walked out at 10pm, and then hid, waiting for Pendry, committed the murders, and picked Debbie up afterwards. As the only corroboration is each other, you can't believe either one of them."

"That's right," answered Don, "and everyone, here's the good bit, Debbie's car is a white Ford Fiesta Hatchback."

Chapter Forty-Eight

Speculation hung meaningfully in the air. The fact was London was full of light coloured hatchbacks; the sighting of a similar car leaving the scene of the shooting was tantalising, but it was not yet evidence.

"Okay." Heidi kept control of her voice, remaining outwardly calm, "I'll chase up the techies first thing in the morning, the image of the white hatchback has just *got* to be enhanced enough to get a make and model, so we can either include or exclude Callum and Debbie. Don, I want you to see if we can get any other trace of that car in the vicinity. I want you all over this like a rash, bus's CCTV, commercial and Transport for London cameras, petrol stations, anything, find that car. That's your only job for now. Okay?"

"Yes, Guv." Don gave a salute.

The remaining topics of the briefing covered the probability that the ex-teacher, Bernard Huxton, was a bully to his pupils, opening up a whole new raft of potential suspects, and the progress of the hunt for anyone who may have held a grudge against Konstanz Bassa and the Union man, Bill Buckle. Sadly, this progress could be described with two simple words, 'not much'. Finally, the officers were assigned tasks for the next twenty-four hours. Paul Winter stepped forward to address the team, giving encouragement and expressing optimism before ending with sobering words.

"Ladies and gents, yesterday we lost one of our team. Panos was one of *us*; he worked here, amongst us. It is a regret that we didn't get to know him better; a coward's hand prevented that from happening. We have a greater incentive than ever to do our jobs, to be professional and vigilant, and I must emphasise again, as with our initial investigation into Sean Crisp's murder, *to do this right!* When we find the person who took Panos from us I want to be able to look him in the eye as the life sentence is given, and know we got him, bang to rights, fair and square, with no wriggle room for a low-life defense lawyer to start bleating about the infringed rights of the maggot he represents." Paul's voice shook with emotion. "Now, please, ladies and gents, let's stand and remain silent for a minute, and think about our friend and colleague, Detective Sergeant Panayiotis Kalamatianos."

Grant bowed his head. Was it only nine days ago that the Task Force members had shown their respect to another dead colleague, PC Sean Crisp? Grant couldn't remove himself from the wave of guilt which swept through him as the room fell into silence, after all, it was his doing, his suggestion, that brought Panos to the investigation, and so to his death.

* * *

The majority of the team had drifted away, and the pace of the enquiry was physically, mentally, and emotionally draining, with early starts, long hours, and full-on intensity in between. Grant found himself, as he often did, seated in the glass box office of DCI Paul Winter in company with DI Heidi Yorke, privately reviewing the case. Grant had declined the ubiquitous offer of scotch from the lower drawer of Paul's desk.

"I can understand Caplan's feelings, who wouldn't?" Heidi said, with exasperation in her voice. "If, as you say, Grant had been rendered impotent by the accident as well as half crippled and in constant pain, it's adding insult to injury to find out your wife is being screwed by a workmate. I know that you shouldn't speak ill of the dead, but I have to confess that I can't see how everyone says how wonderful Sean Crisp was. I mean, really? The man was an alley cat."

"People like cats. Haven't you seen the internet or Facebook? That's all it is, pictures of cats." Grant shrugged.

Heidi ignored him. "Like I say, I understand the feeling, but did he think it wouldn't eventually come to light that he was sending the letters and damaging Sean's car? He's lost everything he had: job, pension, security, and his good name. It's madness."

"Once he found out his wife was unfaithful, perhaps he didn't think he had anything worth keeping. We've already established he must've had a miserable life."

"He feels miserable *now*? Wait until he's banged up, on a segregation wing under Rule 43," put in Paul, "then he'll know what real misery really is. A copper in prison? Shit! Why would *anyone* in our job ever do *anything* to risk that?"

Before a comment or opinion was offered, there was a knock on the door, the DCI called out, "Come." The caller was a tall, slim woman constable who smiled in Paul's direction.

"Excuse me, sir, sorry to interrupt, but the control room took a phone call from a Sergeant Fallon, there's a message for DS Maddox." She waved a sheet of paper.

Grant answered Paul's puzzled expression, "he's the skipper from the Diplomatic Protection Group base, the one who dropped Sean off at the embassy. I went to see him to follow up on Sean's postings." The DCI nodded his understanding. Grant took the note, "Thank you."

"What is it? What does it say?" Heidi asked, her curiosity getting ahead of Grant as he unfolded the message.

"Hold on, I'll get there. Okay, it says, 'I told you I'd remember his name in the end, it came to me out of the blue, Mr 'Dull and Boring' was an admin civvy called... oh fucking hell! I don't believe it."

Chapter Forty-Nine

"What are you talking about? Mr Dull and Boring? What does all that mean?" Paul fired off the questions like bullets, feeding off Grant's excitement.

Grant gathered himself and his thoughts before answering. "I was talking with Chris Fallon, the DPG sergeant, he was a close mate of Sean's, they worked together at Hounslow nick years ago, he told me about something which Crisp and his wandering dick were involved in."

"A wandering dick incident! What a surprise." Heidi couldn't resist the sarcasm.

"Sean was banging an admin woman who was engaged to another admin civvy, a bloke a bit older than her who was 'dull and boring'. He found out, called off the engagement, and confronted Sean in the front office of the nick, had a blazing row, accused Sean of ruining his life, stealing his future, and made all sorts of threats."

"Sounds like he *had* ruined his life." Heidi again.

"Anyway, Sean was in the middle of a really good job he'd organised, taking out a burglary team, which went tits up in court and got thrown out over missing paperwork. Sean eventually found the missing stuff chucked away in the sealed confidential waste sacks, which was one of the admin responsibilities of Mr Dull and Boring."

Paul and Heidi leant forward, eager for the story, waiting for Grant's punchline.

"Obviously, Sean was furious at the sabotage and pointed the finger, but couldn't prove anything. However, the stink was such that Mr Dull and

Boring was transferred to another station and lost out on a promotion he was due."

"Okay, so Dull and Boring is humiliated in front of the whole nick, has lost the love of his life, has been moved stations under a cloud, suspected of evidence tampering, *and* lost out on promotion. Definitely someone who won't be sending Sean bloody Crisp a Christmas card, so who is it?" Paul asked, his patience expiring.

Grant passed over the note, which Paul read, "Oh fuck!"

"Oh fuck indeed," agreed Grant.

"Is someone going to let me in on this?" Heidi exclaimed. Paul passed her the note, which she read out loud. "blah, blah blah…Mr 'Dull and Boring' was an admin civvy called Charles Buller." Heidi's eyebrows shot up like leaping salmon. "Oh fuck!"

"Yep!" Announced Grant. "Oh fuck is right. Charlie bloody One. He's got to be lifted, right now! He's lied and lied and lied, possibly covered up or tampered with evidence, and has a revenge motive to take out Sean Crisp, *and* if he is truly terminally ill with dementia, it explains his hurry. We've been averaging almost one killing a night, it's heading towards 10 pm, we need to arrest him…Now!"

"Agreed! You visited him, Granty, what's his address?" Paul was already reaching for the phone. "We'll get the local uniforms in his area to get there right now, that'll be quickest. Hello, control room, DCI Winter here, I need this actioned pronto…"

Grant passed his notebook to the DCI, running a finger along Charlie One's address, which Paul passed on with his instructions.

"Jesus!" Heidi exhaled. "Can this get any madder?"

* * *

Paul Winter's phone rang ninety minutes later. Heidi had left for home, she'd an early start and much to do in the morning, the identification of the white car in the CCTV film at the top of her priority list. Paul and Grant remained. The call informed them the arrested man, Charles Buller, was five minutes away from the custody suite door. Both men headed downstairs.

Two youths were sitting on the bench opposite the custody sergeant, each with his hands behind his back, evidently still handcuffed. A PC with a bleeding lip and another with a swelling eye stood grim-faced on either side of the prisoners, who looked about nervously, neither expected their evening to end this way. The custody officer turned to face his visitors, "Good evening, sir, hiya Grant. I'm holding your bloke outside in the van while I finish processing these two arseholes, two minutes, okay?"

"No worries, Lance, how you doing?" Grant responded.

"Frankly, my life would be better without pissed up wankers like these two taking swings *at my officers!*" The final three words were bellowed at the two youths ten feet away, who physically jumped with the shock and fury of the audible onslaught. "Twenty fucking years ago, you pair would've been carried in here broken and bleeding, one on a stretcher, the other in a bucket for punching an officer, but we're *nice* coppers nowadays, none of that rough stuff anymore, more's the pity." Grant glanced up at the all-seeing custody suite CCTV camera high on the wall. "Lock the bastards up, take their cuffs off, we'll see how your parents feel about being called in here, eh?" The two battered officers lifted the prisoners by the elbows and led them down the cell passage. Lance Bilton signed a sheet of paper which lay before him with a flourish and addressed the civvy jailor who was standing by the door to the yard. "Okay, bring him in."

A blast of cold winter air invaded the warmth of the custody suite as the heavy door was opened to allow a uniformed constable to lead Charlie Buller into the custody area. Dressed in black jogging bottoms and a thick, black hoody, protection against the cold of the night, Charlie One squinted at the sudden bright lights, scanning the room, looking confused and alarmed. His eyes widened with recognition when he saw Paul Winter and Grant Maddox standing behind the seated custody sergeant.

"Mr Winter, Grant, what's going on? Why am I here?"

Sergeant Bilton interrupted him. "Please listen to what this officer has to say. Go ahead, Jack."

"Sarge, I attended the home address of this gentleman, Charles Buller, at

11.03 pm, he answered the door and I asked, 'are you Mr Charles Buller?' he said 'yes, what is it?' at 11.04 pm I said, 'you're under arrest for the murder of Sean Crisp and cautioned him, he replied, 'what are you talking about?' Mr Buller was allowed to dress in warm clothing; he was searched but not handcuffed. The evidence for the arrest lies with DS Maddox, Sarge."

"Very good, thank you. Mr Buller, I am authorising your detention for the purpose of obtaining further evidence and to interview you."

"May I say something, Sergeant?" asked Paul Winter.

Lance nodded. "Of course, sir."

"Mr Buller has claimed he suffers from early-onset dementia and also a condition called Sundowners Syndrome. At this stage, we only have his word for the veracity of that claim, but I think we should proceed as if it's true until we know otherwise. These medical conditions may be detrimental to Mr Buller's claimed understanding of our procedures and our questioning. Until a suitable appropriate adult and legal representation is available to oversee our actions, I suggest Mr Buller is held without the intervention of the Task Force until the morning."

"Thank you, sir. I still need to go through rights, searching, and normal procedure, and in view of your information, we need a doctor's attendance to certify Mr Buller's fitness to be detained. It so happens we have a lay visitor in the building tonight carrying out one of their random inspection visits. I'll ask if she'll be the appropriate adult for the purposes of the Police and Criminal Evidence Act. Either way, we're into a sleep period, he'll be left until the morning, by that time we'll have everyone in place, then you can get at him."

"Thanks, Lance." Grant patted his friend on the shoulder. "Okay Guv, I think we can bugger off now, maybe tomorrow we'll be able to get to the bottom of this."

Paul Winter laughed, "Tomorrow? Don't you mean today? It's gone midnight."

It was two utterly fatigued officers who pushed the wide door to the Task Force office open and entered, dragging heavy feet. Other than Amber Bennett, furiously scribbling notes at her desk, the office was empty. Grant collected his car keys from his desk drawer as Paul turned the lights off in his office and locked the door. The phone within started to ring even as he pulled the key from the lock.

"Bollocks! Nearly made it." Paul unlocked the door, re-entered his office, answering the phone in the dark. Grant waited, the thought occurring that something untoward had happened in the custody suite to Charlie; instead, the grim face of Paul Winter emerged from the murk of his office.

"There's been another one."

Chapter Fifty

The electrifying effect of Paul Winter's words caused a flood of adrenaline to be dumped into Grant's system, giving him a new surge of energy. Once the basic facts and location of the incident had been established, Grant raised an eyebrow to his DCI, which asked, 'Shall I?' His answer was a nod of the head. Grant called over to Amber Bennett, "Want to earn *even* more overtime?"

"Always," Amber replied, grinning, picking up her personal radio, handbag, and coat. She waved a set of ignition keys under Grant's nose, "Guess what car we've got?"

* * *

The familiar hum of the luminous green, radioactive bogey pool car carried the officers out of central London along the Great West Road to the prominent landmark of the soaring clock tower at Gillette Corner.

"Turn right here," Grant instructed. He'd delegated the driving to Amber; he needed time to think. He'd authorised, that very evening, the arrest of Charlie Buller for the murder of Sean Crisp, and now they were attending another murder scene, which from the information provided seemed certain to be part of the series they were investigating. Charlie One was banged up in a cell eight miles away; he'd been home at 11 pm. He was arrested there. It didn't seem plausible that this latest killing, newly discovered, could be laid at the feet of Mr Dull and Boring Buller.

At the top of Syon Lane, where a mini-roundabout split the roadway, an angled police vehicle blocked the path, its powerful blue lights strobing out over the immediate scene and the scrubland beyond. Incident cordon tape fluttered, crossing the road from a lamppost to a tree trunk. Before them stood a familiar, gigantic figure, arms crossed, staring at their hideous car as it slowed to a stop.

As Grant exited the bogey to be illuminated by the blue light, the uniformed colossus unfolded his arms, his face broke into a wide, dazzling grin, and the air reverberated to the deep timbre of Police Sergeant Babatunde Okafor's bass voice.

"Granty! Meeting in the dark again, people will start to talk." Babs advanced on his friend, crushing his fingers in a vicelike grip as he shook hands.

"Babs…you're hurting me." Grant winced.

Babs laughed, "Man, you're such a pussy, the CID has softened you." He slapped Grant on the side of the shoulder, knocking the recipient a couple of feet to his right. Babs turned his attention to Amber, "Hiya, how you doing? Looking after the old gentleman, I hope, don't let him stay out too late, get him back to the Care Home soon."

"I'm doing my best, Sarge, as long as he gets his afternoon nap and a cocoa in the evenings, he does alright." Amber bantered. "Why are you here, Sarge? It's all over, isn't it, just a crime scene? Do we think the shooter is still in the vicinity?"

Grant answered for his friend, "Any firearms incident requires an armed response; until the scene is released, we've the ninjas standing around looking as hard as they can." Babs fixed a grim expression on his face and nodded solemnly. "What can you tell me, Babs?"

Babatunde shook his head, "It's weird, you'll see, the venue is about forty to fifty metres into Jersey Road," he nodded to his right, "the victim is a kid, well a youth anyway, sixteen, seventeen maybe, come on, I'll show you." The huge black sergeant tapped the window of the ARV, "Oi, your turn to freeze out here, I'm taking the CID to the scene." A figure within gave a thumbs-up and opened the door to take his sergeant's place on the cordon.

"A late-night dog walker found the body about thirty minutes ago, lying face down in the gutter. He thought it was a passed-out drunk, then saw the blood and then the Taser."

"Taser!?" Grant and Amber exclaimed the word simultaneously.

"I said it was weird. The boy was face down with an obvious hole in the back of his head. We've found a 9mm casing in the road; it's bagged up for you."

"That's good, thanks," Grant responded, but his attention was the scene ahead, a small knot of people were gathered in the road, all in uniform, bar one, in a heavy, long coat.

"There's a cycle on the floor, presumably the victims, the back wheel is buckled to fuck. The plain-clothes bloke is a local DC. He put it up to the Task Force; he's waiting on the doctor to pronounce life extinct and for forensics to turn up. You're here good and early for this one, Grant."

Their approach had been noted, and the CID man turned and started to walk towards them. Grant and Amber automatically reached for their Warrant Cards. Babatunde slapped Grant's back, "I'll leave you to it, hopefully you'll let us get off and do something more useful shortly. I can't be out here much longer freezing the bollocks off Mrs Okafor's little boy. Be good, give Lydia my love."

"I will do." Grant turned to face the approaching figure. "DS Maddox, DC Bennett, Major Investigation Task Force." Grant introduced himself and Amber.

"Good to see you, I'm Neville King, the lucky night duty CID."

"Hiya, Neville, what we got then?" Asked Grant.

"Well, firstly, we've got no local witnesses, the nearest house is nearly a hundred yards away, over there." The CID man jerked his head back in the direction of the first in a row of houses. He pointed to his right, "while over here, that there is the yard of a builders' merchants and that there," he pointed to his left, "is open scrub which runs to the perimeter wall of Osterley Park. There's not much in the way of traffic along here, only residents really. I've got a few lads knocking doors," Neville pointed to the row of detached houses set back from the road, "to see if anyone saw or heard anything, nothing to report yet."

"That's good work, Neville, well done for getting on top of that," Grant commented. Amber smiled to herself, Grant was always charming and supportive to local officers, uniformed or CID, 'it pays dividends to be nice, not aloof, supportive, not critical,' he'd said. It was one of a hundred lessons, a little gem from the DS she'd put in her back pocket.

"The one witness we do have is the dog walker who found the body and called it in. He's pretty shaken up, I think the worst thing he was expecting tonight was to carry home a bag of dog shit, instead he stumbles on this horror. It's bloody freezing, I saw no point in hanging on to him here, so he's been taken to Hounslow, dog and all, for a hot drink and to give an initial statement."

"Fair enough." Grant was a little disappointed not to be able to speak to the witness firsthand, but reflected that Neville had probably done the right thing; he was correct about the temperature, it was plunging towards zero. "Can we see the body?"

"Of course. The on-call doctor has been called and is en route from Hammersmith. 'SOCO One' is on its way too and has arranged for lighting, tent, etcetera. The area is cordoned off, and the local authority has been informed it's likely to be for some time too. I'll be honest, Sarge, I'm glad you're here, I'm happy enough to get the ball rolling, but I'm newly qualified and feel a bit out of my depth."

"You're doing great," Grant reassured, "let's look and see if we can work out what's happened, shall we?"

Chapter Fifty-One

The body of the young black man lay face down in the gutter. The entry point of the bullet in the back of the head, six inches above the nape of the neck, was clear to see; the victim's hair was close-cropped, down to the skin. It struck Grant as having the brutally efficient hallmarks of a KGB execution rather than a street shooting in an affluent area of West London. The youth's blood pooled, halo-like, seeming to be a hard, polished, jet black surface rather than the sticky, semi-congealed, livid redness Grant knew it to be. Street lighting did that to blood at night.

About seven feet to the right of the body, a chalk circle three inches in diameter had been marked on the road surface, "shell casing?" Grant enquired.

"Yes, bagged and exhibited," Neville answered. Grant nodded his approval.

"Okay," Grant said decisively, "let's address the most obvious thing, shall we?" Sticking out from between the victim's shoulder blades was a shining, steel object; in the small of his back was a second. From each ran a metal filament whose presence was shown up as the night breeze caught the gossamer thread and stirred it, and in doing so allowed the light to reveal its shimmering track. That track ran twelve feet to the discarded bright yellow X-26 Taser, which lay on the edge of the kerb, where it had been discarded.

"Untouched?" Grant enquired as he bent over to examine the Taser.

"Untouched." Neville confirmed nodding, "awaiting SOCO to be finger-printed."

Grant nodded. "Well, that confirms it." He stood upright. "On the underside, the number fifteen, it's Sean Crisp's Taser, taken from his body outside the Turkish embassy."

"Has this been moved?" Grant nodded toward the white mountain bike, which lay on its side in the road.

"Not by us, it awaits the Scenes of Crime Officer, like the Taser," answered the DC.

"Good. Do we have an ETA for the SOCO?"

"Anytime now, travelling time from Lambeth."

Grant crossed to the cycle. "The rear wheel is stove in, that's a big dent. I don't see any potholes hereabouts that could've caused that." Grant took a small Surefire torch from his pocket, directing the beam on the damaged wheel. "White paint. Look, Amber, can you see?" More supple, Amber bent lower than Grant, her face almost touching the dramatic indentation to the circle of metal and rubber."

"Definitely white paint skip. The dent could have been made by the car's front bumper striking the rear wheel." She stood up, looking around, taking her own torch and shining a beam back and forth across the road.

"My thoughts exactly," agreed Grant. "For whatever reason, it looks like our victim has been rammed by a car, the wheel buckled, he's been thrown to the ground, Tasered, and shot." Grant speculated out loud.

"God!" Neville exclaimed, "that's more than road rage, it's madness."

"It's fury. Pure fury. This was someone who was raging, not planned and prepared with meticulous precision, like the early murders. Our man is getting out of control, Amber. The last two victims, Panos and Cape, they were incidental, to facilitate an escape; this one is rage, pure and simple. What *did* he do?"

"Skip! Look!" Amber bent over, shining the beam at a low angle against the kerbstone. "A paint chip, a flake, white paint, same as the scuff on the wheel."

"That's brilliant, great spot, Amber! It's not dirty at all, freshly deposited, I'm guessing, chipped off the car on contact."

"If we find the car and match the flake to the bumper, if we get a mechanical fit, we've got him, he's tied to this scene. Either way, we've enough for the techies to get a colour match, which can give us a make, model, and even a year for the car. It'll really reduce the search parameters." Amber couldn't disguise her joy.

"You, over there!" Grant called to a PC twenty feet away. "Give me your hat, would you?" The puzzled officer passed Grant his flat cap, which the DS placed over the flake. "To stop it blowing away or any twat standing on it until forensics pick it up with tweezers and pack it away safely and intact." He winked at Amber. It was another little gem which she popped in her back pocket to keep with the others.

As she stood upright, the beam of her torch passed over the road. "Wait a minute, what's that?" She waggled the torch in her hand, the beam dancing across the surface of the tarmac. "Can you see, skip, shining in the torchlight?"

Neville turned his torch in the same direction. "It looks like metallic confetti, it's shiny, reflective." He moved the beam. "It's everywhere."

Grant squatted down in the pool of light, licked the end of his fingertip, and dabbed it on one of the shining objects, and held out his forefinger for the two DCs to examine. "Can you see? It's called an AFID."

"Aphid? Like a greenfly?" Asked Amber, puzzled.

Grant laughed, spelling the word. "A-F-I-D. AFID. It stands for Anti-Felon Identification Disc. It's an Americanism. Each AFID is a fluorescent, multi-coloured disc, less than 5mm in diameter. You can see, they're tiny, but look closer." The officers bent their heads to examine the minuscule, sparkly circle, perched on Grant's fingertip. "Can you see, each AFID has a serial number unique to the cartridge from which it came. Whenever a Taser is fired, thirty or forty AFIDs are blown out at the same instant as the barbs, which carry the electric charge to the target. They can be used to identify which Taser cartridge has been used, the location at which it was fired, and if multiple cartridges have been discharged, identify who did what. Neville, make sure a good sample of these are collected from the scene. If confirmation was needed, this was Sean Crisp's Taser; these little babies and the numbers on them are proof positive, the serial numbers will match the inventory at the DPG base."

"I'll make sure that happens, Sarge." Neville gave a thumbs up as Grant put his hands back in his pocket. Bab's was right about one thing: it was *freezing* out here.

"Have we checked his pockets yet? Any ID on him?" Asked the DS.

"I wasn't sure whether or not to do that, I waited for advice." Neville shrugged.

"S'okay. Glove up and be careful, but let's have a look."

A few minutes later, the officers were examining several credit cards, three jewelled rings, and a gent's Rolex watch. "Well, I don't think he's Mr Wah Wei Ling for starters," observed Grant, holding up one card.

"I suspect he's not Mrs Gloria Castile either," said Amber, holding up another.

"These rings have more ice than a Mojito, and the Rolex is engraved to Dr. Hamish Huntley-Walker. He seems very young to be a doctor," offered Neville.

"My spider-sense is tingling. I suspect he *may* have come by these possessions illegally," Grant concluded, his words dripping sarcasm. "Bag them up, people, I think we may have a murder which is as yet unsolved, but we'll clear up a few burglaries."

Each officer turned to look anew at the sprawled body of the young criminal, lying in a dirty gutter, face down in a pool of his own blood. His end must have been both terrifying and painful. Knocked violently from his bike and shot with a Taser, the two barbs puncturing his back and discharging 50,000 volts into his body before the coup de grâce was delivered in the form of a 9mm bullet to the back of the head. It was a tragically sad, lonely, and undignified conclusion to a young life. Whatever he'd done, it wasn't an end he deserved, but as each officer contemplated the sight before them, each recognised the guilt they felt at caring a little bit less now than they did before.

The shared thoughts were broken as vehicle lights swept the tableau. "Ah, look, wonderful." Grant turned to see the arrival of a small car with a green light atop its roof and a white van with the Met Police livery. "The doctor and the forensics team."

"We may yet get home before dawn, Sarge," said Amber, "light at the end of the tunnel."

"Or a train coming towards us. Come on, let's introduce ourselves."

Chapter Fifty-Two

By rights, both Grant and Amber should've enjoyed the minimum eight hours between shifts that regulations required, but such was their drive to pursue the case both officers pushed open the office door before 11 am to find a bustle of noise and activity prompted by the events of the previous night and morning.

Grant made his way towards his desk, clutching the cup of life-giving coffee, and saw to his astonishment that Paul Winter was also in, his desk covered in papers and the phone, as usual, glued to his ear. He saw Grant and, with a free hand, gestured for him to enter.

"Okay, thanks, yes, I understand the limitations, but do what you can, we'll be grateful. Thank you, bye." Paul replaced the phone as Grant sank into a chair. "Car paint experts, they're all over the paint marks on the bike and the flake Amber found. They always stress the limitations but often pull a rabbit out of the hat."

Grant looked at Paul with wonder. "What time did you get here?"

"I never left," Paul answered, shrugging before swiftly moving on. "Our victim last night was Junior Flight, a well-known toe-rag. Lots of previous for theft from motor vehicles, burglary, credit card fraud, drug possession, and one for assault on police. Busy boy for someone who wasn't even sixteen yet."

"He was only fifteen?" Grant was incredulous.

"Yep, and already a prolific thief. He committed four burglaries last night in the Osterley area, the cards found on him IDed the victims, and they recognised the jewellery and the Rolex. Junior lived in Heston, so it looks like he was heading home when he had his unfortunate encounter. The Taser *was* Sean Crisp's, there was never any doubt of that. We had the results from ballistics, all the bullets from the Rugby club and the industrial estate were from Sean's Glock. By my reckoning, after last night's execution, he has two bullets left."

"Well, someone's been busy." Grant sipped his coffee, "I feel guilty having a whole four hours sleep now."

"So you should, you layabout." Paul laughed as the door was knocked and Amber stuck her head into the office.

"Sorry to disturb you, Guv. Sarge, the custody officer called to say that a solicitor and an appropriate adult have been arranged for 2.30 pm this afternoon."

Grant's head was still spinning with the pace of news and events. A confused response of, "I'm sorry?" was all he could manage.

"To interview Charlie Buller. You know, the man we arrested for murder." Amber gave a cheesy grin.

"Oh God! Yes, of course, I'm sorry my head's still a bit woolly this morning. Yes, that's fine, but I think we may have jumped the gun, literally. There's no way Charlie could've been at Osterley to have killed young…what was his name?"

"Junior Flight" assisted Paul.

"Yeh, him. But we need to interview; he's got to account for his deception and movements anyhow."

"Okay, skip, I'll tell custody that's a date then?" Amber gave a cheery thumbs-up and disappeared from view.

Grant shook his head slowly. "Is everyone on drugs?" He sipped his coffee again. "I'm getting far too old for this."

"If you're up to it, Amber has called the Bingo hall in Shepherd's Bush, they say you can go and review their CCTV any time. Apparently, they also have a camera which covers the car park, that *could* confirm a whole lot of stories and movements regarding Callum and Debbie's whereabouts and identify their car. Heidi called from the Lab at Lambeth, the techie types are working on the film from the industrial estate, which shows the small white hatchback leaving. You never know, this may be it."

"A small white car," Grant mused, "if we find it with a scuff mark and paint chipped off the front that matches the recovered flake…Bingo!" Grant clicked his fingers and grinned.

"Yes. Well done, I see what you did there, 'Bingo', brilliant. Now, can you and Amber get down there? Amber has the address and manager's details."

"Can I finish my coffee first?"

"As it's you, you smell of piss and you're nearly ninety years old, yes."

* * *

Grant slumped gratefully into a chair for the second time inside five minutes. Amber was reading a statement at the desk next to him. "So, we're off to the bingo hall then, clickety click, two fat ladies, eighty eight, two little ducks, twenty two." Grant winked.

Amber looked bewildered, "Are you alright? What're you talking about? Ducks and fat ladies? What do you mean?"

Grant gave up. "Nothing, I'll finish my coffee and we'll go. I suppose we still have the green bogey?"

Amber picked up a set of keys from the desktop and jiggled them. "Our favourite!"

"Oh God!" Grant rubbed tired eyes as Nagur and Craig each dropped a bulging cardboard box on the desk opposite with two large thuds. "Bloody hell. What's that lot?" Grant asked.

"It's Sam Pendry's client list for the past three years. We've just collected it from his estate agent's office in Ealing," answered Nagur. "Bloody hell, skip, you look awful. Late night, was it?" Nags turned to Craig and laughed.

"Very funny," Grant quipped, "wait till you're my age. We were at Jersey Road until the small hours with a dead burglar."

"Yeh, we heard this morning, Heidi did a briefing, you know, while you were still in bed." There was more laughter from the pair of DCs.

"You're really funny guys, you know that. I may have some weeding of paperwork in the basement for you two, should take a month. Still laughing?"

Grant threatened with a half-smile.

"No, no, we're happy enough here," Nagur replied urgently before pausing. He looked thoughtful for a moment. "Sorry, Sarge, but did you say *Jersey Road?*" Nagur questioned, his voice betraying a slight hesitation. "We missed the first couple of minutes of the morning briefing, arranging to collect this lot from the office with Cordelia Lancaster. Was the location of the shooting *Jersey Road… in Osterley?*"

The tone of the question had caused Grant's and Amber's ears to prick up; something meaningful was happening. "Yes, Jersey Road, Osterley, you know it? Is that significant?" Grant's voice betrayed an excitement, he knew it was.

"Yes! We were there yesterday," Craig put in, "at Sam Pendry's house, he lives in Bassett Gardens, it runs off Jersey Road."

"It *cannot* be a coincidence that we've had a shooting so close to the previous night's victim's address," Amber added. "There must be a connection."

Something else stirred, "Did you say 'Cordelia?'" asked Grant. "You said just now that you made arrangements with Cordelia Lancaster. I'm sure you've said before her name was Delia."

"That's right, skip," Nagur answered. "Cordelia, but she's always called Delia, for short, she asked us to call her that. Delia, Cordelia. Same thing."

"I've heard that name. I've heard that name recently. Where? *Where?*" Grant bumped his forehead with his palm. "Come on, you old bastard, where did you hear that name? Cordelia, same name as the nice daughter in King Lear."

Grant stopped bumping his forehead and looked up, "Got it! Three days ago, I was in Newcomen Street, near Guys Hospital in Borough. I was visiting Sean Crisp's post there, the one protecting the M.P. Marlon Tredegor, d'you remember Amber?"

"Yes, skip, I remember you telling me, what's that got to do with it?" Amber puzzled.

"I met a man there, he was very friendly, very chatty, he brought a coffee for the officer on post. He'd met and talked with Sean when he was there for a ten-day stint. He had a brain tumour, this bloke, it's why he was going back and forth to the hospital so often, for treatment. He told me he'd named the tumour after his ex-wife, her name was Cordelia. That's *not* a common name. The officer on post called him Luke, and a passing nurse who knew him called him Mr Lancaster. Luke Lancaster."

"Luke Lancaster?" Amber's voice was little more than a whisper.

"Luke Lancaster, with an ex-wife called Cordelia, *that's* the connection." Grant clapped his hands together. *"That's it!* He knew Sean from passing by him day after day, and Sean ends up dead. His ex-wife hooks up with Sam Pendry, and he ends up dead. And last night, something went wrong when he was on the way to Cordelia's house in Osterley. What the other victim connections are, I don't know, but it's him, *it's him*, it must be him."

Amber's face had blanched, and her hand rushed to cover her mouth. "It can't be. Oh God, it couldn't be."

Grant turned to face Amber full on. "What's the matter? What is it?"

Amber reached out, gripping Grant's arm so tightly it hurt. "I know, I know what's happened, Sarge."

Chapter Fifty-Three

Grant prised Amber's fingers off his arm as she slumped back in her seat. Colour was returning to her face, but she still looked in a state of utter astonishment. "Sorry, skip, it's the realisation, it's a shock, I'm in shock."

The DS patted his friend's hand, "It's okay, Amber, take a breath, gather your thoughts, and tell me what you know."

After a few moments, she spoke. "Okay. We *all* remember our first arrest, right? The very first person you nick." There were encouraging nods of agreement at the universal truth. "*My* first arrest was Luke Lancaster. It's nearly six years ago, I suppose, I was brand new out of the box, on my Street Duties Course, and Sean Crisp was one of the puppy walkers, my tutor. We were on an early turn shift, and a call came out to a personal injury accident; a little girl going to school had been hit by a car on a pedestrian crossing, an ambulance was on the way. Sean said we'll take that, and we flew there on Blues and Twos. We arrived at the same time as the ambulance, and they treated the girl for minor injuries. The car driven by Luke Lancaster had stopped at the crossing to let the children over and a van driver who wasn't paying attention hit him up the arse, pushing his car forward into the little girl."

"So the accident wasn't Luke's fault?"

"No, Sarge. Not at all. Luke did everything right; he called the ambulance, he carried the girl to the pavement, and comforted her. The girl told me how nice he was. The van driver was a total arsehole, I remember he said the car in front 'stopped suddenly, I didn't have a chance'. A total cock.

Sean is leading me through reporting a traffic accident, it was my first. You remember the mnemonic, 'PRIMROSE?' Position of vehicles. Record of question and answers. Information to. Marks in road, etcetera, and Sean says we need to breathalyse the drivers, it'll be good practice for me. The van-man came back negative, but Luke Lancaster blows *over* the limit. I was amazed, it was 8.30 am. Sean says to me, 'nick him.'"

"That's a bit rough, considering what's happened," Nagur commented.

"Yeh, the accident was the arsehole's fault." Craig concurred.

"Shush, guys." Grant admonished. "Carry on, Amber."

"I was really uncomfortable; it didn't seem fair. I think Luke Lancaster saw my reluctance and started to plead with me. He said he was a chef, he'd got the chance of a lifetime, a job with a Michelin-starred chef, he had to get into London on time, it was his first day. He begged me to let him off, but Sean shook his head."

"A Michelin-starred chef. Konstanz Bassa?"

"It must be, Sarge. It fits, and Sean was stabbed with a chef's knife. So, I made my first arrest. Lancaster was close to hysterical, in tears." Amber paused, shaking her head at the memory.

"What happened at the station, Amber?"

"It was bloody awful, like a Greek Tragedy. He blew on the intoximeter, and his lowest score was just one point *above* the legal limit. *One!* He wasn't drunk, apparently unimpaired. The machine detected the residue of alcohol in his system after a heavy session the night before. He was charged, taken to court that afternoon, and disqualified from driving for twelve months, the statutory minimum. The look he gave me and, worst of all, to Sean, when he walked out the courtroom, well, you can imagine. I said to Sean afterwards I was really uncomfortable with the way we'd dealt with it. He said it was 'good experience and a box ticked'. That was the last I heard of Luke Lancaster, but obviously, he never forgot Sean Crisp."

"And when he found out he was terminally ill," Grant surmised, "he decided to settle the score…and not just with Sean." Grant patted Amber's hand. "Well done, Amber. It's circumstantial for now, but we'll find the solid evidence and all the connections, too."

Grant slammed his hands down on the desktop decisively. "Right! Nags, phone Cordelia, *right now*, find out where she is, I'll get someone on the way to her, and arrange for armed protection. And Nagur…"

"Yes, skip?"

"Ask her what Luke's address is; she may know. Find out from her anything you can about Luke, where he's been, what he's been doing, anything about his character, temperament, their separation. Does she know what sort of car he drives, anything. Okay?"

"Yes, skip."

"Amber, call the cancer unit at Guys hospital, see if they'll give his address in case Cordelia doesn't know it. They might refuse, patient confidentiality and all, but see if you can find out when his next treatment session is. Stress that they're not to tell him we called. Do a name check on Luke Lancaster, see if we have anything on file about him, an address, previous convictions. Okay?"

"Yes, skip. On it."

"I need to speak with Paul Winter."

Chapter Fifty-Four

The radio crackled. "In position."

"Received, stand by." Sergeant Babatunde Okafor turned and nodded to Grant. "Okay, the rear of the property is covered. Are you ready?"

Grant grinned; it was like old times on an armed operation with his friend Babs. "Yep, you do the dangerous, heroic stuff, I'll wait here behind this thick, brick wall." He winked at Babs, who gave him a wide grin. "The electoral roll shows only Luke and Mildred Lancaster registered here, which tallies with what Cordelia said, he lost his house after the divorce and moved back in with his mother."

"Useful that she knew the address, the hospital weren't forthcoming with any details."

Grant shrugged, "You can't blame them too much, there's issues of confidentiality."

"I suppose so," Amber admitted. "If he's in there, what do you think he'll do? He doesn't mind killing police officers, does he?"

"If his mother is in the house, I don't think he would endanger her…but you never know." Answered Grant.

Babs patted the Glock pistol in his holster, "You never know."

* * *

Fifty yards away, Grant and Amber sheltered behind a wall, watching as three armed officers, led by Babs, lined up at the door of the mid-terrace house in Harlesden. At the signal, an over-emphasised nod of Bab's head, a dark-clad figure emerged from behind a hedge and moved swiftly to the door. A single blow from the heavy weighted 'enforcer' the shadow carried smashed the door wide open. The radio chirped into life with Babs' voice. "All units, entering...*now!*"

"They're in." Amber's voice was near Grant's ear as she peeked over his shoulder. The officers rushed inside and were lost from view. The temptation to speak into the radio, to ask, 'what's happening?' was overwhelming as first a minute passed and then another, in silence.

"All units from Trojan Three, stand down, stand down. No suspect, one occupant, suspect's mother. DS Maddox, target is clear, target is clear."

"Bollocks!" was all Grant could bring himself to say.

* * *

Mildred Lancaster was *not* a meek and mild little old lady. Apparently, she was also not a cheerleader for the Metropolitan Police.

"Fuckin' hero ain't ya eh? Fuckin' heroes, with your guns and everything, come bargin' in here, scaring a' old lady out of her fuckin' wits for no fuckin' reason. Look at my fuckin' door, who's goin' to pay for that, cos I fuckin' ain't. Fuckin' vandals."

Grant held up the piece of paper, "Mrs Lancaster, this is a warrant authorising us to enter and search this property. We're looking for your son, Luke, he's got himself in some serious trouble, we need to find him. Where is he?"

"He ain't done nuffin', you can all fuck off. You just pickin' on him. Fink your fuckin' hero's don'tcha, well you ain't."

Grant turned to Amber, "I'm starting to think this lady isn't going to help us. What do you think?"

"I'm having trouble hearing you, skip, my ears are bleeding," Amber glared malevolently at Mrs Lancaster, "but I think you're right."

"Okay, Bab's, can you get her out of our way while we search Luke's room?" Grant nodded towards the foul-mouthed harpy before walking away, sadly shaking his head and muttering, "From the land that produced Shakespeare, Chaucer, and Dickens."

"No worries, Granty." Bab's contained his amusement.

Mildred turned her fury on the gigantic, black sergeant, "an' you can fuck off an' all, you black bastard, you lot are only a fuckin' generation away from fuckin' eatin' each other."

"Watch out I don't *eat you, lady!*" Babs lurched forward, open-mouthed, teeth bared. To everyone's delight and raucous hilarity, Mildred Lancaster screamed and fell back into an armchair. The huge sergeant rubbed his hands together in mock expectation, licking his lips in apparent anticipation of a good meal. "You better stay there, lady, 'cos you look like good eating."

Grant and Amber ascended the stairs and pushed open the door to Luke's bedroom. "Sergeant Okafor has an unorthodox way of dealing with racists… threatening to eat them. Not a standard coping mechanism. But I like it." Amber commented as she rifled through a chest of drawers.

"He's one of the best human beings I've ever met, and he's been taking shit like that as long as I've known him, he's always found a way to deal with arseholes like her, usually with humour and always by being a better person." Grant lifted the mattress of the single bed, searching under the pillows and finding nothing.

"The chest of drawers is clear, so's the wardrobe, not even a dark hoodie."

"Maybe he's wearing it. Lift your end of the mat."

"No, nothing."

Grant picked up a pair of training shoes, shaking them for hidden contents and checking the inner label. "UK size 8, which is right, but not Umbro 'Clean Tech' trainers." He dropped the shoes in frustration. "Okay, nothing, no gun, no hoodie, no knife, nothing." Grant shook his head in frustration, "We *need* something to put him irrevocably at a crime scene. Okay, let's go and speak to the delightful Mildred again, shall we? That's if Bab's hasn't got her simmering in a pot by now."

Grant stood by the door, giving the room one last scan, and turned to leave. He stopped. Turned back and stood by the door once more and looked down to the corner of the room. He took three steps and squatted down, his excitement erasing the discomfort to his clicking joints. "Well, what do you know? Got ya!" Grant's grin was so wide it almost hurt. "Amber! Back in here, please, and bring me an exhibit bag." He held up a training shoe, waving it towards a bewildered Amber, and in his best Al Pacino 'Scarface' voice said, "Say 'ello to my leetle friend."

* * *

"We found this, Sarge," an armed officer waved a sheet of paper, "On the table, a sales receipt, any use?"

Grant read the scrap of paper and beaming passed it to Amber, "It's of *great* use. Look, Amber, it's for a nine-year-old white Nissan Micra hatchback; he sold it *this morning*. A local dealer got a real bargain, £150. Seems like Luke was in a hurry to ditch it for some reason. Call Nags and Craig, get them to that dealer double quick, before he repairs what I suspect is a chipped and dented front bumper, and seize that car."

"Will do, I'll bag the receipt and list it for exhibits." Amber could barely contain her excitement.

"So...Mrs Lancaster, will you tell us where your son is, please? It'll be easier for all concerned. I know he's a sick man, we need to end this...now."

Mrs Lancaster's response was predictable, although she looked fearfully towards Babs as she shouted her profanities.

"Don't bother, skip, look here." Amber pointed to a calendar, stuck to the fridge door, "Look at today's date, '3.30 pm, chemo'. He'll be heading to Guy's hospital for his cancer treatment; it's nearly three now."

Grant looked to Babs and raised a questioning eyebrow, and received an instant answer. "You bet, Granty, let's go."

Chapter Fifty-Five

Grant recognised the pretty nurse he'd seen calling to Luke in Newcomen Street. "It's Maggie, isn't it? I saw you a few days ago," he held up his warrant card. "I was with the policeman down the road, talking with Luke Lancaster."

Recognition dawned, "Yes, that's right, Maggie, Maggie Mason, and I remember you, I saw you where the M.P. lives, who's been in the news."

"Yes," smiled Grant, "that's right, exactly. Look, Nurse Mason, I'm really sorry about this, but we've a situation here which we need to deal with and I need your help." During the next few minutes of explanation, the nurse's expression journeyed from its initial smile to surprise, shock, fear, and finally to resolve.

"Our first duty is the safety of our patients, all of them, including Mr Lancaster, and to our staff, I need to speak to the ward manager. We have some time on our side, Mr Lancaster's treatment is scheduled to finish in an hour, unfortunately, there are two other patients in the room with him, also receiving chemotherapy."

"I see." Grant's mind was working fast. "When will their treatment finish?"

"One finishes before Mr Lancaster, the other afterwards. We have three more patients due for treatment arriving in the next hour."

"Well, the first thing is we don't let any new patients in. Can we move the two out?"

The nurse thought for a moment, "Mr Singh will be finished in thirty minutes, Mr O'Kelly thirty minutes after Mr Lancaster, but he's very frail, a bedbound inpatient, he can't be moved during chemotherapy. The treatment room is through there," Maggie pointed to the door. "I really must speak to the manager."

"One more thing, does Mr Lancaster have a bag or rucksack with him?"

"Yes," she answered, "a black rucksack, it's on his lap."

"Right! It would be."

"I *need* to speak with the ward manager; she needs to know what's happening. Please stay here in the corridor."

"Okay, nurse, I understand and appreciate your priorities, thank you very much." As the nurse departed, Grant turned to Babs and Amber. "Okay, we have some time on our side; whatever happens, Lancaster *does not* leave that room, except under arrest, but this is a nightmare scenario from a tactical firearms perspective."

"You know the Glock is going to be in that bag, don't you?" Grant nodded at Babatunde's observation. "In thirty minutes, Mr Singh leaves, but Lancaster will expect to be up and on his way *before* O'Kelly. If I charge in, pointing a gun, who knows what he'll do? O'Kelly is at risk if he starts shooting.

"I've an idea." Said a trembling, nervous voice. The two sergeants turned to look at the apprehensive face of the speaker, DC Amber Bennett.

* * *

"She's a brave girl, that Nurse Maggie." Grant nodded in agreement with Babatunde's assessment. The nurse had been back and forth into the treatment room several times, attending and monitoring the three patients in full knowledge that one was a multiple killer and almost certainly in possession of a loaded gun. The treatment time was nearly up for Mr Singh; once he'd departed, only Lancaster and Mr O'Kelly would remain. The new patients, scheduled to enter the treatment room, had been diverted elsewhere.

Babatunde and Amber were secreted in a staff rest room on the opposite side of the corridor to the treatment room, leaving Grant, the most inconspicuous, dressed in a suit, watching the door. Other uniform back-up was in the lobby, thirty yards away, along with two armed officers.

The door opened as Nurse Mason, with a guiding arm around the patient, Mr Singh, walked tentatively out. As the door slowly pulled itself shut, there was a fleeting moment when Grant caught sight of Luke Lancaster sitting on a high-backed chair surrounded by the accoutrements required to administer chemotherapy, about thirty feet from the entrance. On his lap was a black rucksack. The room was as he'd pictured from the sketch the nurse had produced, he thanked providence once more for her presence, and providing her with a calm, level head.

"You're a brave girl," Grant said sincerely as she passed. "I'll see you get recognition for this."

The nurse smiled and nodded, addressing her words to her patient, "You're doing very well, Mr Singh. How about a cup of tea and a biscuit?"

* * *

The moment was near. Lancaster was expecting his treatment to end imminently, and to leave the room, that couldn't be allowed to happen. In discussion, the proposal to falsely inform Lancaster that his treatment needed to be extended beyond that of O'Kelly, allowing the latter patient to leave, was dismissed. Lancaster had received chemotherapy so often and was so familiar with all its procedures, he'd immediately be suspicious. Already, he'd enquired of the whereabouts of the rest of the patients; normally, he'd have more than one companion. Grant had to make a decision right now: should he follow Amber's plan?

Chapter Fifty-Six

Grant looked left and right. The corridor was empty. Satisfied, he tapped the staff room door, which immediately opened. Babs exited, followed by Amber, dressed in a nurse's uniform. "That really suits you, who knows, if policing doesn't work out." Grant smiled weakly at his feeble attempt at humour. Amber returned the weak smile with one of her own.

"Are you ready?" Grant placed a paternal hand on her shoulder, deadly serious now. "You don't have to do this. You know he's already…" His voice trailed away, leaving the obvious words unsaid.

"Let's get it done." Amber's voice was steely with determination. Grant recognised that tone, it was the same as her response only a week ago, when Panos asked her what was to be gained by viewing the slaughtered body of her friend, Sean Crisp. 'Motivation, ' she'd replied. He'd been impressed then; he was overcome with admiration now.

"Amber, we've paced the distance and timed it, it's fifteen seconds, that's the time from the door to Lancaster, at the instant you reach him, that's when Babs will come charging, he'll be there very quickly, in five seconds. Fifteen seconds there, contain him for five, keep the gun in the bag and his hand away from it, pressed down hard for five seconds. *Five seconds.* Okay?"

Grant kept his voice steady, his eyes fixed on Amber's. Inside, he was full of fear; the man sitting with a handgun on his lap, only thirty feet away, had mercilessly killed eight people in ten days, two of them police officers. Every cell in his body was screaming, open the door, shout a warning, and at the slightest twitch, fill him with holes. But three words haunted him, as rightly they should, hovering over the actions of every police officer, *'Duty of Care'*. An innocent man, desperately ill, was seated a mere five feet from Lancaster; everything that could be done to protect him *had* to be done. There was another aspect to Duty of Care: if Luke Lancaster could be taken alive, then every reasonable attempt must be made to do so. No one, no matter what their crime, could be shot dead out of hand. But at that moment, Duty of Care felt more like an inhibiting curse than a safeguard for a civilised society.

"Okay," replied Amber. "All good, let's go."

The group stood back from the entrance. Amber took a breath and pushed the door.

* * *

15 Seconds.

"How are we doing, Mr Lancaster, not getting lonely, I hope?" Amber said breezily as she paced unhurriedly towards Lancaster, noting with alarm the rucksack on his lap had its top zip undone and Lancaster's hand hidden inside. As the door opened, he'd immediately turned his head ninety degrees, staring at Amber as she stepped into the treatment room. Amber saw his stare, forcing her face to smile, for the muscle tension under her skin to not visibly seep out. Even without hair, she recognised him; he was thinner, gaunt, and ravaged by illness, but she recognised the first man she'd ever arrested.

11 Seconds.

"Where's Maggie?" Lancaster held the stare. Amber kept walking, straight towards the prostrate man.

"She got held up and sent me to check on you."

8 Seconds.

"This doesn't seem right," Lancaster broke the stare, looking swiftly left and right as if noticing for the first time that only he and O'Kelly were in the room, surrounded by empty chairs which were normally occupied. He looked again at the nurse; she was close now. Amber broke her locked gaze with his eyes and looked down at the hand, hidden inside the rucksack.

4 Seconds.

She saw the moment he recognised her, the minutest widening of knowing eyes, the merest raising of the eyebrows…*He knew.*

1 Second.

She pushed off with her right foot, as she did so, praying that her shoe wouldn't slip on the shiny, polished floor and leave her floundering and helpless. The shoe held, giving her the purchase she needed. She dived the last few feet, her arms outstretched before her, reaching for the rucksack; it was the *only* thing in the world, the black bag. Keep what was in the bag where it was. Don't let it out.

She was too late. Forewarned by recognition, Lancaster was swiftly withdrawing his hand; she saw the black grip of the pistol, saw his forefinger inside the trigger guard as the Glock was extracted, turning to point directly towards her.

Zero.

The fingers of Amber's right hand grasped the barrel of the handgun, her forward momentum pushing it upwards and to the right, her left hand flailing, slapped Lancaster's face in a weak, uncoordinated contact. It didn't matter, holding the gun was the only thing that did; her inner voice screamed, *'don't let go, you must hold on'.* Her knees hit the floor beside his chair, her arms extended above her, still gripping the gun. Amber felt him pushing back, driving the muzzle of the gun downwards, towards her, twisting it closer to her face. So near she could see its tiniest detail, even the rifling of the barrel, now only an inch from her right eye, in a moment he could pull the trigger…a flash of light…then darkness, forever.

At some point, every police officer pictures the manner of their own violent death. The voice in her head roared, *'This is **not** how I die. '* Amber screamed with effort, pushing the gun away, locking her left hand on top of her right, the gun moved, she sensed his weakness, heard him grunting with effort, but he was losing. The cancer, the drugs, the fatigue…his body was enfeebled. Then it was over, a huge black hand loomed across her vision, and she found herself being physically lifted, hoisted up from the floor, hanging from the weapon, as the Glock was wrenched from Lancaster's grip.

"I got it, Amber, you can let go." The deep baritone of Babatunde's voice. "I got it."

Chapter Fifty-Seven

A uniformed PC stepped away from Luke Lancaster's side, having completed a search, "Nothing, Sarge, he's clean."

"Thank you," Grant smiled gratefully, "can you wait outside for now?" The click of the officer's boots sounded through the treatment room and were lost as the door closed behind him, leaving Grant and Amber standing before Luke Lancaster, slumped and sweating in the high-back, winged treatment chair. He was still hooked up to the drip, still receiving his life-extending treatment. "I think the honour is yours, Amber."

"Police Constable *Amber,* is it? We meet again, Amber." Lancaster sounded calm and unconcerned, the life-or-death tug of war of minutes earlier seemingly forgotten.

"It's *Detective* Constable Bennett." Amber paused, taking stock of the moment. "Luke Lancaster, I'm arresting you for murder. You do not have to say anything. But it may harm your defence if you do not mention when questioned something which you later rely on in court. Anything you do say may be given in evidence." Amber's voice was strong and steady.

Lancaster began to laugh. "*Court!* You think I'm ever going to appear in a court! Get real, Amber. I'm free, I've been free since the words 'inoperable' and 'I'm sorry' were uttered to me. You can't touch me, I'll never even see the inside of a cell."

"That's not my concern or responsibility, Luke. We found you, we stopped you, we nicked you. We've done our job."

"*How* did you find me as a matter of interest?"

"The usual way," Grant answered, "detective work, coincidence, and a bit of luck. You helped us, you told me you'd named your tumour after your ex-wife, Cordelia. When you killed Sam Pendry, it seemed quite a coincidence his partner's name was Cordelia Lancaster. Our bit of luck was Amber was on the team, she recognised your name and the link to Sean Crisp. But it was all circumstantial until I found one of these, a little friend; it was *this* that finished you. Game, set, and match."

Grant fished about in his pocket for a moment, then held up his thumb and forefinger. "Can you see that? It's very small."

Lancaster squinted, "I see something shiny, what is it?"

"It's called an AFID. They're discharged whenever a Taser is used, and they all have a serial number. I found this one, along with dozens of others, on the ground near to the fifteen-year-old boy you shot in the back of the head." Grant didn't try to disguise his disgust. "When we searched your bedroom, I was about to leave, and I looked back and saw a glint from the bottom of your training shoe. Guess what was stuck in the tread of the sole? A *single* AFID, wedged in there. An AFID with the exact same serial number as those scattered about the murder scene. That led us to you and Sean's Glock. Ballistic comparison will prove the rest."

Lancaster nodded. "Well done, so we've come full circle and we've started and finished with you, *Detective* Amber, arresting me." Lancaster wagged a finger towards Amber. "Only this time you *wanted* to arrest me, the first time you didn't, did you? It was that pretentious prick Crisp, with his bright red moustache and beard, who made you do it. Honestly, what did he think he was, a cavalier or something?"

Grant intervened, fearing Lancaster was on a mission to bait Amber by taunting Sean Crisp. "It may be true, you may never get to court, so tell us, explain what happened and why. You may never get another chance." Grant glanced meaningfully at the chemotherapy apparatus.

Chapter Fifty-Eight

L uke Lancaster seemed to be deep in thought for a few moments. "I *did* have a rather dramatic end in mind, but that would've left my story untold. You may be right, perhaps I will tell you." He paused, gathering his thoughts. "I had perfect preparation and precise plans, all laid out, like a complex recipe, you know, I'm a chef, I presume?" Grant nodded. "I *should* have been a great chef, one of the greatest; it was all I ever wanted to do, from a very young age. At school, I had what *some* viewed as the audacity to drop woodwork in favour of domestic science. I was the only boy in a class of girls, but I shone; I was good. It cost me, though."

"Bernard Huxton?" Offered Grant.

"Bernard? Was that his name? Funny, isn't it, even as an adult, you only think of your teachers as a 'Mr,' 'Mrs,' or 'Miss.' Yes, Mr Huxton, I dropped his woodwork classes, but he still took me for maths. He made my life a misery. He called me 'Fanny Craddock' or 'Lady Luke Lancaster, spinster of the parish', or simply 'Nancy Boy.' He was the worst sort of bully, cruel and mocking, taking pleasure in undermining your confidence, dreams, and ambitions. The other pupils loved it, as long as he was picking on me, he wasn't picking on them."

"So you shot him in the mouth," Amber stated bluntly.

Lancaster chuckled. "That was pure luck, the fact the bullet went through his disgusting, abusive mouth was providence, I'd say. After school, I got various jobs over the years, working in pubs, restaurants, learning my trade, trying to gain a reputation. I applied for an apprenticeship under the *great* Konstanz Bassa in Park Lane. I was shortlisted, interviewed, and accepted.

I was ecstatic, a Michelin-starred chef was going to train and tutor me! For a chef, it's like winning the lottery. The day before I was due to start, I received a call, Konstanz had changed his mind, another candidate, *female*, was more suitable. I was devastated and did what men do at times like that, I got drunk, seriously drunk. At seven in the morning, I got another call from the restaurant manager. On reflection, it was decided my treatment had been unfair, the apprenticeship place was still on offer. I was told to start *that* morning."

Amber shook her head. "And on the way, the van driver hit your car, pushing you into the girl on the crossing."

"I was horrified, the girl was thrown onto the bonnet of my car, I saw her face, then she slipped from view, I thought she was under the wheels. It was horrible."

"It wasn't your fault," Amber said, "and thank God, she wasn't seriously hurt."

"That was your view, not your 'Cavalier' friend, Sean Crisp's. I heard him tell you at the station, 'You're a probationer, this is good experience and your drink/drive arrest box is ticked, besides, he was over the limit, *fuck him.*' Is that an accurate recollection of what he said… Detective Amber?"

Amber felt herself blushing, as far as she could recall, it was word for word what Sean had said to her in the custody suite after Lancaster was charged.

"You used me for practise, didn't you?"

Grant intervened again. "And Sean deserved to die because of *that?*"

"He stole my future!" Lancaster exploded. It triggered Grant's memory of Amber as she'd spoken of Sean Crisp's murder. 'Is there *anything* worse than stealing someone's future?' At the time, he'd mused that being killed wasn't the only way to steal a future, evidently, Luke Lancaster felt the same way and justified his actions accordingly.

Lancaster continued, calm once more, "Konstanz wanted to sack me on the spot when I arrived in the early evening. I begged, I cried, I didn't mention the arrest, just the accident. He gave me one last chance. It was less convenient, but I travelled by tube and things were going well, until two weeks later. The union man, Bill Buckle, called one of his sudden strikes. No warnings, no reason, a 'flexing of industrial muscle' he called them. I arrived at the restaurant late on a day we were catering a high-profile conference. Konstanz sacked me instantly, very publicly, very cruelly. I was finished. Forever after, I was the man who'd been blown out by the great Konstanz Bassa…not once…but twice."

"So they had to die, too?" Asked Grant. "The man who called a strike that made you late and the man who sacked you because of it."

"Between them both, my dreams were destroyed, and none of it was my fault, *none* of it!"

"Carry on." Grant spoke through gritted teeth, "What happened next?"

"I took a job in a small restaurant, run by a family, but my drive, my spark, had been extinguished. I met Cordelia, we married, and between us, we bought a house. Do you want to guess who our estate agent was?"

"Sam Pendry by any chance?" Amber suggested.

Lancaster flicked his finger at Amber, "The Detective gets it in one. Give the lady a prize. Yes, Sam fucking Pendry, literally fucking. Cordelia left me for him, so my home was sold, she moved into Pendry's big house in Osterley, and I ended up in my old bedroom, living with my mum. How fair is that?"

"So Sam Pendry had to go, too? And in the process, Gavin Cape and Detective Sergeant Kalamatianos slaughtered as well. So much for your precise planning; it was just murderous self-indulgence. Even the warped and twisted reasons for killing those you consider had wronged you can't justify the butchery." There was controlled fury in Grant's voice. "It was the act of a coward, a maggot."

Lancaster remained composed, "Don't think you can say or do anything which can hurt or insult me, policeman. We've established I'm way beyond your touch. But it's true, they weren't planned, it's unfortunate, the bullets they took were meant for the others, in the rucksack, you'll find the full list. It'll never be finished now, time's raced away. I was in a hurry, and when you hurry, things can go wrong. By the way, at the time I'd no idea the fat man was a police officer, you may like to know he stood in front of Mr Cape, trying to shield him from me. Failed obviously."

Lancaster looked to Amber, "dressed up as a nurse, but a CID officer now, eh? You've done well, from the little mousey thing that wouldn't say boo to a goose or stand up for what she thought was right all those years ago to this. I wonder what would've happened if you *had* stood your ground against Constable Crisp? Interesting thought, isn't it?"

"Finish your story or I'm leaving." Amber's voice was devoid of emotion.

"Okay, Detective Amber, we're nearly done. The doctor told me the news: 'brain tumour', 'inoperable', 'I'm sorry'. It's funny. They're the only words I can remember, isn't that strange? I went to the pub, and whilst I was drinking, I was looking at all the people going about their business, living their lives, in isolation from mine, untouched, unconnected from me, and what I'd just found out. I thought about the people who *had* touched my life, who'd damaged me, sometimes deliberately, sometimes without even knowing it, but they *were* responsible, and there should be some retribution. It came to me in a flash, I was free, the tumour, which I'd named Cordelia, had freed me. I was untouchable, I could live without consequences. It was an almost God-like sensation, a real epiphany. Can you understand?"

"I can't understand how being told I'm going to die would make me want to kill, so no, I don't understand," Amber answered.

"Hmmm. Perhaps you had to be there. I was back and forth here to Guys for treatment, and I saw Sean Crisp in the street. I recognised him immediately, the red pointed beard, the ridiculous moustache, curled up at the ends. He didn't recognise me, why should he? I chatted whenever I could, bought him coffees. I saw he had a gun, I asked him about it, how it worked, and he told me. He said he normally spent most of his time standing outside the Turkish embassy on night shift. The rest is history, as they say."

"You staked out the embassy until you saw him there, stabbed him, took his gun and Taser, and then went on your vengeance spree. Maybe you could tell me how shooting a fifteen-year-old boy in the back of the head fitted in?"

"Ah, yes, the cyclist."

"He had a name, Junior Flight, and he was only fifteen." Grant was controlling his anger once more.

"Oh, please!" Lancaster scoffed, "he was a yob, if he wasn't a criminal yet, he would have been soon."

The words tweaked the guilty feelings Grant had experienced on learning of Junior Flight's burgeoning criminal career and the subsequent dilution of his sympathy for the murder victim, he despised Lancaster even more for his intuition.

Lancaster looked regretful. "Between him and my temper, my grand finale was totally screwed up. I was on my way to dispatch my darling ex-wife. I had a melodramatic vision in mind, one bullet through her treacherous heart and another as a coup de grâce through her pretty face. Then, as Cordelia the woman expired, my final bullet would destroy Cordelia the tumour in my brain, blowing that vile lump to a million pieces. Don't you think that would've been almost poetic? Destroying the two Cordelias that had blighted my life?"

"The boy."

"Ah, yes, the yob," Lancaster corrected. "I was driving to the roundabout, I had right of way, and the yob rode straight out in front of me. No lights, dark clothing, straight out in front of me. I slammed the brakes on, and in doing so, I saved his life. What did he do? Gave me the finger and shouted, *'Fuck you!' He* was in the wrong, and *I* get the abuse. I lost my temper, Officers, I really did. It's been happening more often. Anyway, please don't tell me that you've *never* endured something similar and just had to swallow it. But when you're free, like me, you *don't* have to take *anything* anymore. It's freedom. Can't you see?"

"The boy." Grant repeated.

Lancaster sighed with disappointment. "Okay, I drove after him, rammed his bike, and as he lay on the floor, I fired the Taser at him. God, he wriggled and twitched; it was wonderful. I had thought to leave it at that, I suspect he'd have moderated his subsequent behaviour, but do you know what? I thought 'bollocks', so I shot him. Honestly, Officers, I really think I've prevented so many future crimes, you should thank me."

It was Amber Bennett who spoke. "You've brought terror to my city and killed eight people, two of them were my friends. I've heard enough of your poison. I'm glad you're dying. I want to leave now, Sarge."

Grant turned to look at Luke Lancaster once more as the uniformed officer took his place next to the prisoner, the door closed, and he was lost from view.

Nine Weeks Later

They'd agreed that the compunction they both felt to attend wasn't out of any desire to show respect or reverence for the dead man. There was no such respect or reverence, but there was a need to close a book. This was the final chapter in a story of eight other, intertwined lives, which over many years had catastrophically collided with Luke Lancaster.

The two officers didn't enter the crematorium's chapel, instead stationing themselves on the other side of the Garden of Remembrance, giving a clear view of the wide double doors which were now opening. A white robed vicar stood at the exit, shaking hands, dipping his head to speak with the mourners, uttering platitudes. What can he possibly be saying, Grant wondered, about a man who'd so ruthlessly let his thoughts and feelings manifest and run out of control?

"There's Mildred." Grant nodded his head in the direction of the small group by the doors, choosing not to take his hands out of his coat pockets on the freezing winter morning. " I find it hard to even sympathise with her, a hideous woman."

"Fucking horrible," agreed Amber. She turned away from the scene, forty yards distant, to look at Grant. "Sarge. All those people, Sean and Panos and the rest, all of them." Her voice cracked with the emotion she had been bottling up for over two months.

The big Detective Sergeant turned to face his friend; he knew what she was thinking. "You shouldn't go there, Amber."

"We could have parked his car, kept the keys at the nick for him to collect later. We could have let him get on his way. There was no real question his driving was impaired, *he* stopped at the crossing after all, the stone-cold sober tosser behind was the one who didn't. Back at the nick, Luke blew a single point over the limit; if we'd left him just three minutes, he'd have come back *under* the limit. Sean Crisp rushed the process to maximise the chance of a charge and a conviction. Luke was right, we *did* use him to practise on." Amber sighed deeply, and Grant saw there were tears in her eyes. "I don't know how to feel about all this. If I'd been stronger and stood up to Sean, if I'd said, 'No, this isn't fair, this isn't right. ' It could've been so different. They'd be alive."

The dam burst, and the tears flowed freely down Amber's face. Grant hesitated for a moment, then reached his arms around his colleague and hugged her. He felt her body convulse with the tears, and his heart went out to her. The loss of her friend, the tortuously long hours, the stress and responsibility, the mounting body count, and the final struggle with a mass murderer for possession of a loaded gun had all taken its toll on the young woman he was holding.

He whispered softly, "Amber, Amber, listen to me. You can go mad thinking like that. The variables are too big for our little minds to work out, so what we do is, we carry on, we do our job, we do it to the best of our abilities. What else is there to do?" He kissed the top of her head as he'd kiss his own girls when they were hurting. "Come on, you, let's go, I tell you what, I'll buy you a coffee and a bun."

With Grant's guiding arm around her shoulder, they walked towards the car park and the fluorescent green monstrosity which was parked there, waiting for them. Grant had collected it from the car pool that morning; apparently, it was all they had.

About the Author

Steve Packwood grew up in the industrial Midlands of England, moving south to London to become an officer of the Metropolitan Police in 1984.

He served in many departments and in many capacities until specialising as one of the British Police's very few firearms officers, ultimately qualifying as an Armed Protection Officer. There followed several exciting years safeguarding Prime Ministers, including Margaret Thatcher and Tony Blair, as well as visiting Heads of State.

Steve was invited to join the Royalty Protection Group, initially on Prince Charles's team (now King Charles III) and ultimately with H.M. Queen Elizabeth II at Buckingham Palace, Windsor Castle, and, in Scotland, Balmoral Castle. In 2014, Steve retired from the police relatively sane and reasonably intact after providing "thirty *years of exemplary service.*"

Steve has been very happily married to Sue for eleven years and has two daughters from a previous relationship. It was Sue who encouraged him to start writing when he retired, mainly as a creative outlet after so many years of living a disciplined and regimented life but also, he suspects, to keep him from getting under her feet.

Steve and Sue are passionate about the theatre and love to travel, having so far ticked off the Far East and the Indian sub-continent as well as most of Europe. But they take special joy in crossing the pond to visit the USA, which they adore. The couple have relatives in Florida and good friends in New York, so these are the most frequent destinations, but they have plans to explore the rest of the country.

Steve has an adventurous spirit. As a qualified scuba diver, he has a passion for swimming with sharks, much misunderstood creatures he adores. He has also sky-dived, para-glided, abseiled and bungee jumped. Sue keeps a substantial life insurance policy in her back pocket. Steve considers himself amongst the luckiest of people and loves his life, often exclaiming with a satisfied sigh to anyone who will listen, *"Where did it all go so...right!"*

https://www.levelbestbooks.us/steven-packwood.html

Also by Steve Packwood

The Dissection Murders